The Night Was Soft and Beautiful, and They Might Never Meet Again . . .

Alexandra and Fraser neared the small thatched hut, and desire flamed between them as they sank to the soft rushy floor still entwined in each other's arms. "God, but I've missed you, my Alex!" Fraser said, "I've been out of my mind with worry for you these past weeks, not knowing if you were alive or dead."

"It's been the same for me!" Alexandra murmured. "Not knowing was the worst of it, dearest. Wondering if I'd ever see you again."

He tipped her chin up towards his face, his long sensitive fingers making her flesh tingle.

"You must always have faith," he whispered.

Alexandra trembled as Fraser ran his hands over her body as if to imprint every touch of her into his brain. He pulled her close to him. . . .

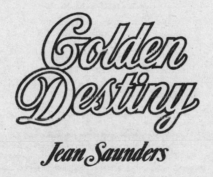

Golden Destiny

Jean Saunders

Pan Books

First hardback edition published in Great Britain 1990 by
Severn House Publishers Ltd of
35 Manor Road, Wallington, Surrey SM6 0BW

First hardback edition published in the U.S.A. 1990 by
Severn House Publishers Inc, New York

This edition published 1997 by Pan Books
an imprint of Macmillan Publishers Ltd
25 Eccleston Place, London SW1W 9NF
and Basingstoke

Associated companies throughout the world

ISBN 0 330 37016 2

Copyright © 1986 Jean Saunders

1 3 5 7 9 10 8 6 4 2

A CIP catalogue record for this book is available from
the British Library.

Printed and bound in Great Britain by
Mackays of Chatham PLC, Chatham, Kent

Chapter One

THE MAY MORNING HAD BEEN DULL, BUT NOTHING COULD dim the excitement of it for Alexandra, and as she had confidently hoped with a child's optimism, the sun eventually began to break through the clouds. It was as though the whole of London had chosen to be on its best behavior for this splendid day, the opening of the city's most magnificent spectacle of the century, the Great Exhibition.

How could it fail to be wonderful, when it had been devised and created under the direction of the elegant Prince Albert himself! The prince would be at Hyde Park that very day, with the little queen and the royal children, to declare the Exhibition open.

Alexandra's parents referred to Victoria as the little

1

queen, with fond and loyal affection. To Alex, at twelve years old, Victoria was as far removed as the moon and stars. It was one more thrill of the day, that she would actually see the royal personages.

Even more wonderful to Alex was the fact that all her family would be together for the occasion. That was what made it doubly special, and she waited with impatience for the hour of departure from the white-porticoed Paddington house, until at last her natural childish irritation erupted.

"Why aren't we leaving yet, Aunt Maud?" she asked impatiently.

Her aunt laughed. "Dear child, you must learn to be patient! Your parents are not ready yet, so there's no point in fussing. The Exhibition will be there for months yet—"

"But Mother and Father will not! And no other day will be quite like today, will it?"

She caught her aunt's reproving glance. She was still a child, but Maud Truscott was already seeing the growing maturity in her niece. The soft plumpness of childhood was already reshaping into more adult pro-portions.

One day Alex would be a lovely young woman, Maud surmised. A prize for some young man to claim as his bride—just as long as Alexandra could curb the ready wit and occasional bursts of temperament that no well-brought-up young Victorian girl should display.

At last, the drawing room door opened, and the rest of the Truscott family appeared. Alex ran to her parents at once, a glow of happiness radiating from her as she held a hand of each. The family was apart so much that Alex always felt this impulsive need to touch her parents physically, as though to prove to herself that they were really here.

"Can't we go yet, Father?" she pleaded. "I seem to have been ready for hours."

Felix Truscott smiled at his daughter. Her wide blue eyes were as lustrous and beautiful as her mother's. Felix himself was a darkly handsome man, tall and commanding, in complete contrast to his wife, Constance, whose delicately featured fair skin had never succumbed to the fierce Indian sun the way his had over the years.

"If you've been ready for hours, my darling, then it's your own fault for rising so early," Felix said genially.

"I have to be awake so early at school, it's impossible for me to lie abed," Alex flashed back at him. "If you would only let me come back to India with you and Mother, I could go to school in Delhi and get up at a more civilized hour"—she made an oft-repeated plea.

"That's hardly likely, since the British schools in Delhi are a good distance from the bungalow," Felix said dryly.

"Alex, you know it's not possible," Constance put in, not allowing the brief sympathy she felt for her daughter to show and giving a small sigh as she saw the mutinous look on Alex's face.

"Because of some old request in Grandfather Truscott's will, insisting that I'm educated in England!" she burst out. "It's not fair, Mother! Why can't I be with you both? It's where I want to be—"

"And so you shall, when your education is finished, Alexandra." Felix's voice was steely now, his use of her full name telling her the discussion was over.

There was never a real discussion on it, Alex raged. There was only the deadlock between her parents and herself whenever the subject was mentioned. And because of the whim of some gray-bearded grandfather she barely remembered, who had held all the family purse strings, she must do as Alexander Truscott had wished. Even her own name, the female counterpart of his, was a constant reminder.

Because of old Alexander and her father's wish to honor his memory, Alex was obliged to remain in England at the expensive and exclusive boarding school for the daughters of gentlemen instead of joining her parents in that most magical, romantic land of India. It just wasn't fair.

"Alex, you promised me you wouldn't spoil your parents' visit with any tantrums," Aunt Maud said discreetly.

Poor Aunt Maud, who might have had a brood of children of her own by now, if her soldier fiancé hadn't been killed in some battle or other . . . useful Aunt Maud, Alex thought with childish cynicism, providing the English home that had been Truscott property for several generations. Giving her strong-willed niece the stable home background. Alex didn't mean to be ungrateful but just lived for the twice-yearly visits home to England by her parents.

She saw Maud's anxious look and bit back the petulant retort. It was foolish to spoil this day when for now, at least, she was with the three people she loved best in all the world.

"I knew it was no use arguing, anyway." She spoke with artless candor to her mother, the scowl changing to a mischievous smile. "But I have to try, don't I, Mother?"

Constance drew her daughter to her side in a soft-scented embrace.

"I suppose you do, darling, and we do understand how you feel. The time will come, I promise you. And you do enjoy my drawings, don't you?" She subtly changed the conversation. "By the time you come out to us, you'll be able to identify every dome and minaret in Delhi, as well as I know them myself!"

Constance was an accomplished artist and delighted Alex by sending her pencil drawings of all the places of interest in Delhi and the surrounding area. There were sometimes swift pencil sketches too, of the big occasions the Truscotts attended, which were becoming more frequent now.

There were dinners and receptions and important functions, and Constance's drawings brought the color and glitter of them all to her daughter. Felix was a rising figure in the Honourable East India Company, known simply by all its employees as the Company.

"We shall be a complete family again, my love, so you just behave yourself and the time will pass all the quicker," Felix added, glad that the small storm had passed.

Alex couldn't think how good behavior would help the time to pass. It was one of the illogical remarks that were made to children. Neither she nor her parents noticed the brief pain on Maud Truscott's face at that moment. For all these formative years, Alex was her family. When the child joined her parents in India, Maud would have no one. Guiltily, Maud knew she was the only one thankful that that day was still some years ahead.

"Here's Henry with the carriage at last," Maud said quickly, as the wheels sounded outside.

She chided herself for the moment of brooding, for nothing must dampen the spirits on this wonderful day. They would soon be mingling with the expected crowds in Hyde Park for a day of pageantry they would long remember. It must surely compare with anything that India had to offer, Maud thought, with a little burst of national pride.

She knew little of the splendors of fabled princes and white marbled palaces, the majesty of bejeweled elephants riding in procession and all the other hardly credible things her brother and his wife had told her about. Maud was a practical woman, and highly skeptical of the existence of some of them.

It made her uneasy at times to know how gullible Alex was on that score. Though perhaps "gullible" was not the right word. The child was a romantic, a dreamer, for all her occasional outbursts. And that romanticism was lovingly fed by her parents, who had filled her head with all the fabulous nonsense about India.

To Alex, India was clearly comparable only to the promised land. It was peopled with many rich Europeans like her parents, living well and happily alongside the wealthier of Indian society, and on intimate terms with princes. Europeans who could call on the gallant officers from the garrisons to escort them and their ladies to the beautiful summer palaces or to the cool hills where tall pines and rhododendron forests grew in glorious profusion.

Whenever Maud read the wordy letters the child received from her parents, there was never mention of squalor or dust or undue heat and discomfort, or the reason why the Company maintained such a large and vigilant fighting force in a country that was supposedly almost entirely under British rule. Those were things the Truscotts preferred not to discuss with their pretty young daughter.

But Maud was old enough and canny enough to know that where there was so much light and beauty, there must also be dark shadows. She wondered privately just how much disservice her brother and his wife did to Alex by not preparing her for the worst as well as for the best.

But now was not the time for reflection . . . and by the time the Truscott carriage had lumbered its way towards Hyde Park, the child's spirits were reaching fever pitch. There was such a crush of vehicles and horses and people . . . and dominating everything, beautiful and glittering against the blue sky, was the huge, magnificent building made of glass, called the crystal palace because of its shimmering symmetry. It dazzled in the sunlight, a triumph of architectural planning and attention to detail.

Alex adored pageantry. She so longed to go to India, to see for herself. But today, there was wonder enough here . . . and they soon realized that not only Londoners were visiting the Exhibition on this May day.

Trainloads and carriageloads of country folk had arrived, gawking in disbelief and speaking in their strange, slow voices. Olive-skinned foreigners gesticulated with excited, waving hands as they perused their Exhibition catalogues. Ladies and gentlemen of fashion, wanting to see and be seen . . . the Truscotts were swept along with the crowds, part of them, exhilarated by them.

Inside the building itself, crowded with exhibits and humanity, Felix too felt dwarfed by the sheer conception of such an edifice. Outside, the flags of every nation flew. Inside, they all waited expectantly for the royal party to arrive.

It seemed an age to Alex before they entered to a fanfare of trumpets. It was a lengthy procession, but the most regal figures of all were the little queen, the handsome Prince Albert and the royal children. A choir sang Handel's Hallelujah Chorus, speeches were made and at long last a gentleman announced as Lord Breadalbane spoke the words everyone waited to hear. He spoke with great pomp and dignity, and thankfully few words.

"Her Majesty commands me to declare the Exhibition opened."

He spoke loudly, but his voice was almost drowned by cheers and more trumpet playing. Soon afterwards, the royal party left to return to Buckingham Palace, and a little of the day's sparkle dimmed . . . but only a very little, for how could it be otherwise? Alex's mind retained the imagery of it all, and especially the beautiful and elegant Prince Albert's appearance and his loving attention to the queen, his immensely attractive foreign accent when he spoke and his dark expressive eyes.

This year of 1851 was very special indeed, Alex thought, as the Truscotts, along with everyone else, milled about the vast interior of the crystal palace and marveled at it all. There was Minton china, Crown Derby, exquisite silver, lace mantillas from Spain, great weaving machinery from France, the fabulously beautiful Koh-i-nor diamond on display for all to see . . .

"Isn't it the loveliest thing you ever saw, Alex?" Felix said. "Once, when a jeweler was asked to value it, he said he could only compare it with half the daily expenditure of the whole world!"

And that was just the kind of emotional remark that was turning the child's head, Maud Truscott thought in exasperation. But Alex was already moving on, as though trying to see everything at once, and suddenly pointing to the tea chests from India and Ceylon, the various teas fragrant and aromatic. Quite prominent among the glass containers displaying the fine dark leaves was one labeled Krubah Tea, in which Felix Truscott had shares.

When Felix and Constance had first gone to India ten years ago, they had dallied with the idea of becoming tea planters. Then Felix was offered a good post with the East India Company, with excellent prospects, and Constance had fallen in love with the small, stylish bungalow they were offered near Delhi, and the idea of tea planting was abandoned. Instead, they had invested a good deal of old Alexander Truscott's legacy in Krubah Tea, which had flourished beyond all expectations and provided a healthy yearly dividend.

"Oh, Mother, just look—" Alex suddenly breathed, bored with the more mundane tea chests. Her eyes were held by more feminine attractions.

Brilliant and jewellike were the bales and bales of beautiful Indian silks, draped in shimmering cascades of peacock colors from their display stands. Alex couldn't resist fingering the fabric, feeling the exquisite richness and sensuality of the fabric. Something deep inside her responded to its touch against her skin, as though warm ripples of silken sunlight ran through her veins . . .

"Aren't they glorious, Alex?" Constance's voice broke through the spell that seemed to hold her daughter transfixed for a few minutes. "The highborn Indian ladies wear garments made of such silk. And the princesses—you never saw such flowing, gold-encrusted silks as the princesses wear—"

"Constance, you'll be filling the child's head with envy if you go on so!" Maud protested, alarmed to see the almost glazed look on Alex's face. "You'll undo all the good her tutors do in teaching the girls that envy is a sin—"

Her sister-in-law gave a soft laugh. "How can it be

sinful to enjoy beautiful things, Maud? I would not want my Alex to grow up so insensitive that she cannot appreciate beauty. If I have one wish to bestow on a daughter, it would be that all her senses are alive to every God-given pleasure on this earth."

Listening to her, Felix thought it no wonder that Alex adored her mother so much, as he did. Still, he was aware that his sister had a difficult job at times, dealing with a growing girl she looked upon as a daughter, but who was not her daughter. A child she was destined to lose . . . At Maud's flush of embarrassment at the small rebuke from Constance, Felix spoke heartily.

"Shall we go outside for a picnic, my dears? I'm told there are stalls with tea and lemonade and ginger beer, and we can buy pasties and pies or bread and cheese, and I suspect there will be fresh fruit and ices too. What do you all say to it? We'll come back inside later on, but a picnic in Hyde Park sounds fun to me. And I'm sure you'll be receiving a pencil drawing of the occasion in due course, Alex, to remember it all by!"

It was exactly how they presented life to the child, Maud thought uneasily, as she heard Alex's squeals of delight. Life was a picnic to be lived in permanent sunshine, light and frothy and ever golden. But Maud knew only too well that life could not always be like that.

The pencil drawing of a picnic in Hyde Park was one of the last items that Alexandra Truscott packed in her trunk on her final day at Lady Margaret's Academy for Young Ladies. The drawing had graced her wall ever since her mother had sent it from India several months after the day they had all visited the Great Exhibition in

Hyde Park. The drawing was a little faded now, its edges slightly roughened, but it was still one of Alex's most prized possessions.

Among all the expensive clothes and fripperies and the trinkets and jewelry she owned, she held two things most dear. One was the reminder of such a splendid day, when she had seen the queen and the beautiful Prince Albert; the other was the string of flawless pearls that had belonged to her mother and which she always wore around her neck.

Alex looked around the room that had been home to her for more than five years. It would be so strange to leave it. The girl with whom she had shared the room had already left the academy to join her own family in Ireland, where they bred horses. She and Alex had wept on each other's shoulders, wondering if they would ever meet again.

This day should have been as wonderful as that sunlit May morning of 1851 . . . Alex blinked back the threatening tears. In the mirror, her reflection looked back at her, wan and pale and lovely, despite the sadness in her face.

She had grown to be everything her Aunt Maud expected in a beautiful young lady. She was slenderly made, with softly rounded curves and the tall straight carriage insisted on at Lady Margaret's. It gave her a proud look, until one looked into the liquid blue gaze from her eyes and met the warm, generous smile from her full, sensual mouth.

Alex did not treat most onlookers to insight into her character. The proud bearing was sometimes a cloak to hide behind when she didn't want her feelings known. It had stood her in good stead three years ago, when, her spirits crushed beyond anything she could ever have imagined, she had heard the news that her lovely, gentle mother had died swiftly and horribly from the cholera.

And because it had happened in India, at a time when the days were furnace-hot, the burial had had to be quick, almost without dignity in its haste, so that Alex's father had been stunned half out of his mind, feeling himself robbed of a proper time to mourn for his adored wife.

Consequently, his harsh, relentless grief had continued for a long time, and his next visits home to England had been painful on both sides. Alex reminded him so poignantly of his beloved Constance that he could barely bring himself to look at her. And Alex, who needed him so desperately, had felt doubly rejected at his apparent wish to keep the visits home as short as possible.

Out of her own sorrow, Alex had discovered a new frustration, confided only to that roommate at Lady Margaret's, when an outsider was so much more of a confidante than a close relative.

"How can death make strangers of people who love one another?" she had raged, weeping. "Father and I can't talk to one another anymore, and Aunt Maud goes puce if I even try to bring Mother's name into the conversation, as though it's suddenly taboo. I can't bear it. I just can't!"

But she had had to bear it and found a strength she hadn't known she possessed. In time, Felix had borne it too, having to accept the inevitable, part of which was a promise made long ago, when Alex was a tiny baby and bound by an old man's will. When her education was complete, she would go to India, and the Truscotts would be a family again.

The promise would still be kept, but the circumstances had changed. Alex's father, older, his hair tinged now with distinguished gray, would be the only one waiting to greet her when the ship docked in Calcutta. And Alex would be accompanied by her Aunt Maud, more waspish than before, who had done much soul-searching before deciding that the child must not travel all that distance alone. Nor live in that barbaric foreign land without the protection of a chaperone.

Felix had smiled without humor when reading the strident words in Maud's letter to him. He no longer lived in the bungalow Constance had so loved, although it still belonged to him, and he had been quite unable to dispose of it. It was a retreat whenever he needed it or could bear to stay in it. It wasn't often, because he still saw the ghost of Constance wherever he looked.

Home to him now was truly going to astound his sister Maud and enchant his daughter. They knew of it, of course, but could have no comprehension of its exquisite beauty. Ever since the East India Company had begun to annex more and more of India, there had been protests among the legions of princes with their own small territories. To some of these princes, from whom no treason was suspected, certain rights had been allowed.

They were nominally allowed to remain rulers of their own lands within the Company's directorship, but they had no access to foreign or political dealings. They had to abide by Company ruling as to the extent of their own armed guard, maintained purely for the princes' prestige and status.

More significantly, each prince so honored had to have a resident British officer of the Company's foreign and political department, who saw that the Company's wishes were carried out. Felix Truscott was the resident officer in the beautiful palace of Prince Shunimar, to the southeast of Delhi.

He wished he had been able to bring Alex here when she was still a child, to have seen it anew through her young, awed eyes. But Alex now was a lovely young woman of seventeen years, and he knew it was that fact that had made his sister Maud determined to accompany Alex to India, and Felix had gladly arranged for both their passages to be paid.

The old family home in Paddington had been sold, and Maud was to meet her niece at Tilbury docks late in the afternoon of the day that Alex left Lady Margaret's Academy, and that day had at last arrived.

It was raining softly as the hackney carriage took Alex through the London suburbs and towards the docks where the great ship awaited its cargo of passengers bound for Calcutta, India. On the billboards, the advertising posters announced that the steamship *Arabella* would sail via Gibraltar and around the coast of Africa, northwards again through the Indian Ocean and finally into the Bay of Bengal and Calcutta port on the Hooghly River.

Felix had gone to great pains to choose a ship that would give the ladies the least discomfort on the long voyage. The *Arabella* cost more in passage money than many others, but fortunately that was an expense Felix could disregard. There would be no riff-raff on board, and it was worth much to him to know that.

Awaiting her aunt at the dockside, Alex looked anxiously through the drizzling rain. The sky was overcast, and other passengers hurrying aboard had little time to spare for the rather haughty young woman looking as though she could well take care of herself. It may have looked that way, but Alex was becoming more and more tense inside. There was a group of rough-looking seamen nearby, and she couldn't miss the ribald remarks they made about the pretty girl standing alongside her trunk and hand baggage.

Where was Aunt Maud? Alex was alternately irritated and anxious. She didn't scare easily, but the swift closing-in of the day, the lounging seamen and the distinctly sour smell rising from the tidal waters of the Thames was making her heart thud uneasily.

Without thinking, she stepped back a pace, imagining that their attitude was one of menace, and she almost stumbled over a coil of sodden rope at her feet. Her rain-blurred eyes took in the swift horror of the gray, heaving water far below the ship's bow, and a surge of nausea swept over her.

"If you're trying to kill yourself, lassie, I can think of better ways of doing it than throwing yourself into the miserable waters of the Thames!"

The harsh male voice beside her had an accent she didn't readily recognize. At the same instant, her wrists were held in a tight, hurting grasp as she was pulled unceremoniously away from the coil of rope.

Alex smothered the brief fear and blinked her eyes in momentary relief, despite the gall of the stranger's insinuation. She opened them again quickly, meaning to thank her self-styled rescuer icily enough to repel any further contact, sure that he must be one of the rough seamen. And then she felt her entire nervous system begin to prickle with stunned disbelief as she looked into the handsome, elegant features of Albert of Saxe-Coburg, the Prince Consort.

Just as quickly, Alex realized that of course it wasn't the prince. Albert had been her idol, as was the case with many of the girls at Lady Margaret's. This man at Tilbury dockside in the gray, slanting rain bore a certain similarity to the prince and that was all. The dark waving hair plastered by the rain to his well-shaped head, and the neat moustache above a firm mouth and jaw were comparable, but this man's manners had none of the courtesy of a royal prince's. Thankfully, he was no rough seaman either . . .

"Thank you, sir," Alex said stiffly. "If you will kindly let go of me now, I'm quite capable of standing by myself, and I assure you I have no death wish!"

The man stared down at her. He was undoubtedly handsome, though there was a hardness about his mouth. There were laughter lines about his eyes, although they weren't laughing now. His skin was well bronzed by the sun, the way her father's was, Alex thought. He released her abruptly, a look of mocking carelessness on his face.

"Thank you for telling me. I've better things to do with my time than rescue rich men's silly daughters—"

Alex felt her temper blaze. Her blue eyes flashed furiously. The little matter of not speaking freely with a stranger was totally dismissed from her mind as she glowered up at him.

"How dare you! And how did you know—?"

She clamped her lips shut. She wouldn't give him the satisfaction of telling him he'd correctly deduced that her father was rich. It was the assumption that she was one of the so-called butterflies of the day that infuriated her.

He laughed now, creasing the lines beside his eyes, an oddly humorless laugh. At any other time, it might have intrigued her. She wouldn't admit, either, that she was a mite piqued by this dour stare when she was more used to admiring glances . . .

"Why else would you be traveling to India unless it were so? You *are* traveling to India? Or do you always

16

stand in the rain with all your baggage alongside a Calcutta-bound ship?"

His tone was thick with sarcasm, as though thinking her a simpleton if she thought he couldn't work it out for himself. Her cheeks burned. He was a hateful man.

A gust of wind snatched at the rain cape he wore, glossed with the bad weather. Alex got a glimpse of bright hose above well-polished boots, and the blue-green plaid of a kilt. Now she knew his accent. He was a Scot. Maybe belonging to one of the Highland regiments her mother used to find so charming and gallant, the officers only too willing to escort the European ladies about whenever their duties permitted. There was a heavy valise at the man's feet, so he must be traveling too. Alex's chin tilted. There was little of the gallant about this one!

"I won't detain you any longer, sir," she said coldly. "My aunt will be joining me in a very few minutes—"

"Then I shall wait with you until she does," he said, to her fury. "Unless you prefer the company of our sea-going friends yonder, who seem to be eyeing you with some interest."

Alex looked at once to the group of seamen. She decided instantly that the Scotsman's presence was preferable to theirs, gave the smallest nod of her head and stood with her eyes fixed on the roadway.

She and the stranger were together and yet not together. The flicker of amusement that finally softened Fraser Mackinnon's eyes was entirely lost on Alex as she stared away from him. For his part, he noted the proud stance of the girl and the effortlessness with which she seemed to exclude both himself and the seamen from her mind.

Arrogant, he decided. Arrogant and rich, the worst combination in a young lassie. Fraser stared just as deliberately in the opposite direction. A few minutes later he heard the girl give an audible sigh as a hackney drew up and a thin-faced woman alighted from it, directing the driver to put her baggage down beside the young lady's.

"Aunt Maud, I've been so worried!" At last the mask slipped from Alex's demeanor, and the soft trembling of her mouth betrayed her anxiety.

"That wretched traffic!" Maud Truscott grumbled. "Never mind, my love, I'm here now, and we had best see about getting our things on board the ship. Are there any porters about?"

Alex heard the snort of amused laughter from the Scotsman. She would have ignored it, but for the fact that he suddenly turned to her aunt with a charming smile.

"If you will allow me to assist you, ma'am, I'll see that all your effects are safely stowed on board," he said. "Your niece and I have not been properly introduced, but I trust you'll forgive the informality when I tell you how I rescued her from a premature watery grave!"

"Bless my soul!" Maud's eyes widened in horror, while Alex was too outraged to speak.

"If that's the case, then we truly thank you, Mr.—"

"Fraser Mackinnon, ma'am, at your service. And you are—?"

Maud was too flustered to refrain from answering. "I am Miss Maud Truscott, and this is my niece, Miss Alexandra Truscott. We are traveling to India, and the sooner we get out of this dreadful rain, the better."

Fraser Mackinnon clicked his fingers, and several men appeared at once. On his instructions, they began hauling the heavy trunk and all the baggage up the gangway and onto the ship.

"Thank you, Mr. Mackinnon," Alex said frostily. "We are quite able to manage now—"

"May I escort you, ma'am?" he said gravely, holding out a hand to place firmly beneath Maud's elbow. She accepted his offer, glancing reproachfully at Alex, who followed them, fuming. He was insufferable, so polite and pleasant to the spinster lady, when Alex knew just how abrasive he could be. Her eyes sparkled with a sudden thought.

Perhaps this Fraser Mackinnon was charming to the aunt because he thought there might be a fortune in the niece! It was known to happen . . . though he certainly hadn't appeared to show any interest in Alex so far! Hopefully, once they were on board ship, they need never see him again.

As soon as they had been greeted by a ship's officer and taken to their cabin, Alex breathed more easily. The cabin seemed cramped to them, yet was still one of the *Arabella*'s best. The baggage was already there, followed very soon by Alex's trunk. Maud paid the men a few coppers for their trouble.

"Heaven knows if one should do that," she observed when they had gone. "Let's not worry about it. I'm more concerned with how we're supposed to put all our belongings in these impossibly small cupboards!"

Alex suddenly laughed. Dear, funny Aunt Maud! She gave her a quick hug and, pink-faced, Maud asked what all that was about!

"Nothing. Just because you're you," Alex said huskily.

"Perhaps it's as well I am, with Mr. Handsome Mackinnon around. Had you been waiting long, Alex? It didn't take long for the best-looking man for miles to be at your side!" She spoke teasingly and was surprised by the vehemence of Alex's reply.

"You've no need to worry on that score, Aunt Maud! I didn't find Mr. Mackinnon in the least attractive, and I don't intend giving him another thought!"

Maud watched her as she threw open her trunk, her firm young body taut with annoyance, the perfect oval of her face indignant. The old quotation about the lady protesting too much sprang immediately to Maud's mind, but she was wise enough to refrain from saying so.

Chapter Two

FRASER MACKINNON THREW HIS VALISE ON THE CABIN
bunk, the blackness of his thoughts descending on him
again like a heavy cloud. For a few minutes on the
dockside, he had managed to forget his depression, but
the little rich lassie and her prim-nosed aunt had been
no more than diversions to Fraser, and now he unfas-
tened his rain cape and let it slide to the floor without
noticing it. He pushed the valise after it and lay
full-length on the hard, uncomfortable bunk. He put
his hands behind his head and stared unseeingly at the
ceiling.

This last leave at home had promised to be a good
one, and he had been looking forward to the breath of
the Highlands in his lungs again. It was still home, for
all that he felt this need to answer the call of the wild,

21

the exotic, whatever it was that had made him pursue this dream of India instead of being merely content to be a Scottish landowner like his father.

There had been many bitter arguments between them six years ago. Guthrie Mackinnon had been so against his son joining the military. None of the Mackinnons had felt the need to take up arms for more than a century, since the crushing of the clans after Bonnie Prince Charlie's ill-fated attempt to reclaim the thrones of Scotland and England for his exiled father. The Mackinnons had rallied then and been fervent supporters of the cause, and in their own family a legend of those days had been handed down. A legend only whispered from father to son, for the fear of reprisals after the Jacobite Uprising of 1745 had lingered for many years after Scotland and England finally became one nation under King George the Second.

Like every other child in his family that had gone before him, Fraser had heard the story of his ancestors, the rugged and fearless Jamie Mackinnon and his beautiful bride, Katrina, and how between them they had aided Bonnie Prince Charlie in making his escape from Scottish shores and onto a ship bound for France and exile. If the story were true, it was hardly to be wondered at that eventually one of Jamie and Katrina's descendants would have that same spirit of adventure in his veins.

But Fraser's own father had objected so strongly to his son's joining a regiment in a distant land that they had made a compromise. Fraser had obtained the position of civilian scout to the 78th Highland Regiment. That a scout could be in just as much danger as a regiment, if not more, was never discussed.

At the time, Fraser had been young enough to hold death in contempt. Now, death was very real. He had been at the family's Highland home for less than two days when old Guthrie had had a seizure. In less than an hour, he was dead. What had begun as a carefree leave had been extended into a somber visit of funeral arrangements and formalities, as well as Fraser's wranglings with the family solicitors. When they heard of Fraser's wish to sell everything, they had said bluntly that old Guthrie would rise up in his grave if the lad's heritage were to die with him.

"Think, Fraser," the earnest Douglas Rothwell had entreated. "This house and land has belonged to your family for generations. Aye, farther back than in those troubled times when the Mackinnons stood up to be counted in favor of the Bonnie Prince. Would ye turn your back on all of that? There may come a day when ye'll think of Scotland and Mackinnon House as a sanctuary, like the young Stuart did once, one day when ye're sick of that hot Indian climate. 'Tis what your father would want, Fraser. Retain your home, at least. There's kinsmen willing to take care of the place until your return, laddie, so give yourself something to come back to, I beg ye!"

Fraser had let himself be persuaded, still thinking himself foolish to do so for the sake of an old legend. But he knew it was what his father would have wished. All the Mackinnons who had gone before had loved this house and its lands and been fiercely proud of its royal associations. His own father had believed the story implicitly, of how the lovely Katrina had disguised herself in the red cloak of an old crone, fooling the English soldiers, and gone on the dangerous mission to see if the French ship had come to speed the prince away from Scotland forever.

His spirited ancestor, risking the life of her unborn child for the sake of a cause, in an act that had earned

her the princely and romantic name of Scarlet
Rebel . . .

For all that, Fraser doubted that he would ever see
Scotland again. Now that his father was dead, there was
nothing for him there, and he had never felt so alone.

He shifted on the hard cabin bunk of the *Arabella,*
discounting the kinsmen who had never understood his
need to break free of the fetters of the clan system that
seemed to him to represent one gigantic band of
children blindly following one feudal ruler. A man
should be free to choose his own destiny, and he had
chosen India.

Perhaps he was a rebel too, born out of his time, he
ruminated. He tried to shake off his gloomy mood. He
would be glad to get away from these rainy shores and
back to the land he thought of now as home. He
refused to acknowledge that if there had been someone
waiting for him at Mackinnon House, a woman, a wife,
then his feelings might have been very different.

For some reason, he remembered the lassie on the
dockside, and the pale, rain-streaked face of Alexandra
Truscott. He only thought of her because someone had
given her a good Scottish name. For all that, it was still
an arrogant name for an arrogant young woman, Fraser
decided. He had honestly thought she was in danger of
tripping over the coil of rope, and her reaction had
surprised him.

A girl of some spirit, he decided, which was a novelty
these days. Most were simpering young things, looking
for a husband at all costs. God, but he must stop these
cynical thoughts! Instead, he considered the girl's appearance, merely to occupy his mind.

Yes, she was certainly pretty. He recalled the flash of
her blue eyes, beautiful as the brilliant eyes of a
peacock's tail. He saw again that sudden, soft tremble

of her mouth when her aunt finally appeared. When he had caught at her wrists, a musky, womanly perfume had drifted into his nostrils. She had felt warm as he had held her so briefly, warm and yielding until she had bristled and stood taut, in a way that told its own tale of money and breeding.

Just for an instant, Fraser had been aware of not wanting to let her go. The feeling had hardly registered in his subconscious until now. It was a long while since he had felt any kind of empathy with another person. Since his father's death four weeks ago, he seemed to have held his emotions in a cocoon of brittle cynicism, knowing himself racked with guilt that their last reunion had been so brief. It was foolish, futile guilt, but still very real.

Abruptly, he got up from the cabin bunk, realizing he was dampening it with his rain-soaked clothes. He needed a wash and to scrape the stubble from his chin and tidy himself after his journey here. Not for her benefit, of course. There were as many beautiful young women in the world as there were fish in the sea, and he had no intention of letting this one get beneath his skin so rapidly.

The *Arabella* was due to set sail in the early evening. She slipped cleanly out of port and into the English Channel and smooth waters. Captain George Philpott eyed the weather ahead with a feeling of satisfaction. By the time they reached Gibraltar, where it could be trickier, most of the passengers would hopefully have found their sea legs.

Maud Truscott doubted that she would ever find hers. From the moment she stepped on board and felt the sway of the ship beneath her feet, she had known this wouldn't be a pleasant experience. And just how

Alexandra could sit there eating biscuits and sipping tea and watching the receding coastline through the port-hole, her aunt couldn't imagine. Maud already lay on her bunk, a damp cloth to her forehead, convinced she would be staying there for the entire voyage.

"Aunt Maud, you can't be seasick already!" Alex exclaimed. "It's so ridiculous—"

"Oh, yes, I can," Maud said feelingly. "And I'd be obliged if you would refer to it as the mal de mer, my love, without that horrid reference to illness! You may go up on deck, if you wish, but please attach yourself to some nice family group."

"I can't leave you if you're really ill—"

"I'm really ill, and I just want to be left alone!" Maud moaned. "Just be careful who you're talking to, Alex."

"You mean no dark, handsome Scotsmen?" Alex suddenly said mischievously, unable to resist teasing, despite the realization that her aunt did look queasy.

"I'm sure Mr. Mackinnon is perfectly respectable, Alex, and I trust that your finishing year at Lady Margaret's wasn't entirely wasted. You know the correct way to behave. Just remember who you are, and you'll come to no harm."

Her voice faded and she closed her eyes. There seemed no more that Alex could do. She had sent for the ship's doctor, who had said cheerfully that it would soon pass, advising the damp compress, the smelling salts and dry biscuits as soon as she felt able to eat them. A covered jug of water stood ready beside the bunk, and a bowl if required. If all that failed, she would be given some medication, but the doctor thought it would not be necessary. Maud had her own thoughts on that.

After a brief hesitation, Alex left her aunt and went up to the upper deck. The air was cool and welcome after the stuffy cabin, and she pulled her soft woolen shawl around her shoulders. She had changed out of her traveling dress into a more comfortable gown of soft heather hues. Her curls lifted softly beneath her bonnet, and she began to relax in the salty evening breeze.

The great adventure had really begun . . . somehow it had all felt a little of an anticlimax until now. All her life had been leading up to this day, but as well as the heady joy she should be feeling there was also sadness because her gentle mother would not be waiting for her in India. This voyage, wanted for so long, was more of an emotional journey than Alex had expected it to be.

At least, it had been until this moment, when she stepped out on deck, and the soft evening breeze seemed to wrap itself around her, and the stars pinpointed the velvet blue of the heavens. Now, suddenly, it seemed as though a great surge of life flowed through her, and her mother's words from long ago echoed in her head like silvery chords: "If I have one wish to bestow on a daughter, it would be that all her senses are alive to every God-given pleasure on this earth."

At that instant, it seemed as though Constance's arms were enfolding her, keeping her safe, and she was a child again. Then, in some inexplicable way, it was as if Constance was releasing her, allowing her daughter to move forward, to stand alone, to be a woman. The sensation sent a shiver through Alex's every nerve-end.

It was such an extraordinary, almost mystical feeling that Alex could only liken it to the miracle of the butterfly emerging from the seemingly dry, dead chrysalis . . . and wasn't that the way she guessed that

Fraser Mackinnon had been assessing her? One of the pretty, empty-headed butterflies who flitted about the London scene.

It annoyed her to allow his name to enter her mind when she had been so caught up in euphoria. It brought her back to the present, and her aunt's instructions. Attach yourself to some nice family group, Maud had said . . .

There were plenty of family groups on deck that evening, watching the twinkling, fading lights of the English coast. They lined the ship's railings, and they all looked as respectable as they should, having paid well for their passages on this ship. Alex let her gaze roam and felt her heart leap.

She could hardly miss seeing Fraser Mackinnon, because he was the only one looking towards her instead of towards the coastline. He had watched her emerge from the companionway and reversed his earlier thoughts about her. Miss Alexandra Truscott wasn't merely pretty. She was the loveliest thing he had ever seen. In the swaying light from the ship's lanterns, her skin was as flawless as the gleaming pearls that lay against her throat, and the soft, rosy glow of the lights softened that imperious look he remembered.

Those eyes, that he had likened to the brilliance of the peacock's tail, were deep and lustrous now. The shawl that she held loosely around her couldn't disguise the womanly shape of her, and for the first time in many weeks, Fraser felt the stirrings of desire. He watched her glance about with a somewhat desperate look, and then her gaze was held by the way he detached himself from the ship's rail with a deliberate, almost pantherlike grace. He moved towards her, and she wondered if she could expect more sarcasm . . .

"I think I should apologize to you, Miss Truscott," he said abruptly.

Her ready retort was stilled, and she eyed him warily. Slightly shadowed from the lantern-light, he reminded her even more of Prince Albert, but he was more powerfully built. He had the same elegance, though, and the strangely foreign look, which in Fraser's case must come from however long he had been in India. She guessed that this wasn't his first visit. His bronzed skin told her that much. She ran the tip of her tongue around her mouth without realizing that she did so, or that Fraser's eyes followed its progress.

"Why should you apologize to me, Mr. Mackinnon?"

"You know full well why, lassie!" His voice suddenly dropped, and Alex noted it with a little shock that shivered through her senses.

When he wasn't being aggressive, Fraser had a rich, deeply seductive voice. Previously, she had thought it brash. Now she knew that it could be very different, according to the circumstances and the mood of the man. She wondered about the timbre of that voice during a lovers' embrace . . . it would be seductively caressing, Alex surmised . . . and her own reaction shocked her.

"No, I don't!" She turned away quickly, praying that her outrageous thoughts weren't transparent on her face.

Fraser laughed, and as she glanced at him, she saw how the laughter changed his face. He was at once more good-looking and a little vulnerable. And Alexandra Truscott was seventeen and ripe for adventure, and could no more contain an answering smile than she could fly to the moon.

"What do you say to calling a truce and beginning all over again?" he went on. "May I show you the moonlight, Miss Truscott?"

"Without my aunt here as chaperone? I'm not sure I should allow it, Mr. Mackinnon," she couldn't resist teasing.

"How much of a chaperone do you need, with all these families not twenty feet from us? Come to that—do you think I mean to seduce you, Miss Truscott?"

Don't you? At his own teasing words, it was as though a little voice spoke inside her head. It was uncanny, this sudden feeling of helplessness, when she was usually so much in control. She was also aware of a strange feeling of destiny once more, of karma . . .

"Promise to behave then," she said, and could have bitten out her tongue as she heard herself, as winsome as one of the butterfly set. But it was an act to cover her disturbed feelings, rather than an attempt to play the coquette.

He held out his arm, and she put her hand on it. His other hand covered hers for a moment, the fingers large and strong, pressing hers for an instant too long. She could still feel their warmth after he had removed his hand and began to wonder in a panic what was wrong with her. She wasn't foolish enough to be under the spell of a shipboard romance already. They were notoriously not to be trusted. Besides, she and Fraser Mackinnon had not got off to a very auspicious start! She glanced up at his handsome profile and thought fleetingly how easy, how very easy, it must be to fall in love . . . and how carefully a young and impressionable girl must guard against it.

"Anyway, the moon hasn't appeared yet, Mr. Mackinnon, so where's your famous moonlight?" she said prosaically.

"Have patience," he said, like an echo of her Aunt Maud. "Make the most of the twilight—Alexandra. I refuse to be ridiculously formal, since we'll be traveling companions for weeks. My name is Fraser. I'd advise you to enjoy this soft twilight while you can. It's very different in the tropics. Night comes suddenly there. One minute it's daylight, the next it's dark. I promise you it will be a never-forgotten moment, though, especially the first time you experience it, a fantastic merging of reds and purples and golds across the sky. Do you have the sense of the dramatic in you, Alexandra?"

She heard little of what he said, merely drinking in the words. But she registered the way he spoke her name. When she was a child, her father had always used her full name when he was displeased with her. When Fraser Mackinnon said it, the sound seemed to send white-hot flames running through her veins. How odd, Alex thought. How very, unnervingly odd . . .

"My parents always said so," she answered. She wasn't at all sure if she liked Fraser Mackinnon or not. It was too soon, yet she had always been a girl capable of instant assessments of people. This time, she was too confused to make any decision about him.

They leaned on the ship's rail, and it established a kind of intimacy between them. Together with all the other passengers crowding the deck to watch the night and the coastline and the glittering, softly rippling water below the ship's powerful lines, somehow they were alone. It was an acutely pleasurable sensation, and Alex wondered if this was one of her mother's God-given pleasures, to feel this strange awareness, almost oneness, with another person. Standing close to a young man on a gently rolling ship, the moon just rising in the night sky, beneath a canopy of stars . . . would this have Constance's blessing? It was a night filled with magic, but Alex still tried to keep her feet firmly on the ground.

"Will you tell me about India?" She couldn't quite say his name yet. She was annoyed and intrigued at the way he was practically taking her over. She didn't look at him, and she heard his short laugh before he spoke.

"Could I tell you about the universe in five seconds?" he said. "India is beautiful, barbaric, dirty, brash, incredible, fabulous and every dream you ever dreamed. Does that say anything to you?"

Alex looked at him in astonishment. "Everything! It echoes my thoughts. My parents gave me an idealized vision of India, but since then I've become more of a realist. I think I know what to expect—"

"No, you don't," he said harshly. "Don't ever think that you know India, lassie. You won't, not ever. She's an enigma. It's part of her charm, and part of her devilry."

Alex felt resentment at his tone. Superior again, she thought, as he had been on the dockside.

"You speak of her as a woman." She felt a small pique at the realization. Absurd. She hardly knew him. He meant nothing to her . . .

"Perhaps that's the way I think of her," Fraser replied. "Didn't your father speak of her in the same way?"

Yes, he did. And she had never realized it until this instant. She glared at this man, who seemed to know more about her own father than she did even though he had never met him. She didn't answer, feeling decidedly ruffled. She felt young and gauche. Fraser Mackinnon was making her feel that way, and she didn't like it one bit. The person nearest Alex jostled her and turned to apologize. Alex was glad of the interruption into this uncomfortable tête-à-tête and smiled at the woman and the two small boys clinging to her skirts.

"I'm sorry if I nudged you," the woman said. There was a military man with her, and they were both young and pleasant-faced.

"It's quite all right," Alex said quickly. The woman smiled.

"We're the Forbes family. I'm Ellen Forbes, and my husband is Captain John Forbes. These little handfuls are Edward and Victor."

"And I'm Alexandra Truscott, going to join my father near Delhi. I'm traveling with my aunt, who is temporarily unwell." She hesitated, then knew she had best go on. "This is Mr. Fraser Mackinnon."

"Mackinnon?" Captain Forbes queried. "You're attached to the 78th, aren't you? I've heard tell of you."

Alex felt a little irritated as Fraser acknowledged it, feeling that she should have known all about the man with whom she had been standing as cozily as though they had been affianced for months! So much about the man annoyed her! She knew she was being unreasonable but couldn't seem to stop it.

"How splendid!" Ellen Forbes was saying. "We go to Delhi too. I think we may have met your father, Miss Truscott. Is he tall and distinguished, with dark hair just going a little gray?"

"That's right. He's the Resident at the palace of Prince Shunimar." She couldn't help the pride in her voice. "How lovely that you know him. My aunt will be so pleased to meet you."

"Is this your first visit to India?" Ellen inquired.

"And my last, I hope. I plan to make my home there.

It's been arranged since I was a child," she nodded. She felt more relaxed by the minute. The two men were conversing quietly, the small boys delightfully certain they could see fish in every dancing wave and Alex had already made a friend. Aunt Maud had wanted her to attach herself to some nice family group, and here they were.

"Why, Fraser! Fraser Mackinnon! It is you, isn't it?"

A woman's musical voice trilled above the buzz of voices and the slow pulse of the ship's engines. A young voice, light and frothy, and its dark-haired owner was bearing down on Fraser with delight in her eyes. Behind her came an older lady, clearly her mamma, a lady with a high-bolstered bosom and carefully coiffured hair beneath her bonnet.

"Good God, Hilary! What are you doing here?" He was confident enough to be careless about his language, Alex noted.

"One could say the same to you! Oh, how tactless of me, Fraser. We heard about your father. I'm so sorry."

"Thank you," he said. He turned to the older lady. "How are you, Lady Delmont? You look very well."

"I am, dear boy, and all the better for seeing you." She spoke in a richly cultured voice. "Despite the circumstances—"

Fraser glanced at Alex. With a flash of intuition, she sensed that he was about to use her as a defense against these well-meaning friends. He wasn't ready to talk about the circumstances, whatever they were. Alex smiled politely as he introduced her to the two ladies.

"Lady Delmont and her daughter wintered in Scotland a year or so ago when I was at my family home in the Highlands," he said briefly. "We all became good friends."

It seemed obvious enough to Alex that Lady Delmont wouldn't object if her daughter and the handsome Highlander became more than friends. She felt a stab of jealousy, acute and sudden and infuriating. She was sane enough to know that since Fraser was the first young man with whom she'd come into real contact in her life, it would be easy enough to be bewitched by him. And she had no intention of becoming so!

There had been no opportunities for meeting young men at school, and she and her friends had spent much time in daydreaming and gossiping about lovers and husbands and that magical unknown world of love. Away from school, Aunt Maud had cosseted her and guarded her, and both friends and aunt had warned about the dangers of falling for the first eligible man she met.

"Surely you're not traveling alone, Miss Truscott?" Hilary's tone was faintly patronizing and incredulous, her only cursory interest in Alex shown in the lingering, envious glance she gave to Constance's beautiful pearls around Alex's neck.

The Forbes family had drifted away, and Alex flushed at the insinuation, barely hidden, that no young lady of breeding would be so rash as to travel alone. She had met plenty of Hilary Delmonts . . .

"Not at all. My aunt is resting. We go to join my father, who is in foreign administration with the East India Company—"

"Really?" Hilary was carelessly disinterested. "I hope it's nowhere near Delhi, such a miserable, stifling city. Mother and I are doing the Grand Tour this time."

In one instant, Hilary had managed to inform her that not only had she traveled extensively, but that she and her mother were certainly not dependent on the fortunes of the Company. Alex caught the amused gleam in Fraser's eye and interpreted it correctly.

35

Butterflies, it said. Despite her annoyance with the other girl, Alex almost laughed out loud.

"Does your mother not travel out to India with you, Miss Truscott?" Lady Delmont said graciously.

A surge of misery swept over Alex at the unexpected question.

"My mother is dead," she said, knowing she sounded clumsy. "She—died in India three years ago."

"I'm sorry, my dear. So! It seems we are a diverse set of passengers traveling on the *Arabella,* does it not?" Lady Delmont was adept at covering an embarrassing moment.

Alex was angry with herself for being caught unawares like that. Perhaps it was because Constance had been so much in her thoughts that day, and if she tried very hard, she could still pretend that Constance would be waiting for her in Calcutta . . . but would the sophisticated Hilary Delmont have blurted out the words so awkwardly? Alex doubted it. The young lady was smiling up into Fraser's eyes now, reminding him of the pleasures of Scotland's mountains and lochs.

"You've hardly need to remind me, lassie." He used the term that Alex found oddly endearing. "Nor to tell me you think I'm mad to leave it!"

"You'll go back one day," Hilary said breezily. "I predict it from my crystal ball!"

Fraser laughed. His earlier mood of depression had lifted, and he admitted that life could still be good. There were at least two bonnie lassies aboard the *Arabella* to make the voyage more endurable. He had come through troubled times, and he was relieved to know that his passive disinterest in the female sex had only been temporary.

He had never been a roué, nor dabbled with the pretty, doe-eyed Indian girls like some of his compatriots in the various garrisons between which his time was allocated. But he had always had a healthy male liking for the lassies, and perhaps a little light diversion on the voyage was just what he needed to revitalize himself. It need be no more than that . . .

The Delmont ladies decided to make ready for the first meal on board, and Lady Delmont told Alex she looked forward to meeting her aunt later.

"I must go too, and see how Aunt Maud is faring," Alex said when they had gone. She hesitated, and then said what was on her mind. "Mr. Mackinnon—Fraser —I don't want to make any faux pas. Your father—"

"He died four weeks ago," Fraser said in that cold, harsh voice he had used before. For a moment she bristled, until she saw the pain in his eyes and recognized it only too well. They didn't touch, yet for an instant she had the extraordinary feeling that their spirits met in a moment of mutual understanding.

"Don't tell me you're sorry. Leave that to the Hilarys of this world, lassie, who only know the surface meaning of the word," he went on, just as harshly.

"Excuse me, please," Alex said stiffly.

She didn't have to stand here and be censured by him. She didn't have to speak to him at all. She turned swiftly and moved towards the companionway, hindered by her cumbersome skirt as she climbed down, finding that her legs were quite wobbly. Perhaps that silly phrase about finding one's sea legs wasn't so silly after all. She wouldn't think that it could be for a different reason that she felt so disturbed, so uncertain and so young. For some reason, she was very aware of how young she was, when until today, meeting Fraser Mackinnon—yes, and the toffee-nosed Hilary Delmont too—she had thought herself a very grown-up young lady indeed.

On Finishing Day at Lady Margaret's, Alex had been one of the elite. She had been leader of the Alex set, far superior to the newer, younger girls. Suddenly, she felt at the other end of the scale, starting out on a life in which she was the novice, and the Hilary Delmonts, several years older, were the epitome of sophistication. She hated the feeling, and she stormed into the cabin, prickly with irritation at her own lack and hardly knowing why.

"What on earth is wrong, Alex?" Maud was gingerly admitting to herself that she felt better as she sat upright on her bunk and realized that the cabin no longer swam in front of her eyes. "Don't scowl, dear! You'll ruin your looks."

"I'm not scowling," Alex said, knowing that she was. She cleared her face with an effort. "Are you better, Aunt Maud?"

"I shall survive," Maud said dryly. "I refuse to succumb to the mal de mer any longer. I shall simply put it out of my mind."

The stalwart words made Alex smile. Her aunt looked at her sharply, seeing the flush in her cheeks.

"Tell me, love, have you met any interesting people besides the delightful Mr. Mackinnon?"

Alex made no comment on her choice of phrase. She told Maud quickly about the Forbes family and the Delmonts and said they all looked forward to meeting Aunt Maud soon.

"Did they?" she said mildly, knowing it was merely etiquette that evoked the wish. "At least I'm glad to know there is a good class of passengers aboard. It's a comfort to me."

"Oh, Aunt Maud, you can be such a snob!" Alex said teasingly.

"And dear Mr. Mackinnon is so gallant," Maud went

on relentlessly. She had clearly taken to him already. "I knew right away that he was not a rough young man, despite his odd accent."

Alex began shaking out the folds of her aunt's chosen dinner dress for the evening. She didn't want to talk about Fraser Mackinnon. She had thought him rough enough at first, when he'd grabbed her so unceremoniously at Tilbury dockside. He had been curt, his words little short of insulting.

And yet . . . and yet . . . there had been that intoxicating way he had spoken her full name. Caressingly, almost, so that it had seemed the only sound she had heard at that moment. The sound still ran through her head, lilting and evocative. She remembered the touch of his fingers curling around her wrists, masterfully and powerfully, and the memory seemed to fill her veins with molten fire, pulsing and alive. Every detail of his darkly handsome appearance was indelibly imprinted on her mind: the deeply searching eyes; the tight, strong jawline; the wide mouth . . .

Alex checked her wayward thoughts in panic, hearing her aunt begin to complain about the girl's slowing movements and trancelike stare into space. Did Aunt Maud think she wanted to feel the way she did? Alex wondered tremblingly. But probably Aunt Maud would have forgotten just how it felt . . . the foolishness, the insecurity, the rashness and the infuriating vulnerability of being seventeen . . .

Chapter Three

THE HONOURABLE EAST INDIA COMPANY'S HISTORY WENT back to 1600, when it received the royal charter for trading from Queen Elizabeth the First. The British Company gradually grew in importançe, despite French and Portuguese challenges to trading rights. The Company, known colloquially in India as John Company, now held a position of great power.

In recent years, the last few territories had been annexed by Britain, and virtually all India was now under British rule. In faraway Britain, that power was complacently believed to be absolute. In India itself, there were many pockets of discontent, not the least that of the native princes of high birth, fiercely holding on to their rights in palaces and forts against the foreign

Johnnies. Small skirmishes frequently arose, even in those strongholds with a resident British officer of the Company overlording them.

There had been three original British trading posts in India, seen to be of immense value by the Europeans. The first was Surat-Bombay. The latter city had been Portuguese territory until it became part of the marriage dowry of Catherine of Braganza. When she married Charles the Second of England, Bombay came smoothly into British hands. On the far coast of the country was Madras, and finally the great advantages of the Hooghly River and Calcutta, seen as the gateway to the northern and eastern states.

Surat-Bombay was fast established as a trading post, awaiting and holding goods from incoming ships and providing the same service of protection for Indian exports to European destinations. Such posts clearly needed strong security measures to safeguard them and their contents, and the foreigners obtained ready permission to set up their bands of armed guards.

From such small beginnings rose the mighty ruling force of the East India Company. Its own army and navy took control of the country's dealings, gradually annexing more and more states, administering law and order ruthlessly when necessary. There was now a strong military and civilian authority.

The flaw in the jewel was that members of the Company could trade privately as well as represent national interests, which often meant that the greedy and ambitious provoked bribery and corruption for personal gain. Such methods caused much of the simmering resentment in India for the foreign traders.

Coupled with this was unease in the British military at the strength of the native enlistment into John

Company's army. It had been welcomed at first, and for the Indians was often seen as a means to status and prestige, especially for those of lower caste.

In his superior's office in Delhi, fanned by an atrociously ill-working system of air-conditioning, Felix Truscott eyed the swarthy Indian assistant, jack-of-all-trades, Bahru. Felix had always disliked the man, and of late Bahru had become insolent and lazy. It disturbed Felix and should disturb his superior, Sir Peter Wallace, whom he had been summoned here to meet.

Felix had lived in India too long not to know the signs. They spoke of unrest, of a deep-rooted, often primitive desire in the Indians to be rid of their European masters. Even here in this office, where normally Sir Peter, his secretary David Gould, and this scruffian worked amicably enough together, Felix sensed the undercurrents.

In the city, it was more than that. Or else he was imagining things, Felix thought irritably. It was the God-awful heat, relentless, dust-laden, that seeped into the very bones. He felt his own resentment that his English clothes were sticky against his skin, while the dark-faced Bahru looked at ease in his loose-fitting garb.

The man irritated him unreasonably that day. He suspected Bahru of being influenced by the betel nut too. The devils chewed the mild narcotic substance rolled in a bayleaf and called it *pan,* and the evidence was in the stained red teeth and the stupid, insolent attitude it produced.

Felix strode to the office window, fingering the dampness of his collar. It had been cooler at the palace. In Delhi, the oppressiveness of walls and buildings crowded in on him. Outside, the teeming human swirl was a mixture of smells and noise and movement. The cacophony of beggars chanting to Allah; the dire intonings of the soothsayers; the tinkling of bells and shouting of merchants at their stalls; the babble of voices. The stink of bullock dung reached even here, into this so-called civilized quarter, mingling with the tang of aromatic spices and exotic perfumes and the warm, pungent smells of leather.

"For God's sake see if you can find a punkah-wallah," Felix barked out at last. "This bloody heat's enough to drive a man insane, and I'm unable to breathe. And what the devil's happened to David Gould, if Sir Peter was called out? Could neither of them be here for an appointment?"

His resentment at being called to give an account of himself spilled over to near-hatred as he met Bahru's insultingly enigmatic black eyes.

"They will return soon, Sahib. Your wishes for a punkah-boy will be attended to. Is it the honorable guest's wish that I make tea also?"

Felix knew it was undignified to let the fellow's manner rattle him so much, especially his smooth-tongued reference to the British love of tea-drinking.

"Yes, it is," Felix snapped. "It's what you're here for, isn't it?"

"To do just as the Sahib Truscott wishes." Bahru was obnoxiously precise, the *pan* making him bold, while the cloying humility of the words made a mockery of them.

"Then get out and get on with it. And get that punkah-wallah up here pretty damn quick-quick."

Felix knew how the man hated to be taunted with the pidgin English, feeling himself a step above his fellows to be working under Sir Peter Wallace. Felix saw the brief flash in Bahru's dark eyes before he silently left the room. Minutes later a young native boy scuttled in, bearing an enormous fan made of split cane, dried and whitened by the sun. The boy squatted on the floor and began the slow, rhythmic movements of the fan to make a breeze. Felix breathed more easily, knowing he was out of sorts with the world, ready to snap at anyone, and knowing he was far from the amiable man he used to be.

He had better improve his temper before Alex and Maud arrived in the new year, he thought. He hardly went to the bungalow anymore, except to check that the place wasn't overrun with natives squatting. A few trusted servants stayed on, and Felix knew he should do something about the place, but somehow he had been unable to let it go. Constance had loved it so, yet he still couldn't bear to be inside it for long because everywhere he looked he was haunted by her memory.

Of course, Alex would want to see it, to be where her mother had been so happy, and it was an appalling dilemma for Felix. He was more than content to call his Resident's quarters in Prince Shunimar's palace home, and who wouldn't!

He frowned, remembering last week's ugly happenings, the cause of his summons here today. So much bitterness beneath the outwardly serene everyday life . . . but there was no point in fretting over it anymore. He shifted his thoughts back to his daughter instead.

How the years had flown since he had dandled his pretty little Alexandra on his knee and told her of the magic of India, the tiger hunts and the elephants, the magnificence of marble palaces and stately Indian princes. And now it was nearing 1857, and she would see it all for herself. He thought of the wonders he would show her, not forgetting the cool green tiered slopes of the tea estates in the hills where he held such a major shareholding in Krubah Tea. It was far more of a shareholding than anyone in his family realized. He had invested wisely, and it had paid off.

His thoughts broke off as David Gould, his young face red and perspiring, came into the office at last, pushing a hand through his shock of fair hair until it stood on end in unruly spikes.

"My God, but there's a crush of 'em about today, Mr. Truscott, begging your pardon, sir!" he said forcefully. "Some of 'em stinking worse than armpits—"

"Thank you, David. I believe I see the picture clearly." Felix grinned, hardly needing the graphic description. Then he spoke pointedly. "I'm relieved to see someone at last. Is all this hanging about meant as a test on my nerves?"

"I'm sorry, but Sir Peter was called away. You have some tea, don't you? Can I get you some more?" the secretary said diplomatically.

"I'm awash with tea," Felix said irritably. "I just want to get this meeting done with. I've work to do."

David made no comment to the barbed words. As always, each spoke without concern for the punkah-boy. He was of low caste, doing a menial job. Only those in higher positions, the house servants or military men, deserved any real attention. It was the way things were . . . how the British had always believed them to be.

At last, Sir Peter Wallace came in, banging doors in his impatience and apologizing profusely for his absence.

"Do you have those import figures I asked you for, David?" he hollered at his secretary as he motioned Felix into his inner office and sanctum.

"Right here, Sir Peter." David was the perfect secretary, Felix reflected. In a position of authority he would be useless, but as an aide he was invaluable. He put the bulky file on Sir Peter's desk and left the two men alone. Thank God the building's air-conditioning system had juddered into somewhat efficient action by now, Felix thought feelingly. Bahru had sullenly brought in another tea trolley, and now Sir Peter looked keenly at Felix.

"Now then, Truscott, let's have it. What the devil happened at Shunimar's palace to start up the little mutiny among the savages?" He never minced words. His keen gray eyes watched Felix unblinkingly. He was gray from head to toe. Gray hair and whiskers, gray English suit, gray scratchy voice . . .

"It was hardly a mutiny, sir—"

"What else d'you call it when flaming torches are thrown over palace walls and damage done to Company property, heh? I'd call that mutiny, man!"

Felix knew this interview could be explosive and kept his own temper under control with an effort.

"It was no more than a handful of his guard, sir, convinced that Prince Shunimar would be more lenient with taxes if he wasn't answerable to the Company. We've heard it all before. It began with a petition to the prince that he ignored, and the thing flared up out of all proportion. We got them to agree to an audience and made them understand that there would be no advantage to them at all in changing the taxation laws. Nor that the Company would kow-tow to a few miserable native discontents!"

Frustration and anger showed in every line of Sir Peter's face.

"You *persuaded* them to agree to an audience? That in itself smacks of kow-towing to them, Truscott! I don't like it. Where there's one outbreak, there could be others. Any injuries?"

"None, sir." Felix clamped his lips shut. Sir Peter was a fine administrator, but dealing with people wasn't his forte. He could antagonize princes and natives alike and had done so in the past. Felix's job required a lot of tact, especially in knowing when to speak and when to be silent.

"And what do you intend to do about it?" Sir Peter demanded.

"It's already done," Felix said calmly. "It was all under control before I was summoned here. The prince and I have an excellent understanding, and there'll be no more trouble."

"For the present," Sir Peter grunted, and to that Felix had no answer. It was true that all was quiet again now. The natives were mollified by the detailed explanations about Company policy and taxation laws. There was a Company garrison in the area, but if real trouble ever erupted, Shunimar's palace was isolated and vulnerable to attack. As if he was reading Felix's thoughts, Sir Peter spoke tersely.

"I'll suggest to the military that we put more troops in the garrison nearby. Shunimar's palace would be a beautiful, dangerously situated target, if targets are what we're talking about, Felix."

They looked at each other uneasily. Military red tape took its own time, but if real trouble ever did erupt, they all of them would be vulnerable, civilian and military alike. Felix hoped to God that all the signs of unrest were in his head and that it wasn't the height of folly to bring his daughter out here at such a time.

Sir Peter leaned back in his chair and blew a fine spiral of smoke into the air from his cheroot. He smoothed back his thinning gray hair, his habit when he intended changing the conversation, and Felix inwardly smiled, knowing him so well. Sir Peter told him to pour the tea.

"We'll leave the matter for now," he said abruptly. "You've some leave coming up in the new year, haven't you, Felix? Saved some of it from this year, I understand, to meet your daughter in Calcutta."

"That's right, sir. My sister will be accompanying her."

"Ah, yes. We must arrange some entertainments and introduce them to some of the officers, what? Your daughter's of an age to be interested, I believe?" He made an effort to be sociable after the unpleasantness of chastising one of his residents. Truth to tell, he was relieved that Truscott had dealt with it all himself. Good fellow, Truscott.

"At seventeen, I imagine so, Sir Peter." It really hadn't occurred to Felix before. "I just hope she doesn't expect too much of India—"

"Nonsense. How could she?" It was clearly an impossibility to Sir Peter. "She'll be enchanted with Shunimar's palace for a start! She's fortunate to be able to see it so intimately. The prince thinks highly of you."

"One tries to cultivate friendship—"

Sir Peter missed the irony of the remark. "You never cultivated anyone, Truscott, so don't belittle yourself. Now then, if we've got our other little matter out of the way, let's get down to less traumatic Company business." The censure was obviously over, and tempers had cooled.

By the time the steamship *Arabella* had cruised around the southernmost tip of Africa and into smoother waters, the temperature had climbed dramatically. European crinolines and tight-laced undergarments were unbearably restricting, and many ladies on board were obliged to lie down in their cabins each afternoon when the sun was at its most merciless. Maud Truscott was one of them. Free now of the mal de mer, the heat made her faint, and the afternoon's rest refreshed her each day.

British complexions on the *Arabella* now were being shaded by parasols and fans. Gentlemen passengers sported the deep suntans usually attributed to southern climes and looked the healthier for it. Those like Fraser Mackinnon, already seasoned by some years in India, found the climate to their liking and thrived on it.

Fraser admitted to himself that he sought Alexandra Truscott's company. He quickly tired of Hilary Delmont's trilling voice and found it a little irksome that Alex spent so much time with the Forbes family and was so attached to the two little boys. He found her one languid afternoon, leaning on the ship's rail and hoping to catch the smallest breeze to cool her. Fraser moved swiftly to her side, not guessing how aware of him she was. The swift beat of her heart always told her of his presence, though for a few minutes she pretended not to notice him. He stood as motionless as she, breathing in the salt scents of the sea and enjoying the crystal clarity of the turquoise water.

"Why do you avoid me, Alexandra?" he said finally.

"I do not—"

"I think that you do. Did your fine school teach you to tell lies?" He had learned all about Lady Margaret's by now, and Alex felt her cheeks grow hot. He had a directness about him that matched her own. She ignored his question and turned towards him.

"If you will not tell me about India, Mr. Mackinnon, then tell me about Scotland."

He smiled. "You're very refreshing, Alexandra," he commented. "Most young women are either too reticent to ask questions or beat about the bush in idiotic simperings. But you're not one of them, are you?"

"Am I not?" She wasn't sure whether he was flirting with her or not. She had no experience in such things. She faced him properly, her elbows leaning against the rail, the taut young curves of her figure revealed in the cool yellow gown she wore with its tight-fitting waist and frilled skirt. She was innocently provocative. "What am I like then—Fraser?"

He laughed out loud, and she liked the sound. A thrill like a flame ran through her as she saw the spark of desire in his dark eyes.

"You're a little witch. A sea-witch, golden and beautiful, and well you know it, lassie!"

Her chin lifted. "Am I meant to be flattered by that?" she demanded, unsure what to believe.

"That you are," he said dryly. "You bring out the Gaelic poetry of my ancestors in me, and that's a rare thing of late. You remind me of sunlight in that pale dress, with the sun glinting through your hair."

The very words were sheer poetry, yet he spoke them in an oddly distant voice. Suddenly, his eyes seemed to focus more sharply on her, and she couldn't stop herself trembling at that look.

"Maybe one day I'll tell you of another lassie with hair like fire, who began a legend in my family," he said and immediately wondered why on earth he'd done so. The legend of Jamie and Katrina was handed down in his family and told only to a Mackinnon wife or husband for safekeeping. A careless moment had nearly made him betray something precious.

He needn't have worried, for Miss Alexandra Truscott looked a mite put out at the thought of another lassie to rival herself. Fraser smiled at the thought and changed the conversation.

50

"Anyway, if you want to know about Scotland, you must go there yourself," he went on. "Maybe you will, if India doesn't steal your heart completely. There's all the difference in the world between the two countries. Scotland's a land of mountains and beautiful glens, and the winter snow makes a fairyland of it all."

"You make it sound like Christmas. Real Christmas," Alex said, a trifle wistfully, for Christmas was almost on them now, and nothing could seem more unlikely here in the warm waters of the Indian Ocean.

It was certainly the strangest Christmas most of the passengers had ever spent. A green pine tree adorned the dining room, in the new fashion Prince Albert had brought to England. The tree was decked with baubles and tinsel and cones to look festive. By each dinner plate was a small gift provided by the ship's owners.

"And all paid for by ourselves in the extortionate fares," Aunt Maud remarked to her niece.

At Lady Margaret's, it was considered bad form to discuss money matters. In any case, Alex refrained from the comment that it was Felix Truscott who had paid theirs. Instead, she opened her packet along with everyone else. The older ladies had gifts of pretty fans. The younger ones had lace masks for the popular masquerade balls of the day. The gentlemen had necktie pins or snuffboxes. Alex fastened her black lace mask to judge the effect and smiled across the table at other passengers doing the same.

"You look quite wicked, Miss Truscott," Hilary Delmont said coolly. "It's amazing how a tiny scrap of lace transforms one."

"I must use it at the next masquerade then!" Alex wasn't sure if the girl was intimating that Alex was really a little mouse or not . . . she could never quite tell with Hilary.

"It certainly gives an air of mystery to that charming look of innocence," Fraser Mackinnon added. "My compliments, Miss Truscott."

"Thank you, Mr. Mackinnon," she answered gravely.

So formal, when the way he was looking at her made her hands shake as she removed the mask and replaced it in its wrappings. So far from her, on the other side of the table, when she longed to be close to him, away from all these people. Alex was aghast at the way Fraser Mackinnon seemed to occupy her thoughts, and even her dreams . . .

Seeing the warm color in her niece's cheeks, Maud Truscott began to feel faintly alarmed. Had she been lacking in her chaperone's duties? Maud was astute enough to read the frequent glances between her niece and the handsome young Highlander. It might amount to no more than that, but it needed thinking out.

Maud was not adequately equipped to deal with a young woman where certain matters were concerned. Her own experience had been curtailed before it had really begun, and as a spinster lady she had a natural reluctance to discuss intimate details. She had assumed that such things were part of the last social preparation year at Lady Margaret's and had thankfully left it at that.

She might have been horrified had she known of the discussions among the Alex set that went on far into the night, especially when considering the attributes of the ideal man who would be each one's destiny. Some of the girls had brothers and were worldly in telling what little they knew. Others, like Alex, had little male contact and agreed with a romantic sigh that as long as he was kind and loving and, naturally, rich, then it was all they required. Rich was the background they all knew, so it never occurred to any of them to fall in love with a pauper, until Alex's usual provocative remarks had startled them one night.

"Of course," she had whispered wickedly in the cloying atmosphere of an academy bedroom crammed with her contemporaries, "if some fabulous sheik came and snatched me away in the night and wanted to ride off with me on his white stallion and make wild, passionate love to me in a tent, then I'm sure I could be persuaded! In fact, if he looked like Prince Albert, he could be as poor as a church mouse," she finished to her own surprise.

"Alexandra, you wouldn't!" They had all shrieked with laughter at her racy words, realizing they would probably all do the same. All the Alex set were in love with Prince Albert that summer, and they were all more daring and outspoken and recklessly inclined than previous final classes. The tutors of Lady Margaret's gave a delicate sigh of relief when the Alex set left . . . yet for all that, the girls had no real knowledge of men, and their passions burned only in their imaginations.

Now Maud Truscott could almost read Alex's thoughts as she heard the announcement that there would be a masquerade dance on the eve of the new year. At a dance, a gentleman was permitted to hold a lady close. The Scots gave the odd name of Hogmanay to the new year's eve, and Maud had heard tell that they claimed a kiss from the nearest lady as the clock chimed midnight. She didn't need to be a clairvoyant to guess that Fraser Mackinnon would be near to Alex when midnight struck.

Alex, whom he had already called charming and mysterious in her lace masquerade mask, which Hilary

Delmont had said made her look wicked. For the first time in her life, Maud was in a situation in which she felt helpless. She could deal with Alex, the child, but this Alex was becoming a young woman, and growing away from her.

She tried to broach the delicate subject before the masquerade dance, but somehow the words always eluded her. She wondered in a panic how she could have missed the way Alex was maturing so quickly. She saw the soft, rounded contours as Alex paraded in the deep sapphire ball gown in readiness for the dance, saw how the fabric shimmered and rustled with every movement of her supple young body, and knew that Alex was no longer a child.

"Alex, my love, I feel I should say something to you," Maud began again diffidently, and Alex swiveled away from the mirror to face her.

The gleam of the perfect pearls around her neck pulsed a little in the cabin's light. Alex had guarded her skin from the fiercest rays of the sun, but something in her reveled and exalted in the heat on her flesh, which was now a soft, warm honey color, alluring and flattering and framed by the golden fall of curls on her bare shoulders. Any man would be intoxicated by her, Maud thought fleetingly, as she tried again to say what she felt she should.

"Oh dear, I find this so difficult, Alex. It's just that I don't want you to let the—ah—romance of the voyage go to your head in any way—"

Alex knew immediately where all this was leading.

"You mean I mustn't let Fraser Mackinnon take advantage of me, Aunt Maud, and I must be sure to walk off the *Arabella* with my—ah—innocence intact!" She couldn't resist teasing, and saw the shocked look on her aunt's face. "Oh, Aunt Maud, I'm sorry, but I'm not stupid, honestly. I won't let you down. As for Mr. Mackinnon, I thought you approved of him."

"So I do, but that's not to say—" she floundered again, and Alex gave her a quick hug.

"I promise you there's no need to worry, Aunt Maud. Besides, he takes as much interest in Miss Delmont as myself. They knew one another before this voyage, and I think Lady Delmont has earmarked him for her daughter."

She ignored her aunt's tut-tutting at her breeziness and also the pang her own words gave her. It was true that Fraser spent part of his time with the Delmonts, just as Alex spent some of hers with the Forbes family. She had no way of telling if he thought those hours they were apart as wasted as she did. Her own feelings were totally confused. If this was love, she didn't know how to deal with it . . .

"Let's just enjoy this evening, Aunt Maud," she pleaded. "A few hours from now it will be 1857, and we'll soon be reunited with Father. It's so exciting. A new year and a new beginning!"

She fastened the lace mask with a flourish and stood back for her aunt to admire her, twirling as best she could in the small cabin. Alex's eyes matched her gown in their sapphire brilliance, the black lace mask a perfect foil for her skin and hair and the soft, generous mouth. The total effect was stunning and Maud had no doubt that Fraser Mackinnon would agree with that.

"You'll do," Maud said coolly. "I'll leave the compliments to the young bucks. Remember your dance card, Alex, and don't assign all your dances to the same young man!"

* * *

As if Fraser had heard her aunt, Alex found that he didn't intend claiming every dance with her, but his name was on her card before and after midnight. The evening was sparkling and joyous, with music and wine and dancing, and just before midnight there was a fanfare on the drums. The ship's captain called for silence.

"Ladies and gentlemen, we'll begin the counting down towards 1857. The Scottish among you are at liberty to celebrate in your usual way with the clock's chimes, and those who are not Scottish should take full advantage of their custom!" he said jovially.

Everyone began to count under the captain's direction, and after the clock's chimes were heard came the loud clanging of a bell and the captain's voice bellowing out a welcome to 1857. Whatever else he said was lost to Alex as she was suddenly enveloped in Fraser Mackinnon's arms. She felt as though she melted into them, as though she had been waiting all her life for this moment, and it was all happening with exquisite slowness as she raised her face to his, her mouth soft and waiting for his kiss.

The only man she had kissed in her life before was her father, and this was so very different. She felt the rough texture of Fraser's skin against hers and the tickle of his moustache. She tasted his lips, firm, demanding, passionate. His arms held her close, curving her closer to his body. She could feel his heartbeat, and it was her heartbeat too. Her senses were alive and on fire. New sensations flowed through her like warm honey, as though this was the moment her life truly began.

They broke apart, and then other young men were exuberantly taking kisses from every pretty female

56

passenger, and Alex hated them all for breaking the spell. She saw Fraser embrace Hilary Delmont and hated her too. It wasn't until order was restored once more and Fraser had found her again to claim the next dance that her disturbing emotions relaxed a little once more. But not much . . . for now at last she knew how it felt to be falling in love. Foolishly or wisely, she was falling in love with Fraser Mackinnon. He hardly spoke during the dance, but surely his eyes spoke of love when he looked at her . . .

Alex was aware of a new panic. She burned with a fever she didn't understand, yet she was faced with a sudden, appalling truth. She didn't know how to behave with a man! All the racy, late-night whisperings at Lady Margaret's, the giggling, the certainties for the future—all vanished at once. She was an immature child again and angry to know it, for someone like Hilary Delmont would be so self-assured in this situation.

"Do you remember asking me about Scotland, Alexandra?" Fraser said quietly. He held her as close as the dance allowed, and she could feel the vibration of his voice against her breasts.

"I remember," she whispered. "You told me about the winter snow, and I thought it sounded so beautiful—"

"When I was a wee laddie, I used to soar down the snowy mountainside on a plank of wood, feeling the wind in my hair and the sting of snow on my face. It's wonderful to soar down a mountain, Alexandra. It's like going into the unknown, but feeling perfectly safe too, because at the other end there's always warmth and comfort waiting."

She looked into his face, dark and handsome and

princely-proud in the Highland attire and sensed that there was more than one meaning in his words. She felt her heart begin to pound at the look in his eyes.

"Maybe one day you'll soar with me, my lassie," he said softly.

The music stopped, and he held her hand lightly as he led her back to Aunt Maud. Their fingertips touched politely and then parted as he left the ladies with a little bow. As he moved away, all the drumbeat of India was in Alex's head, and the poetry of Fraser Mackinnon was already in her heart.

Chapter Four

By the time the *Arabella* arrived in the bustling port at Calcutta, Alex had made a firm friend in Ellen Forbes. The Forbes family was staying in Calcutta a while, but they all intended meeting again in Delhi, exchanging addresses with that in mind.

Alex hoped fervently that she would not see Miss Hilary Delmont again, and for more than one reason. She felt the familiar irritation as Hilary made her effusive good-byes to Fraser Mackinnon before they all left the ship. Alex tried to keep her face expressionless as the young lady glanced at her triumphantly when Fraser said warmly that he hoped their paths would cross whilst Hilary and her mother were in India.

But she was comforted by the fact that Fraser had already said he wished to accompany her and Aunt

Maud and Felix Truscott on the overland journey to
Delhi and remembered Aunt Maud's enthusiastic reaction. She reminded herself that Fraser and the Delmonts were old friends and that courtesy alone
demanded he should express a wish to see them again.
She admitted to herself that she hoped fervently that
was all it was.

But now that the ship had finally docked, she was
longing to see her father, and her eyes strained against
the bright sunlight. It almost scalded her eyes as she
scanned the milling crowds awaiting the passengers. It
was early February by now and the cooler part of the
year, yet dramatically hotter and more humid than the
English climate. She was jostled on all sides by the
crush of people, felt a moment's panic, and then Aunt
Maud was gripping her arm.

"I see your father, Alex!" she said excitedly. "There,
look—he's waving to us—"

Alex craned her neck, and then Fraser's voice
sounded close to her. He could see the gray-haired man
standing head and shoulders above those nearest him,
as Maud waved furiously.

"Stay where you are, ladies, and I'll make my way to
him and bring him nearer. Your baggage will be waiting
for collection, so once you're safely reunited with Mr.
Truscott, I'll away and organize it with a carrier."

"We're so grateful, Mr. Mackinnon." Aunt Maud's
voice was lost in the crowd as Fraser moved away from
them. Alex felt like a small fish in a vast ocean as the
bodies pressed in on her from all sides, stifling the
breath out of her.

There were skins of all colors, but the caste marks
Alex had expected to see on Indian foreheads were
missing, since it was now forbidden by the British
authority to make such distinctions, another source of

disquiet. Women's brilliant saris vied with loose, white male garments, wide-skirted European dresses and the garb of gentlemen and military men, a fair sprinkling of which were the colorful Scots tartans.

Within minutes, the two men were back with the ladies, Fraser to turn away immediately to attend to the baggage, Felix to clasp his lovely daughter in his arms and feel a surge of love that had been missing in his life for too long. It was as though with Alex's presence here at last, some of the missing pieces of his life were knit together again, and the sweet ghost of Constance was calmed once more.

"Oh, Father, it's so good to see you!" Alex's voice was thick with tears as she too thought of Constance. This was the day she had dreamed about. She hugged Felix close to her, aware of the slight tremble in his strong arms and of her own emotion. They held each other tightly, and then it was Maud's turn to be embraced, both women laughing and crying a little and feeling the poignancy of this meeting.

Alex realized that Fraser Mackinnon had returned to their small group and was watching the reunion. She wanted to draw him in, to make him part of it, remembering that he must be feeling his own loss now, since hearing of her own story. They had both lost someone dear to them. It was another link between them. She gave him a watery smile and stretched out her hand to him.

"Please join us, Fraser," she said huskily. "I want to introduce you to my father properly."

She watched as the two men shook hands with British formality. She spoke with a breathlessness that told its own tale to her father and her aunt.

"Mr. Mackinnon has been so kind to us, Father, and he travels to Delhi as well."

"Then I'm sure we would all be glad of his company on the appalling train journey we have to make before we hire a carriage for the remainder of the route," Felix said briskly in his forthright manner. "I can't promise you much comfort until we reach Prince Shunimar's palace, my love, but I've no doubt Mr. Mackinnon's presence will help to pass the time more congenially, unless you have other plans, sir?"

Alex held her breath. She couldn't bear it if Fraser was to walk out of her life so soon. As though he read her thoughts, she saw the little quirk of a smile on his mouth. He didn't look at her, but she knew his first words were directed at her.

"I would be delighted to accompany you, Mr. Truscott. I feel as though I know you already and will be interested to hear of any political developments in the several months I have been away." He tried to keep the significance out of his voice, but he saw Felix Truscott give a little nod and knew that such talk was for male ears alone.

He too had wondered about the wisdom of Alex's coming here at a time when there was a restlessness in the country that was almost tangible. Was it wise for ladies like the Delmonts to be doing the Grand Tour? But if one listened to every whisper on the wind, one would never move from one's own fireside, and the British had never been a race to turn tail at the first hint of danger. And if Alex hadn't come to India on this particular voyage, they might never have met.

He preferred to stop listening to reason at that point. He had stopped several weeks ago, if the truth were told, and begun listening to his heart instead. It was as though the ice there had melted with every warm, innocent glance from those beautiful eyes of Alexandra

Truscott. He had known women before but never one who had occupied so much of his mind, as though she was always destined to fill a place there, to be a part of him.

Fraser was acknowledged to be a brilliant scout, a canny Scot with a quick brain and the ability to assess a situation quickly. Why should he deny that what he felt for this young woman with the oddly haughty air that belied the passion in her nature was love?

His eyes spoke of love whenever he watched her unconsciously sensual movements. He wanted to possess her as he had never wanted anything in his life before, and yet he was prepared to go slowly, to let the flower unfold in the sun, knowing instinctively that she was still as virginal as a newborn bairn. He wanted her love, but he wanted it to be given freely . . . and if nothing else told Fraser Mackinnon that he truly loved a woman for the first time in his life, it was that feeling, that need to cherish.

In the cold hours of the early morning, he could laugh at himself incredulously for thinking like a lovesick fool, a mere boy, when he was filled with all a man's longings for his woman, his lassie. But he only had to see her, to breathe in her sweet scent, to touch her soft skin, to know that he would never harm her, never rush her, and it was a strangely humbling knowledge for a man who was a man in every sense of the word.

That they were destined to be together he somehow never doubted. No more did she. There were some things in life that made mere words superfluous.

The Indian carrier had reached their side with all their baggage piled high on a handcart.

"You'll walk ahead of us until we reach the railway

station," Felix told him curtly. He spoke to his daughter and sister as Alex's eyebrows rose in some surprise at his tone.

"They're just as likely to scuttle off with the baggage and sell it at some street bazaar," he said, uncaring that the boy could hear all he said. "They have to be watched all the time. Some of them think of the British as being just rich pickings, and most of 'em resent the railways. They prefer the stinking bullock carts to civilized transport, but I daresay this wallah will help us push our way through."

Her father had changed, Alex thought immediately. His attitude was that of brash British official, imperious towards the natives . . . or perhaps he had always been that way, she thought with a little shock. How little she knew of him when she thought about it. Twice-yearly visits home to England with Constance over the years, in the carefree days, even fewer in recent years . . .

Those early visits had been filled with excitement, with dreams, with the delicately painted views of a land burnished with life and gaiety and princes and palaces . . .

There was a small commotion in the crowds moving away from the dockside as a group of young Indian carriers fought to get control of some baggage for their handcarts. Their faces were ugly, the small screams from the British ladies standing nearby totally ignored until order was restored by some officers. Alex was suddenly aware of the smells, the hovering cloud of flies, the taste of dust, the pungent scent of the waterside and of garbage flung from the sides of ships and left to float in a scummy swell alongside, trapped by the bulk of each ship.

"Can we get away from this place?" she muttered. "I can hardly breathe—"

"You echo my thoughts exactly, Alex, dear." Aunt Maud was already holding a lace handkerchief to her nose. "Do we board the train directly, Felix?"

Her brother grimaced, his still-handsome face more set in the furrows of middle age than of old.

"We do, if any trains in this God-awful hole can be said to go directly," he said tersely. "They leave when the spirit moves them, and God help us if we're in any particular hurry."

He gave his arm to his sister, who clutched it gratefully, and Alex felt her hand tightly gripped in Fraser's as they moved in a body behind the baggage carrier, weaving his way in and out of the crowds with surprising speed. Alex's thoughts were mixed. To get to Delhi in a hurry would mean parting company with Fraser Mackinnon, yet this teeming mass of humanity and the dross that usually hung about any waterfront was far from palatable.

"Stay close to me." She heard Fraser's rich burr next to her ear. "Some of the devils can smell money a mile off, but the beggars usually steer clear of the military. Most of them assume that a Scots kilt means a soldier anyway, so just keep looking straight ahead, Alex."

She thought he had been mildly blaspheming, but once away from the dockside she saw that the beggars were real. She tried to do as he said, looking straight ahead, but she could hardly avoid seeing the dregs of humanity lining the streets, begging bowls stretched out in skeleton-thin hands, their combined whining an appallingly heartrending sound.

Thankfully, a vehicle was soon at their disposal to take them the rest of the distance to the station, the carrier keeping closely in front as instructed so that Felix could watch him at all times.

Maud glanced back at her niece and saw her pale

face. Wasn't this just what she had always predicted? she thought savagely. Neither Constance nor Felix had prepared the girl for any of this, and she was being plunged into it without warning. And without her mother here to soften the shock.

Though, she had to admit, the presence of Fraser Mackinnon seemed more than enough for Alex in any circumstances. She didn't miss the way their hands clung together when there was no further need for it, and it would have been more seemly now for Alex to sit demurely by the young man's side.

Obviously, it was the done thing to ignore the beggars. She trusted her father and Fraser, who had seen it all before, and if this was the way to behave, then she would blot the sights and the sounds out of her mind.

But her fingers had curled more tightly around Fraser's as they had hurried along in the gigantic movement of humanity from the docks. She had been aware of being pressed close to his side, of the protective way he pulled her to him whenever she was in danger of being crushed by any unsavory character. She had glanced up into his face, and he had leaned towards her.

"I must see you again, Alex," he'd said, so quietly that only she could hear. "I can't let you out of my life now that I've found you."

Her breath caught. He had said the words she longed to hear. They sang in her blood. He wondered if she had any idea of how transparent her feelings were as she looked up at him. He felt a sudden, savage need to keep her safe, as though that need were imminent.

"We still have some time together," she'd said shyly. "Father says it will take more than three weeks to reach Delhi. We'd be glad of your company, Fraser. Aunt

Maud and I are truly two innocents abroad. I realize it more with every step—"

" 'Tis not your father I'm wanting to see, lassie, nor your stalwart aunt! But clearly 'tis your father I'll need to win over if I'm to be calling on you."

She betrayed her joy in the glow of her smile and the sudden flush that warmed her cheeks.

"Will your duties permit your calling on me?" she asked, sensing that he would move heaven and earth to ensure that they did. The knowledge intoxicated her, despite the fact that Aunt Maud seemed to be frowning at her from time to time.

"Be sure that they will," he smiled back. "As long as I have your father's permission."

You have mine, Alex thought passionately. *After these weeks together, every minute we're apart will seem like a year from now on . . .*

The words throbbed in her head until she almost thought she had said them aloud, and the hard pressure of Fraser's hands on hers was like an unspoken confirmation that their feelings were identical. It was a heady, spectacular avowal of love.

The train journey was every bit as bad as Maud suspected it would be. It was a crush of people, cross, hot, thankful to be away from Calcutta and into the interior of the country, some to be going to the cool of the hills, where Felix Truscott promised his womenfolk he would take them soon to visit the Krubah Tea estate, his pride and joy, and his sanctuary when things got too hot in the city.

"Father has an interest in Krubah Tea, Fraser," Alex told him as the train rattled along, stopping frequently, only to start up again with a jerk and throw people against one another, a sensation not entirely unpleasant to some. At least Aunt Maud could hardly complain when it was the train's erratic movements that allowed Fraser Mackinnon's arms to steady her niece! And it was a delight that both participants didn't deny.

"Really? I understand they can be a magnificent sight," he commented.

"You're right, my boy," Felix said with satisfaction. "And preferable to the stink of the city. The tiered slopes of gray-green bushes are soothing to the eyes after so much red stonework and garish attire and the endless animals roaming the streets. Even the splendors of a prince's palace can become tiring after a while, and one longs for the green of old England."

Alex turned the conversation back to a more useful direction. She spoke directly to Fraser.

"You mean you've lived in India all this time and never seen a tea estate?"

"There's never been the opportunity," he said. "It's not something you can just do without an invitation!"

Oh, but he was wonderful! He knew exactly the right thing to say! Alex could hardly contain her smiles as her father said at once that it would be his pleasure to have Fraser accompany them to the Krubah Tea estate and that he hoped they could all spend a few days there.

"A part of the house is always put at my disposal when I want to take guests," he said. "I rarely do these days, but you must come with us, Mackinnon. A party is always more interesting and makes the traveling safer. We will arrange it, if you're interested. And since you have been so kind to my ladies, perhaps you would care to come for tea at the Residency very soon?"

"I would like it very much, sir," Fraser said with such alacrity that Maud said dryly that she didn't doubt that for a minute. Alex laughed.

"Don't be so stuffy, Aunt Maud! It was you who kept telling me what a gentleman Fraser was, don't you remember? You were the one who was charmed by him, even before we left England! I thought you'd be pleased that we're not to lose contact with him," Alex said mischievously. Her aunt gave a mild snort. She looked keenly at her niece and said what was on her mind, regardless of the swaying train carriage and the interested glances of fellow passengers. Her voice was brusque.

"I'm well aware of Mr. Mackinnon's good points, my love, and I just hope you remember that you're a well-educated young English lady, and don't let your fascination with India go to your head!"

Fascination with Fraser Mackinnon was what she meant, and Alex was well aware of it as she was jolted against him in yet another impromptu train halt. Her hands went involuntarily against his chest, and suddenly she was conscious of his heartbeats, vibrant beneath her fingers.

His arms had closed around her to steady her, his face unavoidably touching hers, the texture of it rough against her, making her soft skin tingle. For no more than a few seconds she was imprisoned in his arms, held captive by him, warmed by him, and the maleness of him was suddenly very real to her.

The contact was brief, etiquette forcing them to break swiftly apart, but enough to make Alex realize that she ached to stay in his arms. She wanted him to hold her, his hands to caress her, his mouth to possess hers. She wanted to know him as a lover . . . the words that no well-bred Victorian girl should even think were in her head before she could deny them.

Alex breathed more quickly, as sensations new to her

swept through her like a flame, flickering and burning, exquisitely powerful and pleasurable, stunning her senses, as though they would envelop her.

She moved quickly away from him, almost afraid to look at him lest he read everything there was to know in her face.

And oh, Aunt Maud, this was so much more than just fascination . . .

She was wildly, headlong in love with Fraser Mackinnon. She was seventeen and a novice at love . . . but never more sure of anything in her life than that this was her one love, her only love . . .

In many ways, the three weeks of traveling between Calcutta and Delhi were long and tedious. In others, it was a frustration and a delight. There were still days to share with Fraser until they would inevitably have to part, he to return to the 78th Highland Regiment in the garrison outside Delhi, she to begin life in Prince Shunimar's beautiful palace to the south, in her father's Residency quarters.

The hotels in which they stayed en route were the best available but hardly up to British standards. Aunt Maud constantly complained, until Felix barked at her that if she was determined to be so tetchy, then it was a pity she hadn't stayed at home.

Despite the fact that their last hotel was the best so far, Aunt Maud retired to bed in a huff on the final night of their journey, while the other three took an evening stroll in the safety of the grounds. The scent of flowers was heavy on the air, the brilliant colors of the peacocks startling as they strutted about displaying their feathers and uttering their strange, piercing cries, adding to the exotic unfamiliarity of the scene.

The twilight was every bit as beautiful as Fraser had once told Alex. The daylight seemed to hover for final moments in a glory of color across the sky—reds, golds, purples—until everything merged into the softness of night beneath a canopy of deep blue velvet. It was always throat-catching in its beauty, and never more so than when shared by lovers.

As though aware of the tension between the two young people, Felix Truscott concluded his guarded conversation with Fraser concerning the instability of the native guards at Prince Shunimar's palace and the feeling of unrest generated by pockets of violence that flared into life in various cities and towns from time to time.

Because of Alex's presence tonight, he had toned down the general anxiety felt everywhere of late. He and Constance had always sought to shelter their daughter from the realities of life. All the same, ever since the moment of meeting her at Calcutta, he had realized she was no longer a child but a woman. He had felt a sudden shock to see how mature and how lovely she had become. She was so like Constance . . . even seeing Constance's beautiful pearls lying so lustrously around Alex's throat had twisted his heart . . .

He needed to be alone with his thoughts, and even on so brief an acquaintance with the young Scot, he felt instinctively that he could trust Fraser Mackinnon.

Felix was abrupt. "I'm in need of my sleep. May I leave my daughter in your care, Mackinnon, and bid you both good-night?"

"You'll never leave her in safer hands, sir," Fraser said gravely.

Alex leaned towards her father and kissed him with great warmth.

"Good-night, Father. And thank you for—for giving me India!" She spoke self-consciously, but she knew he understood.

They watched his retreating figure until the shadows swallowed him up. They stood closely together in the scented garden, the English-style arbors giving them seclusion.

"Strange words," Fraser said at last. She looked up at him, seeing him almost in silhouette as the darkness deepened, but knowing already every line and plane of his face.

"Perhaps they are," she said. "But I can't think how else to thank him for making a dream come true. This was always my dream, Fraser—"

She spread her arms, as though to encompass the world.

"Despite all that you've seen so far? It hasn't always been pleasant, or even too sanitary—"

She gave a soft laugh. "Don't deny that you love it too! I haven't forgotten how you described India to me on the ship. You said it was beautiful, barbaric, dirty, brash, incredible, fabulous, and every dream you ever dreamed. I couldn't believe how sensitive you were to what I've always believed. You spoke as though you were inside my head, thinking my thoughts, sharing my dreams—"

One moment they were a heartbeat apart; the next she was crushed in his arms, as though he could no longer bear to have even the smallest breeze between them. She swayed against him, unable to protest, pushing aside every convention, needing his touch, needing him. Her face lifted, waiting for his kiss, to feel again that surge of pleasure that was so wondrous to her.

He spoke against her mouth long after that first touch, his lips moving softly against hers, sending shivers of desire through her. She recognized them, acknowledged them, and was no longer afraid or shocked by them. Leaping from childhood to womanhood in the exalted realization that passion was not only part of a man's world, that desire could be fanned into a flame just as easily for a woman . . .

"I think I loved you from the first moment I saw you, my sweet lassie," Fraser said gently. "Maybe I didn't recognize it as love just then, for you were more of an irritant beneath my skin! But 'twas love all the same, and it grows more with every passing day. Will you tell me you feel the same?"

She spoke with a breathless quality. "Do I need to tell you, Fraser? Don't you know it? You must know it! I feel as if the whole world must know it—"

He tipped her chin up to his with his finger, tracing the curve of it and sliding his hand down her slender white throat to feel the pulse beating wildly there. He could feel the tautness of her firm young breasts, the peaked nipples telling him of her awakening sexuality. Passion and tenderness burned in him.

"I know it, my sweet Alex, but I ache to hear you say it. Don't ever be afraid to say the words, my dear one. 'Tis the most beautiful phrase in the world for a man and a woman to share."

The poetry of his Highland ancestors enchanted her as his voice seduced her. She whispered the words she had never used in her life before.

"I love you, Fraser. I love you. I love you—"

He folded her in his arms.

"God, I want to hold you like this forever," he said, suddenly harsh. "I don't ever want to let you go back to that virginal room that's banned to me. I want to be with you all night long, to breathe every breath you take, to share every dream you dream."

"Fraser—" Alex said faintly, realizing that here was a situation as unnerving as it was exhilarating. She was on the brink of something new and wonderful, and she was suddenly afraid. She despised herself for being so, when her free spirit yearned for adventure, for the love of a passionate man . . . and yet there was still enough of a Lady Margaret's Academy young lady in her to make her halt the surge of passion flowing between them before it was too late.

She heard Fraser give a soft, rueful laugh that held a hint of desperation in it. His kiss on her lips was less intense, his embrace a little less possessive. She could feel the restraint in him and knew that, until these moments, she hadn't been fully aware of the effect of a woman on a man. Her education had been far from complete after all.

"Have no fear, my sweet lassie. I would never force you to do anything against your will, and if my tongue runs away wi' me at times, betraying all that I feel, then 'tis no more than my wild ancestry asserting itself. The Highlanders were ever a passionate race, but Alex, 'tis more than I can bear to see you every day and not touch you—"

"Perhaps it's as well that this is the last time we'll be in constant company then!" she began to tease, and then the words were numbed on her lips, for to be separated from him was the last thing on earth that she wanted.

"We may be apart from necessity," Fraser said gravely. "But you'll stay in my heart, dearest one."

"And you'll stay in mine," she said, in a rush. "I'm—I'm sorry I seemed so foolish just now—"

74

He spoke softly against her mouth. "Don't be sorry. Your reaction told me a great deal about you, my love, and this was not the time for us, that's all."

She gave a small shiver, as though a goose had walked over her grave. Time had no meaning for her when she and Fraser were together, but there were conventions to follow, and a proper courting time . . . if, indeed, that was what he intended . . .

As if he read her mind, he pulled her close again for an instant, the rich timbre of his voice like music to her senses.

"I will speak to your father soon, if you agree to it, Alex. He may think this no more than a shipboard romance, so it may be prudent to wait a month or two before we make our intentions known. Or do I assume too much?" He broke slightly away from her, looking down into her flushed and lovely face, made even more beautiful by moonlight. She could feel his heartbeats, swift and erratic, matching her own.

"Alexandra." Her very name on his lips was a sweet seduction. "You are going to be my wife, aren't you?"

Chapter Five

ALEX LAY SLEEPLESS LONG INTO THE NIGHT IN THE STUFFY heat of the hotel bedroom. How could she sleep? She and Fraser Mackinnon shared a dream, a secret that was theirs alone, and the reality of love was more spectacular than all her wildest imaginings.

She loved him. More than life itself, she loved him . . . and he loved her in return. Life was so beautiful, and it was even more beautiful that it had all happened here in India, where destiny had always intended her to be.

"If only you could see him and know him, Mother," she whispered to the bright square of moonlight outside her window. "I know you would love him too."

Her one regret was that Constance couldn't know and share her daughter's happiness. Her mother's remembered words rushed into her head as they had done once before, enveloping her with their perception: "If I have one wish to bestow on a daughter, it would be that all her senses are alive to every God-given pleasure on this earth."

Alex knew now that there were more earthly pleasures that she had yet to experience. Many more, that Fraser would show her. . . . She felt the sweet, shivering tingles run through her, remembering the hardness of his body against hers and the way her own body had pulsated in response.

The next time she would not behave so immaturely. Her heart soared, knowing there would be a next time, and a next . . .

Had there ever been a time when she didn't love Fraser Mackinnon? The lovely, drifting thoughts spun in and out of her head. It seemed as though she had always loved him, and she marveled that out of all the people in all the world, their lives had been thrown together on this sea voyage to India. Theirs was truly a destiny of dreams . . .

At last she slept, enveloped in the knowledge that she was loved and wanted . . . and the physical needs of her young, responsive body that was so ready for love knew fulfillment in sensual sleeping fantasies that were the promise of reality.

In her sleeping state, she floated into Fraser's arms as uninhibitedly as an innocent child, but there was nothing of the child in his sweet arousal of her, nor in her erotic responses. All that she couldn't wakingly express through her lack of experience became an instinctive flowering of love between them in her dreams, culminating in a release of passion so intense and explosive that Alex awoke with a start, finding herself damp with perspiration and in a wild tangle of bedclothes.

"Fraser, my love—" Weakly, she breathed his name. The dream had been so real, his tenderness and passion so perfectly attuned to her needs, that she knew she would trust him to the ends of the earth. When the time was right for them . . .

Next morning, Aunt Maud fussed about, ensuring that Alex had packed every last thing in her baggage for the final stage of their journey to the Residency at Prince Shunimar's palace. Never having set eyes on a royal personage before, nor certain of how to behave in such circumstances, Maud was nervous, and when she was nervous she got a headache and became a cross-patch.

Although the euphoria of the previous night still lingered in Alex's mind, she couldn't forget that soon she and Fraser would have to part company, and the thought was enough to fill her with misery.

Fraser himself seemed preoccupied with organizing their departure—and with the sudden, careful attention to keeping his and Alex's association apparently platonic.

Her father was openly irritable, arguing with the hotel owner on his exorbitant charges and refusing to pay for food that was cold and served without due courtesy to British guests. He cared nothing for the fact that the staff muttered behind his back and wished the John Company man to purgatory and back.

The truth was, Felix was none too keen on having his ordered life disrupted by the presence of two English ladies, however adored, and it was only now, when they had neared the end of their journey, that he realized how it was going to change.

While Constance had been alive, it had been their cherished wish to bring their daughter out to India to share their lives. But with Constance's death, everything had changed, including Felix himself. He was no longer the tolerant man he had once been, and the thought of trailing around with two women on their sight-seeing excursions and shopping expeditions was almost more than he could bear to contemplate.

His gaze followed the handsome Highlander, Fraser Mackinnon, overseeing the baggage into the carriage taking them to the Residency. Constance would have been charmed by the man. She had always taken a fancy to the colorful Scots officers with their bright tartans and their willingness to act the gallants with the ladies, gracing any social occasion.

He would need to sound the man out, of course. Maybe this Mackinnon wouldn't want to act the nursemaid to his daughter and sister . . . but if the man were willing, then strings could be pulled.

Mackinnon wouldn't want to feel emasculated by leaving a man's job to escort two women about, but maybe he could be relieved of his duties for long spells when requested. There was no war brewing at present, and a scout was not of the utmost necessity . . .

Felix ignored all the warning signs of unrest that had soured his own mood lately, the summonses to his superior's office that had become more frequent of late, the discussions and arguments with Prince Shunimar, who, although personally loyal to the East India Company, was fully aware of his own guards, whose allegiance could swing away from him in a moment should trouble flare up again.

They all seemed to live on a knife-edge of disquiet lately. Even the Indian devils had begun laying down their own laws, some refusing to cross the sea when required for military service, because to cross the sea meant to lose caste. Contrary swine, Felix thought savagely, and strove to push them out of his mind, thinking for once of more personal matters.

The solution was obvious. His sister was taken with the Scot, and as for Alex . . . he had wondered briefly if she was becoming enamored of the man, and if he should say something. It was one of those times he missed Constance's female presence most acutely. Constance would know what to say, what to do. He wouldn't want to put his daughter at risk of having her heart broken by a rogue.

Somehow he couldn't think of Mackinnon in those terms. And certainly today, as the last carriage ride began, the two of them conducted themselves very properly. One might almost say, with studied indifference. Felix made up his mind.

"Perhaps you would like to call on us next Sunday afternoon, Mackinnon," he grunted as the carriage jolted along the dirt roads, the usual cluster of flies hovering ahead of them like a dark cloud. "I may have business at your base garrison a few days prior to it, and if so, we may have a word or two then. If not, can we say that you'll join us for tea on Sunday?"

"It will be my pleasure, sir," he answered, as politely as though he were going to a vicarage garden party.

Maud forced her stiff face into a smile, although the appalling ride jarred her head alarmingly.

"We shall all look forward to seeing you, Mr. Mackinnon. I confess that a familiar face will be very welcome."

Alex said nothing, keeping her gaze on the dusty road and trying not to betray how her heart leapt joyously at her father's words. Let the others discuss it. As long as she and Fraser knew how important this was to them both, it was enough, and both avoided glances that might be interpreted correctly.

The carriage took them through wild country where animals roamed freely and the brilliant plumage of birds flashed and darted in the trees. The peacock was India's national bird, and already it was a familiar sight to the English ladies.

They went through poor villages where indescribable hovels housed entire families of doe-eyed Indian children, running behind the carriage and begging for rupees. They skirted wide, flooded rivers and trickling streams. Holy men squatted enigmatically by the roadside wherever they went, often as motionless as statues. The periodic call to worship from distant mosques seemed to drift across the countryside like some eerie, wailing plea, unnerving, foreign to their ears.

As the afternoon grew late, Felix pointed out the glimmer and gleam of minarets and domes a long distance ahead of them. In the dazzling sunlight, the city of Delhi glowed like a huge golden orb, and Alex felt a tug at her heart. At last she would see so many of the places her parents had known so intimately. The drawings that Constance had so lovingly sent to her would come stunningly to life in all dimensions.

"We don't travel as far as Delhi, of course," Felix said abruptly, as though his thoughts followed hers. "Shunimar's territory is to the south of the city. I take it that you'll continue in the carriage to your base garrison, Mackinnon?"

Fraser nodded. This terrain was as familiar to him as it was to Truscott, and thankfully not so stiflingly hot as Calcutta. He had seen it all before, and yet there was something about Delhi's ethereal quality in the sunlight that never became commonplace to the eye. The entire city seemed brushed by the hand of some giant artist, as though to gild it especially for the benefit of visitors seeing it from a distance. It was a burnished city in a burnished land. And now he was seeing it through Alex's eyes, as she exclaimed with wonder at the vast panorama unfolding in front of her.

He wished selfishly that they were sharing it alone, that her father and aunt would vanish in the air and that there were only the two of them in this wonderland. Such thoughts were almost blasphemous, and he as instantly wished them away.

"But we shall see you on Sunday," Alex said, unable to resist saying the words out loud.

It made them real. It would bring him close for the few days until she saw him again. They hadn't been apart for one day since that fateful meeting at Tilbury docks in London, she realized with a little shock. Their lives had been bound together from that moment. No wonder she felt bereft at their parting. But Sunday would inevitably come . . .

Her sadness at leaving Fraser was tempered by her growing excitement as the carriage swung slightly eastwards. In less than half an hour, Felix was pointing out another mass of buildings on the horizon that grew and took shape as they neared them and became the elegant walled palace of His Highness Prince Shunimar, the palace known as the Pearl of the Plain.

As they traveled nearer, through village and hamlet, the domestic animals of the dark-skinned people roamed freely where they would, causing the carriage to make frequent stops.

"Damn nuisances," Felix swore loudly. "They treat them like gods, cows and bullocks and every damn four-legged beast in creation, let alone the screeching peacocks! It's a pity they don't pay more attention to their own needs. They'd let their children starve rather than slaughter a cow, if you ever heard anything so idiotic!"

"You can't be serious, Felix!" Maud protested, seeing the pathetically thin children scampering alongside the carriage, hands clawing out for gifts in a way that was becoming all too familiar and somehow disgusting.

Felix snorted. "When you've been in India as long as I have, you'll believe anything of the dark devils, Maud."

It was all a very different picture from the one he and Constance had painted for Alex over the years, Maud thought. She had always guessed it would be so, but what she hadn't expected was to be thrust into the midst of it! The whole country smelled. It was dirty and squalid and every bit as bad as she had anticipated. She wondered just how disillusioned her niece was feeling right now.

Glancing at her, Maud was affronted that Alex seemed to notice nothing of the wretchedness of this endless, bonebreaking journey. Nor of the heat, which was making Maud suffer appallingly. Nor of any of the small discomforts in being away from home. Of course, Alex was too taken up with young Fraser Mackinnon to notice much else as yet!

Maud wasn't as blind as they seemed to think she was, and privately she thought it wasn't a bad thing that the two of them should be separated very soon. If anything serious was to develop between them, then they should be given the opportunity to conduct a proper courtship.

In England, that meant meeting at decent intervals, little tête-à-têtes that were supervised, at least until the couple were officially affianced and given time to get to know one another. Maud, for one, didn't trust an attachment that grew quickly because of two people being thrown together by circumstances. It rarely lasted.

And just because they were far from home, Maud saw no reason for her niece to behave in any way less English. Indeed, the British in India should wave the flag at all times, bring some culture to the savages and instill civilized behavior into the minds of these—these—

They had arrived at the red sandstone wall of the palace. Beyond it, the bastions rose towards the heavens, majestic and beautiful, pink-hued against a cloudless sky. A warm and gentle breeze filled the air with the scent of blossoms, in stark contrast to the mingled smells of cow-dung and worse that had assaulted Maud's nostrils. It came from behind the high wall, as though a different world lay beyond it, and she prayed fervently that it was so.

Felix called for the driver to halt the carriage at the enormous wooden gates set in the wall. He and Fraser got down stiffly, and as Felix pulled on a long rope, a bell jangled, and a small opening appeared, revealing a dark face. Felix barked his name at the man and stood back.

"The chowkidars—sentries—take their orders seriously," he commented to Fraser. "We all alight here, and my own carriage will take us the rest of the way. I'll give orders that you are to be admitted whenever you give your name, Mackinnon, and we shall look forward to seeing you again on Sunday, about three o'clock. But as I said, our paths may well cross again before then."

He and Fraser helped the ladies down. The driver sat immobile all the while and then scurried around lifting baggage. He was forbidden to enter the gates, and it was one of the chowkidars who carried the baggage through to Felix's carriage.

It was all like a dream, Maud thought. Her brother was treated almost as a prince himself. She could see the landscaped gardens of the palace, and her unsettled nerves began to relax a little. At least there was some civilization here, despite the appearance of the many strutting peacocks that her brother seemed to despise and which both she and Alex found so beautiful.

The baggage was all loaded onto the other carriage, and there was no more need to delay. Alex looked at Fraser, wishing desperately that she dared to throw her arms around his neck and say good-bye properly. Or better still, that she needn't say good-bye at all, ever . . .

She felt him take her hand in a formal handshake and knew that she must go through the proprieties.

"I thank you for your company, Miss Truscott, which has made my return to India less harrowing than I had expected," he told her gravely. She inclined her head a little, remembering his recent bereavement.

"I am glad my idle chatter diverted you a little, Mr. Mackinnon."

Once again they were so polite, so formal, when to both of them it seemed as if the very air between them must shout of their love. Fraser turned away to say good-bye to Maud and Felix Truscott, as if he couldn't bear to prolong the moments. Within minutes, he was back inside the carriage, and it was disappearing away from the rest of them in a cloud of dust.

The sense of loss Alex felt was sharp and instant. He had been gone no more than a second, and yet he might have been gone from her for a year. The anguish was the same.

"Let's get inside our quarters," her father was saying

testily, hurrying them into his carriage and calling for the driver to move on at once. "You'll want to see your rooms and have a rest, I daresay, and I'll have business to attend to. A man in my position can't be away for two weeks without troubles piling up in his absence, and I'm sure to be needed to sort them out. Besides that, we have an audience with Prince Shunimar after dinner this evening."

His words threw the two of them into a panic at once. An audience sounded so frightfully formal.

"We're not to join him for dinner then?" Maud said thankfully, sure she would be unable to eat a thing in a royal presence. Her brother laughed harshly.

"Good God, no! The man's a prince, Maud. He may not be a Victoria or a George, but he's still a royal and doesn't dine with ordinary folk. He'll take tidbits and wine with them when he entertains at a ball, and a banquet is naturally a different matter, but his daily meals are taken strictly alone. Even if he chose to do otherwise, his astrologers have forbidden it."

Now it was Alex who looked at her father in astonishment. She had been charmed by the lovely grounds of the palace, the fountains and waterfalls, the serenity of formal flower beds, the impressive statues and white trellis-work arbors around which entwined strange, vividly exotic blooms. She had been content to let her father and her aunt bicker mildly as they often did, until her father's last remark.

"You mean Prince Shunimar consults astrologers?"

At Lady Margaret's Academy, such persons had been spoken of in whispers as being not quite trustworthy, charlatans or frauds. To hear that Prince Shunimar was forbidden in his actions by them, and obeyed their instructions implicitly, was startling to say the least!

Felix glanced at her half-smiling face.

"You'll find many things different here from what you knew in England, my dear. Everyone consults his astrologer, and many a man won't begin the day until he knows what the stars foretell."

"But that's pagan!" she exclaimed.

"It's India," Felix said dryly.

The carriage drew up beneath the canopied stables, where several loose-garbed servants appeared at once, to stand silently while the visitors dismounted. Maud's legs felt as wobbly as when she had first embarked on the sea voyage, and she longed for a bath and a sleep, presuming that there would be civilized arrangements for such things in this place. She swung between awe and irritation, her tiredness making her fractious, and longed for some time to be alone. There had been too much noise and bustle for Maud. She longed for quiet.

The baggage was left for servants to take to the Resident's quarters. Alex saw how deferential the men were towards her father and relaxed a little. How she would feel in the presence of the prince she had no idea, but for the moment it was clear that her father was king!

The palace was vast. Felix pointed out the zenana, the women's quarters where no man over the age of twelve was permitted to visit unless he was a close relative. The way of life was very different from home, Alex thought, with a burst of nostalgia that surprised her.

They were shown to their rooms, which were large and spacious, each with a bathroom attached, to Maud's pleasure and relief. She felt as though she had been traveling forever. Her room and Alex's were adjoining, with a small alcove and connecting doors between, and when Felix had left the two women to settle in, Alex took her aunt's hands in her own.

"Thank you, Aunt Maud," she said gravely.

"Whatever for?"

"For making this journey, when I know you'd much rather be at home in London—"

"Nonsense," Maud said briskly. "Why would I rather be there, when I can be here with my sweet girl? You and your father are my whole family. Where else would I choose to be but with the two of you?"

They hugged each other, and then Maud turned away in swift embarrassment. She wasn't by nature a demonstrative woman. She prodded her bed and nodded with satisfaction.

"At least we shall live in some comfort here, my love, even if the prince has some very odd ideas. Living by the word of astrologers, indeed!"

"This is India, Aunt Maud." Alex repeated her father's dictum. "We're the foreigners, remember—"

"We're British!" Maud said indignantly. "Everyone else is foreign, but not the British!"

Alex felt laughter bubbling up inside her. Aunt Maud could be so doggedly outraged at any affront to her nationality. Wherever she went, she would always surround herself with a little piece of England. A gentle tap on the door stopped the laughter, and she went to answer it. A well-proportioned Indian woman stood there, her head slightly bowed as she spoke in a servile way to the lovely young English lady.

"I am Pandira, missy Sahib. It will be my pleasure to wait on you and the Mem'sahib at all times. If you will please state your wishes."

For a moment, Alex couldn't think of anything to say. The woman was more composed than herself, dressed in a dark, elegantly floating sari edged with embroidery, her sleek black hair just visible beneath its swathed folds.

"I know what I want!" Maud said. "And that's a hot bath. Do you have hot water?"

"Of course." Pandira turned her dark eyes onto the older of the two women, as enigmatic as all her race. "Is it your wish that I prepare it, Mem'sahib?"

"Yes, it is," Maud said imperiously. "And I daresay my niece will require the same."

Alex smiled at the Indian woman.

"When you're ready, Pandira," she said. "My aunt's needs are more urgent than mine."

The woman nodded slightly.

"The waiting will be as brief as possible, missy Sahib, and the enjoyment worth any small inconvenience. I took the liberty of placing scented bath oils in your boudoir. Is it your pleasure that I sprinkle them in the water to release the oils, which is the best way, or would you prefer to do it yourself?"

"Oh, you do it, please!" Alex said hastily. "I'm sure it will be wonderful."

She could see that Pandira's composure was beginning to unnerve Maud now, but Alex was enjoying herself already. The anticipation of lying in a beautifully perfumed bath, pampered with the scents of exotic oils and the sensuous feel of them on her skin, was suddenly even more desirable than an audience with Prince Shunimar, exciting though the prospect was to her.

Pandira moved silently away to prepare the individual baths, and Alex tried hard not to giggle as Maud said apprehensively that she hoped the woman understood that an English lady took her bath alone.

Whether Pandira heard or sensed Maud's modesty, she said smoothly that she would see to unpacking the ladies' baggage while they attended to their toilet, but that she would be close at hand should either of them call for her assistance.

Alex went into her own room and began to undress from the heavy traveling clothes. They had seemed ridiculously lightweight in England, but here they were cumbersome and she longed for the unrestricting Indian garments. It would be the first thing she would buy in the bazaars of Delhi, she promised herself. A beautiful silken sari, like the ones the princesses wore, as her mother used to tell her.

She sank into the richly smooth bathwater, feeling its warm caress on her skin, and gave a sigh of pure pleasure. The perfume was pungent and musky, a mixture of so many scents she couldn't distinguish one from the other. They filled her head.

The bathroom was luxurious, with mirrors all around its walls and a small pillow-shaped projection for her to rest her head on. She did so, closing her eyes blissfully. She spread her arms, and her fingers touched a button along the side of the bath. She pressed it experimentally.

From a dozen places, small jets of lemon-scented water swirled against her body, the warm spirals sending a frisson of enjoyment through her flesh wherever they touched. It was somehow wicked, Alex suspected, and perhaps one shouldn't relax in its warmth quite so wantonly. The ripples of pleasure were akin to those she had felt when Fraser Mackinnon's hard male body had pressed against hers, making her aware of the differences between them, her woman's softness, his male power . . .

She wanted him . . . the thought swept over her like a dam released. She had never known this feeling of wanting before, this aching need to complete the pattern that God had fashioned. One man, one woman, united in the most intimate way of spirit and flesh . . . each fused with the other, the perfect being . . .

"Alex, are you quite well?" her aunt called from the other side of her bathroom door. "You've been in there an unaccountably long time, and I thought I heard you moan a little while ago—"

Alex struggled to sit up, splashing water from the side of the bath in her haste. The shock of her own thoughts had been interrupted so rudely, it was just as though her aunt could see the darkening of her eyes, the flush on her cheeks, the strangely abandoned way she looked. Reflected in the surrounding mirrors of the bathroom, Alex thought how very unladylike she suddenly appeared, with the lingering pleasures of imagined love still a beautiful fantasy in her mind!

"I'm just getting out, Aunt Maud. I'll be with you in a little while." Quickly, she pressed the button again to stop the jets of water, wondering if Aunt Maud had also discovered its delights.

If she had, Alex had no doubt that she would have stopped them at once, finding them a heathen intrusion into her privacy. She smiled with secret pleasure. How differently one viewed the world when one was seventeen and in love . . . and how awful to be a dried-up spinster who could never recapture the sweet subtleties of every new experience . . .

She dried herself quickly with thick, warm towels, slipped a dressing-gown around her and stepped back into her bedroom. Pandira waited patiently in the small alcove between the two bedrooms. Had she too heard the little involuntary moans from Alex's bathroom, she wondered? And if she had, Alex had no doubt that she would not interpret them as innocently as her Aunt Maud!

91

"What do we do now?" Alex said quickly. Her aunt was already dressed again, face red from the bath and the struggle back into her corsets.

"May I suggest some tea?" Pandira put in. "It will be my pleasure to bring it to you, and if you would care to take it on the verandah, you will enjoy the beautiful rhododendron vistas of the palace grounds. Sahib Truscott says they remind him of England. Dinner will be served to you and Sahib Truscott in about one hour. So if you will permit me."

She was large, but she still seemed to glide across the room on slippered feet, throwing open the long windows and letting a warm breeze drift inside the room. There were bamboo chairs and a small table on the verandah. It was early evening, and the night scents were just beginning to suffuse the air. Alex thanked the woman.

"Tea would be delightful," she smiled. "Thank you, Pandira."

"Your wish is my wish, missy Sahib," the woman said unemotionally.

She left the room, and Alex dressed quickly. Maud frowned, pursing her lips.

"Servants should know their place, but some of these are insolent in their very servility," she stated. Alex laughed, leaning over the verandah to see the acres of grounds stretching away from the palace walls, a veritable paradise of brilliant color to please the eye.

"You're never satisfied, Aunt Maud! Here we are, surrounded by luxury, and still you complain! Think about poor Fraser. Do you think he lives in such elegant quarters in his military garrison? Just enjoy it the way I intend to!"

Maud heard the soft way she spoke of him and surmised correctly that it wasn't merely the palace luxury that produced her well-being. Alex was learning quickly how very pleasurable it was to speak the beloved's name at every opportunity, bringing him near, holding the memory of his voice, his touch . . .

Alex leaned farther out on the verandah, hiding again the secret smile that curved her lips, feeling the caress of the breeze on her flesh, and wishing it was Fraser Mackinnon's arms that warmed her.

Chapter Six

FELIX TRUSCOTT HAD BEEN AGREEABLY SURPRISED WHEN there had been a recent reshuffling of administrative staff among John Company men and he had been allocated the services of David Gould as his new assistant. He'd been impressed by the boy's efficiency each time he'd seen him in the offices of his superior, Sir Peter Wallace, and now that David had been installed in Truscott's Residency quarters for a month, the partnership was working well.

Relieved to be back in familiar territory again in his own office, he went briefly through the stack of paperwork that had accumulated in his absence, while his daughter and sister settled in.

"Your ladies arrived without undue discomfort, I

hope, Mr. Truscott," David remarked. Felix nodded briefly.

"As well as could be expected, to quote a guarded phrase," he said. He looked at the fresh-faced boy. "Will you join us for dinner tonight, David? My daughter would enjoy meeting you, and she's had the company of two old 'uns for long enough. What d'you say to it?"

The young man's face flushed red with pleasure.

"I'd be honored, sir—"

"For God's sake, don't be honored, just be sociable," Felix said irritably. "The girl wants natural conversation, not a lot of questions about the voyage and the weather!"

Even as he spoke, he knew it would be all that David could muster. The boy was an excellent assistant but not much of a ladies' man, usually getting flustered and tongue-tied as soon as some determined English mama looked him over as a possible suitor for her daughter.

There was no risk of that here, of course, and Felix hardly knew why he'd asked him to join them, except that it might make the meal more entertaining and stop any lingering complaints that might be forthcoming from Maud.

And it was true enough that Alexandra would probably feel the lack of young company now that Fraser Mackinnon had departed for his garrison. Prince Shunimar and his entourage were old and staid . . . he supposed he should have prepared his daughter for the prince, but it hadn't crossed his mind. She'd find out soon enough now, anyway. He brushed the thought aside.

"Any more trouble since I've been gone, David?"

The boy shrugged. They were all becoming complacent about the small flare-ups inside and outside the palace and territory of the Pearl of the Plain. Once, it would have been Felix's first question, but he had been content to go through Company papers first and leave the query until later.

"No more than usual. More like petty bickering than trouble, I'd say, sir. Some of the guards had a set-to in the grounds a week ago and set fire to one of the pagodas, but they won't bother us again."

Felix didn't reply. Shunimar had his own methods of dealing with troublesome guards, from cutting off their hands to immediate execution. Like many of his contemporaries, Felix thought it was better not to know. Prince or no prince, the man was without heart. It would not surprise Felix if his own guards turned on him completely. He just prayed that his daughter and sister weren't around when and if it happened. He turned back to his papers, glad to be back in his own little world.

Away in the garrison of the 78th Highlanders, under the command of the white-haired General Havelock, Fraser Mackinnon was attempting to reestablish himself in his particular world after some months' absence. He still felt strangely detached from it all—the convivial army life in which he shared, albeit on the fringes as a scout; the camaraderie of fellow Scots who brought a breath of home to an alien land; the easy company of men, which was frequently relieved by the demands of the British social set. All in all, it wasn't a bad life . . .

But Fraser was keenly aware of a change in himself, and he was canny enough to know it all stemmed from his meeting with Miss Alexandra Truscott.

He recalled how he had struggled with the depression and guilt following his father's death. His father had so wanted him to remain in Scotland on Mackinnon land, following the old Mackinnon traditions of laird and landowner and raising Mackinnon children to enrich the clan. It hadn't been Fraser's wish. He'd felt the need for travel, adventure, for seeking out pastures new . . .

Yet, after breathing in the pure, clean Highland air, seeing the glory of the glens and mountains, the crystal-clear burns and tumbling waterfalls of his homeland, there had been an undoubted tug at his heart. Vulnerable in his grief, he'd thought then that if he had a lassie, a wife to come home to, he'd be content to roam no longer.

And now he had met Alexandra Truscott, who had had a dream of India as compulsive as his own, with passions as strong as his own, and who would probably want to remain in India for the rest of her life. He smiled ruefully.

Her enthusiasm had echoed his own feelings, but the pull of his own heritage was surprisingly deep in his veins. He had never anticipated it, nor thought he'd be willing to act the laird in preference to the dashing figure he knew he cut here.

But the idea of forging a new dynasty of Mackinnons was becoming increasingly attractive to him. And the thought of making the lovely lassie Alexandra Truscott Mackinnon, even more attractive.

For an instant, he imagined her sitting with her long, fair hair unpinned. In his mind, he caressed her slender shoulders as she leaned over a wee bairn, created from their own love. He pictured her nursing his child, holding it to her soft, full breasts and crooning a soft lullaby, and he felt a shaft of desire so acute that it was almost a physical pain. All the feelings and emotions he'd kept so firmly under control in his grief were released at last, and with the knowledge came the ability to love once more. He owed Alex more than she knew, and as sure as the sun rose and set, he meant to make her his own.

In the beautiful palace known as the Pearl of the Plain, the two English ladies glanced at one another nervously. Dinner was over, introductions to the young and earnest David Gould had been made, and Felix was well pleased with his womenfolk. They were fair and elegant compared with the dark-skinned servants moving silently about the Residency dining room, and Felix felt justifiably proud of his beautiful daughter and gratitude to his sister for taking on the role of substitute mother all these years. He would be prouder still to present them to His Highness, Prince Shunimar . . .

From somewhere deep in the recesses of the palace, the muffled sound of a great gong could be heard, and Felix gave a small nod, scraping back his chair.

"We're summoned to the presence, m'dears," he said jovially. "We'll say good-night to you, David."

The young man bowed as the ladies stood up, resplendent in their dinner gowns, Maud's of silver-gray shot taffeta, Alex's a shimmering blue that matched the color of her eyes.

David Gould hadn't been able to stop looking at her all evening. He was already besotted, although Alex hardly knew he was there and was merely as polite as etiquette demanded. Once, she might have thought him a charming enough young man . . . but he seemed only a boy, when her heart was already given to a man . . .

A manservant was already waiting at the door to lead the Sahib Truscott and his ladies to the prince's presence. They walked through what seemed like endless corridors of marble columns and screens inlaid with precious gems, great tapestries on the walls and filigree ceilings. Alex began to feel hopelessly lost as each corridor seemed more magnificent than the last, as if to impress on visitors the wealth and status of the owner of such a palace. Her nervousness grew.

At last, the servant halted beside two tall doors made of more exquisite gold filigree work, seemingly fragile, yet they must have weighed an enormous amount. Outside, two guards stood with crossed swords, moving aside when the visitors approached.

Knowing the history of the East India Company, the reason for her father's installation here and the fact that Prince Shunimar remained virtually no more than nominally powerful at British discretion, Alex would have found it all slightly farcical had not the chowkidars looked so fierce and warlike.

The doors opened, and at the end of a vast room an enormously fat man sat enthroned upon a dais. Suspended above him was a great mat of brilliant turquoise peacock feathers, waving gently to create a breeze to keep the elite one cool. He was clothed in a garb that was mainly scarlet, so dazzling in jewels it made the eyes ache to look at him overlong. On his head was swathed a turban of softest cloth of gold, and in its center a huge ruby burned with all the fire of the desert sun. The only movement came when his fingers glittered with more jewels as he motioned the visitors to come forward.

Alex noted that all around the enormous room, exquisite in its decor, more chowkidars stood motionless. Between them, flaring torches in elaborate gilt holders cast unnerving shadows over faces and stances. It was like some great carved tableau, with only the three British people having life and substance. Alex could hear the sound of her own breathing and felt a sudden healthy irritation at being made to feel this way. The prince wasn't a god, but he obviously meant to give that impression to those who sought an audience with him!

Like her niece, Maud had been transfixed by Prince Shunimar, his dark, enigmatic eyes unblinking as they approached. But now her gaze, as well as Alex's, shifted slightly to where, on either side of the prince and slightly behind him, two other men stood poised and staring.

"The astrologers." Felix breathed the words out of the corner of his mouth, as if sensing their curiosity. "Shunimar doesn't move without his shadows!"

The words dispersed some of the awe Alex and Maud had been feeling. If the man couldn't think for himself without the aid of such people, then he wasn't so godlike after all!

Near the dais, the perfumed air became heavy and more noticeable. Alex saw the astrologers lean towards the prince, one by one, and whisper in his ear. She began to feel slightly hysterical. Were they condemning these British women who braved this sanctuary? A sliver of unease ran through her. She seesawed between wanting to laugh, and wanting to run . . .

"We greet you, Mr. Truscott." Prince Shunimar spoke in perfect English, scorning the Indian deference in favor of the British mode of address. "We greet your ladies and trust that they find their new abode to their liking."

Alex opened her mouth to speak, then closed it again. She remembered that she wasn't to address the prince until he addressed her, and as yet his eyes were solely on her father.

"They are most happy, Highness," Felix said coolly.

"How could it be otherwise in this most harmonious of residences?"

The prince grunted. The astrologers whispered again. Alex felt unexpected pity for a man who had everything in the world and yet felt unable to make the slightest move without his advisers. It was they who had the power, not the prince, Alex thought suddenly. And they who could cause trouble . . . she blinked as Prince Shunimar looked directly at her and smiled slightly.

"There is an aura of purity about you, Miss Truscott, that we find most pleasing. You are welcome. The older Miss Truscott, too, has our most happy greeting."

He spoke again to Felix without requiring a reply.

"You will know that we do not care for frequent entertaining, Mr. Truscott, but that we make an exception for our royal birthday, which falls auspiciously at the time of the next rising moon. We have graciously decided to hold a ball in the state apartments, to which you may invite as many trusted British friends as you desire, to mingle with the highborn Indians. There will also be an elephant parade, which I am sure your ladies will find most amusing. We will consult the horoscope and inform you of the details in due course."

The jewels gleamed as he folded his arms across the bulk of his body, and the audience was over. Following her father's lead, Alex stepped backwards for the entire length of the room, feeling as though none of this was real. She could sense Aunt Maud's apprehension that she would trip over her gown at any minute, and it was a great relief when they were outside the audience chamber and the huge doors closed behind them.

Alex felt a wild desire to laugh, but she had to contain herself until the servant led them back the way they had come and Felix showed them into the Residency drawing room. Only then did Alex explode into laughter, tears of incredulity welling up in her eyes at the impossibility of the last half hour.

"He can't be real, Father!" she gasped out at last. "Is he a strolling player puffed up with his own importance and acting a part?"

"I assure you he's very real, my love." Felix was relaxed and smiling now, enjoying the reaction of his daughter and the unwilling smiles of his sister.

"Why didn't you warn us? You should have done! Especially about those terrifying men by his side, with their piercing eyes! Is he allowed to do anything for himself?"

Felix shrugged. "He can do anything he wishes. He's the prince of all the heavens, Alexandra. But he chooses not to make a move until his astrologers have cast a daily horoscope. You must understand that this is an ancient continent and we must not laugh at their customs—"

She couldn't stop, her eyes damp with mirth and the release of tension. "And he thinks we shall be *amused* by an elephant parade! Does he think it's an everyday occurrence in London? I've never even *seen* an elephant, except in paintings!"

Felix laughed now. "Then I promise you you're in for a treat," he said in his dry way. "This won't just be a string of beasts waddling about and shaking the ground beneath them, darling. The prince's birthday parade is an excuse to dress up the royal elephants in their finery and display some of his jewels and precious ornaments. It will be an occasion to remember and a fitting end to the ball, since it's usually conducted after dark to make more of an impact by torchlight."

Maud's mouth seemed to be permanently open, as she listened to the calm way her brother spoke of such things. And the ball . . . that would be another ordeal,

she supposed, with highborn Indian ladies and gentlemen and their own British acquaintances, few of whom
would be known to her and Alex. Alex's thoughts had
already winged ahead, and suddenly her young face
was alive.

"Can we invite Fraser—Mr. Mackinnon, Father?
And the Forbes family, whom we met on the ship?
They were such nice people, and Captain Forbes
thought he may know you. I have their address in
Delhi, and I mean to call on Ellen Forbes as soon as she
arrives here from Calcutta."

She rushed on, seeing the way her aunt's brows
arched at her mention of Fraser Mackinnon, and she
mentioned the Forbes family almost as an afterthought.
Her immediate joy was that it would be another excuse
to see Fraser again and to let him see her. Not in the
dusty traveling clothes of the last week or so, but once
more in the elegance of silk, her hair washed and
fragrant and shining . . . she glowed at the thought.

"Of course we'll invite Mackinnon," Felix said indul-
gently. "And your friends will be welcome. I don't
recall a Captain Forbes but may well have met him
briefly. There's a strong kernel of British socialites who
will be wanting invitations, so the two of you can
consult with young David Gould sometime and write
them out, if you wish for something to do. I have plenty
of work to do in the next few days, so you will have to
amuse yourselves. I imagine it won't be difficult."

Alex was elated. The future was no longer a little
uncertain. India was hers for the taking, the dream of
her life, and Fraser Mackinnon was part of that dream.
Life couldn't be more wonderful.

They quickly settled into a daily routine at the
Residency. They were still tired from the long journey

and needed these few days to revitalize themselves, to explore their immediate surroundings before venturing into Delhi, which they couldn't do unescorted, and to draw up the invitation list for Prince Shunimar's ball with the help of David Gould.

He was only too delighted to pore over lists and to give suggestions, with the lovely Miss Truscott beside him in his little office. The freshness of her was like a breath of home, and David realized that there were times when he truly missed England and all that Alexandra Truscott represented with her educated voice and impeccable manners and the undoubtedly spirited nature she kept so well under control.

He was not a man for pushing himself with the ladies, preferring to admire from afar, but Alex was so eager for his assistance in her task that it went straight to his head. For her part, she likened him to a young colt, immature and sweet and not to be taken seriously. Not sensing this fully, he daringly put a request to her on the second day after her arrival.

"Miss Truscott, I would be honored if you would reserve a dance for me at the ball, although perhaps it's not quite fair to steal a march on the gentlemen who won't see your dance card until the day—"

Scarlet-faced, he bumbled his way through the words he'd been practicing all morning and stopped abruptly as Alex gave a teasing laugh. She leaned towards him and patted his hand, and he gulped in mingled embarrassment and joy.

"Of course you may have a dance, David!" she said gaily. "I shall rely on you to point out all the rogues and opportunists! You shall be my brother for the evening! It will please my father to know you are looking after me."

It didn't really matter to her. She had every intention

104

of being in Fraser Mackinnon's company for every possible moment, her senses tingling at the thought. She didn't even notice the dumb misery that washed over David Gould's young face at her words. But he was nothing if not stalwartly British.

Besides, deep down, he felt in his bones that he was destined to remain a bachelor all his days . . . in a strange way, it was almost a relief to know that Miss Truscott didn't take his adoration seriously, that he could continue to worship from afar and be her brother. He cheered up. If a brother she required, then a brother she would have.

"It will be my humble pleasure to be your protector—" he began, at which Alex burst out laughing, her blue eyes dancing with mischief.

"Oh, David, don't be so pompous! I don't ask for a bodyguard! And I shan't want to feel your eyes are on me every moment to see any tiny indiscretions, do I?"

She teased him again, and he blushed furiously. Alex tired of the game and pored over the list of invitations once more. Most of the names meant nothing to her, but she had been assured that they were among the cream of the British in Delhi and its surrounding area. Generals and captains and officials of the Company and their ladies . . . Captain Forbes and his family had been added to them.

"You'll add the name of Mr. Fraser Mackinnon, won't you?" Alex spoke with such studied casualness that David knew at once that this was the man who might afford the tiny indiscretions of which she had spoken. He had already heard the name.

"Isn't he the scout attached to the 78th Highlanders?" He didn't look up as he scratched Fraser's name at the end of the list. "Your father mentioned his kindness to you and your aunt on the voyage, and I believe he intended calling at Mr. Mackinnon's garrison today, once his Company business in Delhi is completed."

Alex only heard the words she wanted to hear, her face breaking into a sudden smile, tinged with impatience. Her father was visiting Fraser's garrison! Why hadn't he told her? She might have persuaded him to take her and Aunt Maud on an escorted visit. A few more hours that might have been spent in his company. Unconsciously, her hands clenched together, and David felt a brief envy towards the man who could make Miss Truscott's breathing quicken, causing those delightful rounded curves to rise and fall and the beguiling flush to fill her cheeks . . .

He had toyed with the idea of suggesting to her father that he might escort Alex and her aunt into Delhi for some sightseeing, but he guessed that there was another escort she would much prefer, if his duties allowed. Regretfully, David abandoned the idea and said instead that they might begin writing out the invitation cards if Miss Truscott so desired.

At about the same time, Felix was riding into the army garrison of the 78th Highlanders, having already had a consultation with his superior, Sir Peter Wallace, in Delhi. He had rarely taken the vacation time allotted to him in recent years, preferring to bury himself in work rather than recall the idyllic times he and Constance had shared in off-duty hours.

But his conscience was pricking him. It was hardly fair to Alex, nor to Constance's memory, to expect the girl to sit idly in Prince Shunimar's palace, however luxurious, while Felix went about his normal business. His daughter was no milksop. She had an inquiring mind and a ready wit. She deserved more than the kind of reclusive life led by some of the Indian wives and princely concubines. She was young and lovely, and in time he hoped she would make a good marriage.

Each time his thoughts reached that point, he knew that Constance would want Alex to see the lovely bungalow home that Felix had almost shunned since his wife's death. Alex had expected to live there, had seen Constance's drawings of the place, and would want to visit it. If Constance were still alive, she would expect Felix to give sufficient time to his daughter to make her feel thoroughly at home in her new country.

He would do what he could . . . but he guessed that Alex wouldn't be averse to having the handsome Scotsman on hand whenever possible, and it would ease his own commitment to playing the escort too frequently, he thought half guiltily. To that end, he had made inquiries of Sir Peter Wallace and was now to approach Mackinnon himself and then his superior officer.

Unless any kind of mutiny was imminent, he hoped to conscript Mackinnon's services for his own use. After all, they were all servants of the East India Company, and Sir Peter could probably insist if he so wished.

Felix rode into the garrison, reining in his horse and handing it over to a stable-wallah. He was a first-class horseman and preferred to ride whenever he could rather than use a conveyance, especially through the streets of Delhi, where he would be held up a hundred times by slow-moving bullock carts and roaming animals and the like.

He breathed in the familiar camp smells of cooking and wood-burning fires, tobacco and the inevitable curry. The Scots accents burred pleasantly in his ears as he sought out the scout's quarters without more ado.

Fraser rose from his seat in some surprise when he saw his visitor and called out for some tea to be brought at once. He had just finished his midday meal, and Felix brushed aside the offer of joining him.

"Tea will suffice," he said, and without waiting for the boy to bring it, he made his business known.

Fraser listened impassively, betraying nothing by his expression, and it flashed briefly through Truscott's mind that such a man could be very useful when spying was called for. But he had no doubt that the 78th would already know that.

The tea arrived, the tea-wallah pouring it inexpertly and being waved away.

"Let me get this absolutely clear. You want me to act as official escort to the ladies, is that it? You want me to show them around Delhi, to take them on a brief visit to your bungalow and possibly to the hills to inspect your tea estate. You're sure you don't think of me as a gigolo, Truscott?"

Felix flushed darkly. "Dammit, man, I thought you'd welcome the idea! If I thought you weren't the man I could safely entrust my daughter and sister to, I'd never have suggested it. And you'll correct me if I'm wrong, Mackinnon, but I fancied there was a certain rapport between my daughter and yourself. I don't think she'll object to the arrangement."

Fraser looked at him coolly. "You surmise correctly, sir. And because Alexandra and I have come to know one another quite well during the voyage, I think you should take her to the bungalow yourself, or at least come with us. She'll be missing her mother more keenly there than anywhere else."

Felix felt his face burn. He didn't need this young man to explain his own daughter's feelings to him . . . and yet, perhaps he did. He knew he had been shirking the visit to the bungalow, thinking he could pass his duty off completely to Mackinnon's capable hands. He nodded slowly.

"Maybe you're right. The more of us that go together, the better it will be." He spoke for himself as much as for Alex, and they both knew it.

Fraser went on, speaking firmly. "I've no objection to spending time at your bidding, if 'tis agreed on by the general and the Company, but my first duty is to the regiment. Though my enforced absence has resulted in my assistant taking on more and more of my duties, and I feel like a spare cog in a wheel at times."

Felix grunted. "I've cleared it with Sir Peter Wallace, and I have a note to that effect. We are all under Company rule, remember, and I've no doubt General Havelock will agree to release you when necessary. Naturally, it all depends on you and on the supposition that we're not suddenly thrust into a war! These blasted natives keep threatening to disrupt things—"

"I'd say that was the more important consideration." Fraser could be as dry as Truscott. He looked at him keenly. "You'll be aware of the cartridge problem, of course? First news of it broke out while I was away and caused a pretty rumpus—"

Felix scowled. He was increasingly aware that he was cushioned from much of the bickering and disturbance that went on in the regiments and the major Residencies in the cities. Life in the Pearl of the Plain was a different world from all that went on outside. But naturally, the cartridge problem had been uppermost on everyone's lips for a few weeks, with official papers sent to every Resident and general until it all died down again as these things always did.

"A storm in a teacup, Mackinnon—"

"Don't dismiss it so lightly, sir. Have you not heard

of the burnings across the country? British homes put to the torch, more discontent among the native regiments than ever before—"

"The devils should be pleased with the new Enfield rifles. Damn good weapons—"

"But not if the cartridges are greased with animal fat!" Fraser went on doggedly. "To do such a thing was like putting a match to a tinderbox. How shortsighted can the fools in Britain be to send such cartridges? Don't they know that beef fat is sacred to Hindus and pork fat unclean to Moslems? And that it's an outrage to both religions to eat the fat of dead animals?"

"I didn't know you were so pro-Indian, Mackinnon—"

"Dammit, man, one needn't be pro-Indian to respect the way of life of these people. We live in their country, for all that we're so damned arrogant—"

"There's a good case for bringing Christianity to them, then," Felix retorted. Despite Mackinnon's impassioned words, he was quite enjoying this argument.

"That's a damn fool thing to say, if you'll forgive me, Truscott. Would you want to take away their very identity? I tell you, we haven't heard the last of this cartridge thing yet, for all that it's been subdued. And you wonder why I think twice about deserting my post to escort your womenfolk about like some dandy?"

"I think you're overreacting," Felix snapped now. "And I confess that you puzzle me, Mackinnon. I've heard of your reputation as a first-class scout, but I'd have thought that some weeks in my daughter's company might have compensated!"

Fraser gave nothing away. "If you thought me a philanderer, sir, you'd not have chosen me for the job!"

Felix laughed shortly. "All right, man. Then think it

over, will you? 'Twill only be a part-time occupation, for God's sake. Nobody's asking you to desert, as you so dramatically put it! I'll hope to hear good news from you on Sunday. You haven't forgotten you're invited to tea?"

"I haven't forgotten. I look forward to it," he said gravely, his thoughts still on the cartridge affair he'd only recently learned about, even though the first hint of it had come from the munitions factory near Calcutta over a month ago while he had been voyaging from England to India.

His thoughts still revolved around the possible consequences of such an incredibly stupid incident. Had the fools who decided such things not realized how disastrous it was to an Indian of devout caste to let his lips touch the cartridge paper, as they were bound to do when biting it away? And for their lips to be defiled by animal fat? Did the officials in Britain not realize that nine-tenths of John Company's army was formed by Indian sepoys and sowars, the infantry and cavalry, not the British? Most commanding officers had grown old and complacent in the years of British rule, but the underlying Indian feeling was of resentment, bitter and strong, ready to be fueled by the slightest spark.

Many mistakes had already been made in the mismanagement of the country under Company rule. To forbid the caste marks was one, in the idiotic belief that all men should be equal in a country where such a thing was highly alien. So that even priests might unknowingly commit the unforgivable sin of brushing shoulders with untouchables, those of such low caste that even if their shadow touched another's food, the food would be thrown away. The priests—the Brahmins—wouldn't even hang out their washing lest these shadows fall across them. Did the Company think that such age-old traditions could be dismissed in a single stroke of officialdom? With the cartridge question, Fraser wondered if the final spark had already been struck.

He was tormented by his thoughts for long after Truscott left, and it was a long while before he allowed himself the luxury of fully realizing what the man's proposals all meant. He would see Alex more often than he had dreamed possible . . . and finally he was able to put his restless imaginings, that didn't bear imagining, aside. At last, he forced himself to think only of Alex.

Inevitably, his spirits soared, then became more cautious. If he was the official escort, then he must bide his time before informing Truscott of his intentions towards his daughter. Otherwise, it was possible the man would think twice about throwing the young couple into such close contact, and he'd lose this chance that had come so unexpectedly.

He imagined her face on Sunday when he told her, having no doubt that General Havelock would release him for temporary duty attached to the Residency, since his young assistant was doing so well. Such a pompous piece of red tape for such a delightful task. He thought of Alex's eyes, alight with pleasure, her whole beautiful little body that curved so joyously to his, and hoped that her innocently provocative reaction wouldn't betray them both too readily!

Chapter Seven

FELIX'S INSPIRATIONAL IDEA OF ACQUIRING FRASER MAC-kinnon to escort Alex and Maud for a few weeks, until they had become acclimatized to India, had been like waving a magic wand about the two women. Maud was openly delighted when Fraser arrived for tea the following Sunday, almost more pleased than Alex, Felix thought in surprise.

It was strange . . . had Felix been as perceptive as his late wife, he might have read the signs of averted glances and slightly trembling hands all too clearly. As it was, he was merely amazed at his own cleverness in arranging things to everyone's satisfaction. On two days a week, Fraser would be at the ladies' disposal, and for longer periods for any arranged expeditions.

Tea was a carefree occasion that day, a mixture of

British convention and Indian delights, with delicious sweetmeats and rich cream concoctions, thinnest chuppatti bread and fine Krubah tea, which Felix naturally insisted on using at the Residency.

"If it suits you, Mackinnon, we can make a journey to the tea estate during April. It will take four days to travel there and four back, so I suggest an overall time of two weeks. Can you arrange your absence?"

"Just give me the exact dates, and 'twill be convenient," Fraser said, sensing the leap of Alex's heart at the thought, matching his own. Two more weeks of travel and lodging in the fragrant cool of the hills, when the temperature in Delhi would begin to rise. Apparently, this year had been cool by Indian standards so far, though it did not seem so to the Englishwomen. The rains had been heavier than usual, the rivers full and the country therefore greener, but soon the temperature would rocket, so a timely visit to the hills would be welcome.

"Alex wishes to see the bungalow." Felix's voice became more abrupt. "We'll go there quite soon. If you're free from now on to take them into Delhi on their sightseeing, perhaps we could go to the bungalow the week after next."

"Have you told Fraser about the prince's birthday ball, Father?" Alex couldn't contain herself any longer. The vista ahead of her was everything she could have hoped for, and her father was a darling for arranging it all so wonderfully. Her dream was coming true, and she saw no stalking tigers on the horizon . . .

"I have not. I guessed it would soon come from your lips, my love," Felix remarked. "Has the date been arranged?"

"The prince's aide told David it would be on the 29th

of March. So be sure and keep that date free too, Fraser—"

"You do know I have a job to do with the regiment, I suppose, lassie?" he said with mock severity. "I don't intend to dance attendance on you for twenty-four hours a day from now on!"

Felix laughed, saying jovially that it was good to put a haughty young woman in her place now and then, but Maud didn't miss the quick glances between the two young people, nor the way the smiles lingered on their mouths when they were talking about other matters. And she determined not to forget her own role as chaperone to her lovely niece.

It was why she had come to India against all her better judgment, and although she couldn't deny the relief of knowing that Fraser Mackinnon would be around to protect them from Lord knew what heathen customs, she still intended protecting Alex's virtue, come what may.

Once the tea ritual was over and the hard clear blue of the sky began to soften a little, Felix asked Fraser if he would care to show Alex the royal elephants.

"Prince Shunimar has given his permission, and I've seen enough elephants to last me a lifetime," her father continued. "I don't suppose Maud wants to traipse around the compound for an hour, but if you two want to see them, you had best set out before it gets too dark."

Fraser and Alex were on their feet almost before he had finished speaking. They left the comfortable Residency quarters to stroll through the palace grounds before they rode in a small pony-drawn trap, an ekka, of the kind used by women in purdah with its drawn curtains, but useful for short trips around the Residency. They would ride to where the elephants were housed and exercised, a mile away from the grandeur of the palace itself.

Back in the drawing room, Maud looked at her brother in some exasperation. "Don't you think you're throwing the two of them together unnecessarily, Felix? Alex is a vulnerable young woman, and fond though I am of Mr. Mackinnon, I'm not sure of the wisdom of letting them go off together like that. I doubt that Indian women are allowed in the company of a young man alone! I thought we British brought our standards here—"

Felix disliked having his suggestions questioned. If anything was designed to make him even more stubborn, it was petty nagging. He testily dismissed her anxieties.

"I trust my daughter, Maud, and so should you, if you've brought her up correctly! I trust Mackinnon too, and what could happen in the confines of the palace grounds, for God's sake? Show some sense, woman, and if you're in the mood for it, I'll give you a game of chess."

They walked sedately through the exotic grounds of the palace, drinking in the scents and sounds. Peacocks strutted about them, stunning white and brilliant kingfisher-hued. Birds that looked fashioned out of pure fire darted among the yellow-blossomed kikar trees, and in the distance wilder, more primitive cries of jackals and monkeys drifted about them.

They didn't touch, but Alex was burningly aware of the lithe, easy movements of the tall man beside her as the swing of his tartan brushed her wide crinoline. She didn't need to look at him to know every line of his profile, darkly handsome with that startling likeness to Prince Albert she had noticed at their first meeting.

Or was she the only one to see it? No one else had ever commented on it. Was it merely that the thought of Prince Albert had been her first young adolescent dream, and that the slight resemblance Fraser Mackinnon bore to him was enough to make her love for the man a delicious continuation of the fantasy . . . ?

Walking beside her, Fraser was conscious of every silken sound her soft tea-gown made on that dazzling afternoon. He breathed in the scent of her hair, more alluring to his senses than the most exotic blooms in a prince's garden. The sweet femininity of her appearance awakened all his male desire. She was innocence and fire combined, and he wanted her for his own.

They reached the stables and climbed into one of the ckkas. Fraser took the reins himself as they left the ordered confines of the grounds and rode out towards the elephant compound. Once beyond sight of the Residency windows, Fraser let one hand rest lightly over Alex's, and felt the instant curl of her fingers around his. Their thighs touched on the hard wooden seat, and he could feel her warmth through their clothing. God, but he had never ached for anything so much as he ached for Alexandra Truscott.

"I've missed you," he said softly.

Her teasing retort died on her lips as she glanced at his face. "I've missed you too. It's seemed like a year," she said truthfully. He felt his breath catch at her artlessness.

"What are we going to do about us, Alexandra?"

A shiver ran through her. They were no longer two separate entities, but a unit. They were "us."

"My father's already done it for us! Arranging for

117

you to be our official escort!" She glowed at the
thought and then spoke hesitantly. "Fraser, it is all
right, isn't it? You don't feel it's a little unmanly to be
relieved of your regimental duties to look after Aunt
Maud and me?"

He laughed, a rich, warm sound, pushing his unease
about the whole Indian situation out of his mind for the
present. She had forgotten how much she loved to hear
him laugh.

"No, I don't think it's unmanly, my funny, darling
lassie! But escorting you and your aunt is not what I
had in mind when I spoke about us, dearest. What
about us?"

She looked at him a little blankly. His voice deepened. "Alexandra, I ache to be alone with you. Not
merely like this, riding with your father's blessing, but
really alone with you, a man with his woman. The
wanting can be heaven, and it can be hell. Do you
understand?"

Her heart thudded so wildly she thought she would
faint. "Yes, I understand—"

"I don't think you do." He was suddenly harsh.
"When your father first put the suggestion to me, I
hesitated. There were other considerations to do with
my regiment that needn't concern you—" Unconsciously, he was shielding her from the truth, the way
her parents had always done when she was a child.
"But also, I wasn't sure that I could bear to be near you
so much and not do what my instincts tell me to do,
lassie. I don't believe you've any notion of how powerful a man's passions can be—"

Her face flooded with color. "Are you censuring me
because of that? Would you rather I was a loose
woman, who knew every trick to lure a man?"

"You don't need tricks, lassie," Fraser said. "Your own innocence is seductive enough—"

"You make me feel almost ashamed of it," she said angrily. "I don't know what you want of me anymore—"

She stopped, tears stabbing her eyes, because suddenly they were quarreling, and it was the last thing she wanted to happen. Fraser too had hardly expected to be so assaulted by her loveliness that he had come near to losing his head. He was supposed to be the strong one, and he squeezed the tense fingers in his palm and drew them to his lips.

"I just want you to be my Alexandra. If I've said anything to upset you, forgive me, dear one. I want to tell your father of our love, but I dare not just yet, or I fear he'll replace me. So we must pretend to be no more than friends for the present. You see the sense in it, don't you?"

He realized he was answering his own question. What to do about "us." They could do nothing for the present. He tried to keep things light, flirtatious, wondering if he had already gone too far in his avowal of love for her in so short a time, in such troubled times . . .

"I see," Alex said in a small voice. "I suppose I understand it. Just as long as I know you love me, Fraser."

"Be sure of that." His voice became teasing again. "And don't expect me to abide by my own rules if we happen to be alone together, lassie."

"Like now?" she said provocatively. "It will be dark when we return to the palace, won't it?"

"And under cover of darkness, who knows?" he finished her sentence, and her mood brightened. She

119

could twist Fraser's intentions with one word, one glance, and although she didn't know it, it alarmed him somewhat. He had always been fully in control of his emotions, until now. But he had never fallen in love . . . until now.

They reached the elephant compound, and when Fraser explained their visit, the young Indian boys with switches in their hands proudly displayed the elephants to the guests. Alex kept well back from the huge animals, awed by them, respecting them, but screwing up her nose at the smells and trumpetings and the ungainly, lumbering movements of the dozen animals.

"Do the Sahib and missy Sahib wish to see the raiments?" the chief boy said deferentially.

"Aye, we may as well," Fraser said briskly. "We'll be able to tell the others what we've seen."

Alex realized what he meant. If they could describe the raiments, whatever they were, then a slight delay in their return might pass unnoticed. The boys led them to a large wooden building nearby, running ahead and jabbering noisily to one another. It was dark and musty inside, but lamps were lit immediately, and Alex gasped.

The entire central space inside the huge room was filled with metal frames, each one the size and shape of an elephant's back, and draped over them were the raiments and headdresses the animals wore for ceremonial occasions—such as Prince Shunimar's birthday parade, Alex guessed instantly. All around the walls, too, were the howdahs, the decorated seats for the riders, the mahouts. The raiments appeared more costly than anything Alex had ever seen before, save for the prince's own apparel and apartments, silks glittering in the lamplight, jewels sparkling and reflecting the light in a myriad dancing pinpoints of light.

Alex tried to imagine the beasts dressed up so grandly for their parade, and it was all beyond anything she had ever envisaged before. She wished all her friends at Lady Margaret's Academy for Young Ladies could be here on that night at the end of March, at the palace called the Pearl of the Plain, to see the elephants parade. She gave a small shake of her head as Fraser waited for her reaction, when they had walked around every one of the raiments and exclaimed on the gorgeous array.

"It's unbelievable," she said honestly. "I had no idea such splendor existed until I came here."

"Imagine what it was like in the great palaces of nobles of more importance than Shunimar!" Fraser commented. "He's a small fish compared with some of the mightier Mogul rulers of the past. Some of them would feel a burning shame at the stripping of power by the British government and the miserable pride the present-day princes feel in these comparatively paltry displays!"

Alex looked at him in astonishment. The words were totally unexpected, as much to Fraser as to her. He hadn't meant to say them, but to him these great beasts in their splendid garb always epitomized the power and glory of India, and there had once been so much more. He was still disturbed by the rumors of the cartridge affair and its repercussions and attuned to every resentful glance from child and sepoy. Even these laddies here had eyed the visitors with a grudging look. He had sensed it, if Alex had not. She misunderstood him and smiled mischievously.

"If you think it paltry, you obviously haven't seen the prince's audience room, where the ball will be held, Fraser! Talk to me then of paltry displays! You're being invited, of course."

"Am I? Whose idea was that, I wonder?" His lips were tugged into an unwilling smile.

"Mine, of course! And I shall expect you to dance with me occasionally, if only to keep dear David Gould from claiming too many. I fear the poor boy has a hopeless pash on me, Fraser."

She sighed, watching him from beneath her lashes, unconsciously coquettish, and even though he knew it well enough, he felt a rush of jealousy.

"In that case, you had best mark every other dance with my name," he said arrogantly. "I would claim every one, but I doubt your father would think even a trusted escort had the right to so much."

She giggled, enjoying these heady moments, surrounded by the finery and regalia of a prince's kingdom, her love beside her. And suddenly she had seen enough.

"Can we leave now? Such perfection makes my head ache, and the air is cloying in here."

He agreed at once. It would be good to be outside again, in the clean, windless air of evening, and to be together for the short ride back to the Residency. Already, the night had deepened, and they had missed the twilight. And Alex was aglow with all she had seen, with Fraser seated by her side in the ekka. They risked pulling the curtains about them, enclosed in their own small world. His hand holding hers, she was shielded from everything ugly and unpleasant as she had always been all her life, completely unaware of any gathering clouds ahead.

In those first carefree weeks, life for Alex became all that she had expected of India. She and Aunt Maud found their own amusements within the palace grounds on the days when Fraser didn't arrive to take them into

Delhi. There was much to see and do, and Delhi itself was a delight. They made their visits during the mornings, when the sun was at its least oppressive. It was only reckless folk who ventured out in the heat of the afternoon.

When she was a child, Alex had been charmed by Constance's drawings, sent home regularly to bring the city to life, and now it was just as though those old paper drawings suddenly assumed form and substance. It was as though the spirit of Constance guided her through every alleyway and bazaar, to the beautiful views of gilded mosques silhouetted against a clear blue sky, to the massive sandstone walls of the Red Fort itself, shimmering in the sunlight, symbolic of Delhi's magnificence.

She wanted to experience everything, like a child with a new set of playthings. Fraser was charmed by her excitement at every new discovery and shared them through her eyes. Maud was exhausted by her tireless energy and begged for frequent rests.

"We must go inside the Red Fort, Aunt Maud!" Alex protested. "I shouldn't sleep tonight if I hadn't seen it all!"

Maud groaned, and Fraser took pity on her. They had already found the Forbes family home on an earlier visit, and Alex and Ellen had fallen on each other in delight, the children greeting Alex like a long-lost sister. Their bungalow wasn't far from here. He suggested that Maud should go there, while he and Alex explored the wonders of the Red Fort, already familiar to him as one of the tourist attractions of Delhi.

"That sounds like an excellent idea," Maud said gratefully. Alex would be safe with Fraser Mackinnon, and she would have a much-needed rest. They took her to the Forbes' house at once, and within half an hour

Alex and Fraser were ready to enter the most famous landmark of all Delhi.

"I'm nervous," Alex said wonderingly. "Why should that be so? It's just a building—"

"Don't ever let an Indian hear you say so," Fraser grinned. "It's far more than a building. It's an experience, a dedication. It's right that we should share it together."

She took his arm, glad of its comfort as they entered through the covered passageway lined with shops and into the brilliant sunlight and an emerald-smooth lawn.

"All save princes of the blood must dismount here and go forward on foot," Fraser observed. "Ahead of us is the Hall of Public Audience, and behind it are the royal baths, which are said to be breathtaking, but unfortunately, we're unable to visit them. But you'll find the rest of it wondrous enough. Shall we enter the hall?"

They moved forward together, and there was a reverence about the whole area that Alex couldn't explain. Inside the great hall, she drew in her breath, too stunned to gasp out loud. The ceiling was made of silver, the walls inlaid with jewels. They walked slowly, to drink in every sight, and were halted by the sheer glory of the Peacock Throne.

There were two figures of peacocks behind the throne, their tails expanded to display the inlaid sapphires, rubies, emeralds, pearls and other precious gems. The throne stood on six massive feet of solid gold that were also inlaid with jewels. A glowing figure of a parrot stood between the two peacocks, supposedly carved from a single emerald.

Only now did Alex begin to appreciate the vast wealth of a land where such things were displayed for public viewing, and only now did she appreciate Fraser's meaning that the once-great moguls would feel a burning shame at their British victors. For victors they were, however peaceful the daily life of present times. She felt a shiver run through her. She had felt it before, as if she were truly caught up in this great complexity of human struggle for power.

"Have you seen enough for one day?" Fraser's voice pulled her back to the present, and she nodded quickly.

"It's so beautiful it makes me want to cry. It fills me with more emotion than I believed possible. It's so sad—" She looked at him in embarrassment. "Does that sound foolish? Everyone else seems enthralled by it all, but I keep thinking of all that's past, and how empty it all seems by comparison."

"It's not foolish, my love. It's called empathy. Not everyone has it, but you're a very special person, Alexandra, and I do believe you're growing up at last."

She looked at him sharply, through suddenly misted eyes, unsure whether he was laughing at her or not. But his words were merely meant to break the unbearable tension of the moment, and daringly, among the crush of people wandering about the hall, he brushed his lips against her cheek.

"Let's go somewhere less emotive," he suggested. "Back to Chandni Chowk, where I know you love to browse."

"How could I not! It must be the most wondrous shopping street in the world," she said gratefully, glad he had broken the strange spell she'd been under. "And Ellen has invited us for lunch, whenever we choose to arrive, before we go back to the Residency."

They smiled like two conspirators, together in body and spirit, loving the convenient indisposition of Aunt Maud, loving each other, loving India.

They left the beauties of the Red Fort, the fountains

and marbled courtyards, for the more mundane shopping area, which could never be mundane to Alex. They listened to the many street astrologers, marveled at the arrays of shimmering silks and countless embroideries and intricate silver trinkets. They breathed the scents of spices, the cow dung, the incense sticks and pungent tobacco, the exotic fruits and flowers, and it was all India, a potpourri of life. A bullock halted all the traffic as he took his tribute from a stall, and no one cared. It was just India . . .

"I want to buy you something," Fraser said suddenly, "while your aunt is not with us to disapprove, and you must say you bought it yourself."

"All right!" She loved the intrigue of it.

"We'll go native," Fraser went on. "The Indians like to buy several items that are seemingly inexpensive on their own, but together they make up a special meaning for the recipient."

Her face was filled with delight. "Oh, Fraser, that's beautiful," she said softly.

"Not as beautiful as you, dearest. You shall choose—"

"No. I want you to choose. Then I shall know the things have come from your heart to mine." She was suddenly shy, but he nodded as though such flowery words were commonplace to him.

Fraser Mackinnon, hardheaded Scot, canny scout for his regiment, was as besotted as any love-sick boy on that dazzlingly sunny morning. He would have given her the earth. He was a true descendant of those others in his family legend, Jamie and Katrina. One day he would tell Alex their story.

They entered the bustling street and stopped a dozen times, to be instantly surrounded by eager vendors and just as eager ragged children, sure that these fine

Britishers would toss a coin or two into their out-stretched hands.

"Ignore them all," Fraser advised. "If you give to one, you'll have a multitude around you in seconds."

It was hard to ignore them, but she knew it was the only thing to do. It was some while before they finally emerged from the street, to find their way back to the carriage that had brought them. Before they went back to the Forbes' house, Alex looked at the small collection of items Fraser had bought her.

"A small silver trinket to represent all the riches in the world I would give to you," he said now. "A tiny jeweled elephant on which I would carry you away into the night and an embroidered mat that I would put at our own hearth."

"Thank you," Alex whispered. "I'll treasure them always. They mean more to me than my mother's pearls, Fraser."

She touched the perfect string at her neck, and he knew she couldn't have compared his gifts with anything more precious to her. They left the bustle of the city then and reached the Forbes' house, its rooms cooled by gently waving punkahs, the young boys silently pulling on the ropes for the British Mem'sahibs. Ellen greeted them at once and called for tea and a light luncheon.

"We've had ours already, Alex, and the children have already gone to bed for their afternoon nap. But I promised you would look in on them before you left. Have you had a good day?"

"Wonderful! We explored part of the Red Fort, but it was just too much to take in. Later we went shopping, and I bought a few little things as mementos."

She avoided Fraser's eyes, but she couldn't resist showing off the handful of gifts. Ellen admired them, glancing at her quizzically, just as if she knew the significance of the collection. Perhaps she did. She had been in India too long not to know of its customs. Aunt Maud merely said they were quaint but hardly of any value.

"It depends what value you put on them, Aunt Maud," Alex said with a smile. "Personally, I think they're quite precious!"

Now she knew by Ellen's laugh that she understood very well. Over lunch, Alex produced the invitations to the prince's birthday ball.

"Do say you'll come, Ellen. It will be a wonderful affair, and I'll be glad of your introductions to some of the other British community. The list is very long, and I don't know how many important Indian people will be there as well!"

"We shall be delighted to come, Alex!" Ellen said with obvious pleasure. "And I wanted to ask you if you would care to join our Monday Club. The British wives and ladies meet regularly, changing the venue every few months. It's my turn to be hostess for the summer. Please say you'll join us—and your aunt too, of course."

"It sounds wonderful. Thank you." Impulsively, Alex hugged the other girl, feeling drawn even more into this strange, enchanted land, and yet realizing that the roots of home were still strong. It would still be a little part of England that was recreated in the Forbes' home every Monday.

Before Fraser and the Truscott ladies left for the Residency, Ellen took Alex to say good-bye to the small boys, dozing beneath their net canopies but not really sleeping. They mumbled sleepily to Alex, wanting a hug and a kiss, and she readily complied, loving their warm little bodies and their sticky hugs. She straightened to find Ellen watching her.

"You should have some of your own," she said candidly. "How soon before you and Fraser make an announcement?"

Alex went pink. "We hardly know each other—"

"Nonsense. You've always known each other! I saw that long ago on the *Arabella*, Alex. And the tokens from Chandni Chowk today—he bought them for you, didn't he? You may fool your Aunt Maud, but you can't fool me, darling. The two of you have love written all over you, and I'm so happy for you both!"

Alex laughed softly. "Then it would be silly of me to deny it, wouldn't it? Oh, Ellen, it's so good to speak of it to someone!" She suddenly realized the truth of it, wanting to share her feelings. "I love him so much! I never knew how spectacular it could be, this wanting to be a part of someone, to share their thoughts and their life—"

"You'll find there's even more to share when you're married, Alex. To be spiritually and physically one with the man you truly love is the greatest gift of all and can be little short of heaven."

They both laughed a little embarrassedly at revealing so much of their innermost thoughts and then spontaneously hugged one another. Ellen was a very dear friend, and Alex was buoyant at knowing they were to meet often from now on.

Chapter Eight

THEY WERE TO VISIT THE TRUSCOTT BUNGALOW IN THE middle of March. Alex awoke with mixed feelings. She thought of the bungalow as a place of revered memory, and yet how could it be? She had never seen it. But it would be filled with her mother's ghost, and that was something she never questioned.

Fraser came to the Residency early that day, and the four of them each had their own thoughts as they left the Pearl of the Plain in the Truscott carriage. Felix wished this day could be over. Maud was more curious to see this lovely bungalow of which she'd heard so much.

Fraser hoped that the visit wouldn't upset Alex, while she grew more nervous as their route took them through the plains, the day's heat beginning to make the steam rise from the trees and shimmer upon roadway and river. Knowing Alex's background, Fraser hoped this wouldn't be too nostalgic a visit for her to bear.

As the women chattered and Felix pointed out landmarks to them, Fraser let his thoughts roam. He was more than uneasy regarding the mutterings circulating among the garrisons. His base was with the 78th Highlanders, but he delivered any pertinent reports from regiment to regiment, and the unease in all was the same. If mutiny came. The words were like a recurring theme among men and officers alike these days.

If mutiny came, they would realize the frailty of the British regiments, compared with the might of the Indian platoons. The sepoys and sowars may well be under British command, but in revolt, they could crush the British by sheer force of numbers. The British would be appallingly outnumbered.

Rumors were rife in cities and villages, and because of the fiery cartridge question there were those who could turn this into a religious war. Already, the burnings were beginning. Across the plains, stretching north and west from Calcutta, there were incidents of thatched roofs suddenly blazing in the night, of British homes violated, the telegraph station at Barrackpore burned to the ground.

Fraser felt a thrill of alarm in his veins. Already, in his own mind, he was thinking of it as a seemingly inevitable war. The British authorities probably wouldn't back down from using the greased Enfield cartridges until it was too late, and eventually the Indians would totally refuse to use them. They would be at an impasse, from which there was only one way out. Why couldn't the authorities see it? Everyone else saw it.

In Eastern jargon, the inevitability of it all was carried on the wind and written in the stars. That sense of mystique was much in evidence among the sepoys these days. Murmurings of signs in the skies, of omens and portents, normally dismissed and derided by hard-headed British soldiers, were beginning to be noted, listened to and talked about uneasily among the ranks.

If need be, the ancient barbarism of the East would rid itself of the John Company oppressors once and for all. The entire atmosphere in the garrisons of late had shifted from calm confidence to a sense of watching and waiting . . .

"You're very quiet this morning, Fraser!" He started as he heard Alex's voice. "There's nothing wrong, is there?"

He forced a laugh, catching Truscott's glance, and neatly avoided a direct answer. "What could be wrong on such a morning as this, in the company of two lovely ladies?"

"Now I know why they call the young officers gallants!" Maud remarked. "You've enough charm to wheedle the birds from the trees, young man."

Fraser smiled. "But I'm not an officer, Miss Truscott," he reminded her. "I'm a civilian, the same as you."

Alex was careful not to look at him, apparently studying the skimming of two large cranes across the surface of the river flowing alongside the road they traversed.

"Does that mean you're not bound by any commission, Fraser? You could leave the service at any time?"

"That's right. Not that I've ever considered it, although it was my father's dearest wish for me to return to Scotland and our ancestral home."

"Shouldn't you ever wish to do so, dear boy?" Maud said. She knew of his father's death and spoke delicately. "Doesn't one have a duty to one's ancestors as much as to the present?"

"When the time is right, I may return," he replied impassively. Maud went on relentlessly now.

"I should hope so! We should never forget our roots. Our ancestors made us what we are, Fraser, and your father is right. You have a duty to your family—"

"He has a bloody duty here, woman," Felix snapped, bored with her chatter. "Stop nagging at the boy and stick to your female doings."

She glared at her brother. "You can be very coarse at times, Felix. You never used to be this way. Sometimes I think the Indian sun must have touched your brain."

Maud stuck her chin in the air, but Alex understood her father very well. Of course he never used to be as sharp-tempered and acid-tongued as he was now. He had had his lovely, calming Constance to share his life, and now he had nothing. Alex was acutely aware that her presence could never compensate for losing Constance. It even underlined his loss, and today's visit must be an ordeal for him. For her father's sake, they had best keep it fairly short.

It was an hour's carriage ride to the white-painted bungalow, set idyllically among the trees at the water's edge. Alex felt emotion and some agitation wash over her. She had seen it all in Constance's drawings and imagined coming here to live with her parents. Now, it was all so different.

She felt strangely alone and isolated. Even Fraser's presence couldn't lift her from the mood of melancholy descending on her. She had wanted to come so much, and now she was almost afraid to set foot inside the place. Fraser too seemed preoccupied, and Alex wondered suddenly if he was regretting the role her father had given him. The thought depressed her even more, and for the first time she felt there was an odd barrier between them that she couldn't cross.

The bungalow wasn't left empty. A native retainer and his wife took care of it, living modestly nearby. It was foolish to pay them and to keep it on, but Felix had been quite unable to dispose of it, nor to clear out Constance's clothes and the little studio she used for her drawing and painting. Alex guessed she would find everything the same as if her mother had merely gone out for a walk. It was unnerving.

Felix quickly introduced his guests to the old Indian woman, Jaya, and her husband, Chohban.

"I have business to discuss with Chohban," he said abruptly. "Jaya will make some tea while you look around. You don't need me to guide you."

He went outside again, while Maud looked affronted. The white-haired Jaya smiled a warm welcome at Alex.

"You have the look of your mother, missy Alex," she said in her musical voice. "He will find her in you."

"Thank you, Jaya," she whispered, not sure if it was a good thing or not. All she seemed to do was stir up memories to tear at her father's heart. She realized it more and more. At times, it seemed he couldn't bear to be with her. At others, he stared at her as if tormented, not really seeing her at all, but the image of someone else.

"Your father could be more gracious and not leave us to find our own way," Maud said, aggrieved. Alex rounded on her.

"You don't understand, do you, Aunt Maud? He can't be in here very long. It—it stifles him."

"No, I don't understand. If he hates it that much, he should sell it. It would fetch a good price—"

"There's no price he could put on it," Alex muttered.

Maud shook her head impatiently. "I always said your parents filled your head with nonsense about India, Alex. I do believe you're as addle-brained as they ever were. I thought you might have realized by now that it's just another place to live, and without the comforts of home too—"

"How can you say that, when you live in a palace? It's probably more luxurious than Queen Victoria's!"

"It's not home," Maud sniffed doggedly. "And one day, Alex, my dear, perhaps you'll remember what a special word that is. Nothing can take the place of home!"

Alex was annoyed at feeling guilty at her apparent lack of sensitivity, when it was Maud who was lacking in such feelings! All the same, she felt obliged to apologize.

"I'm sorry. I do know all that you gave up to come here with me, and I want you to be happy, really I do. We have so much to look forward to. The prince's ball at the end of the month and the visit to Krubah Tea. Please be happy, Aunt Maud!"

Maud spoke grudgingly, seating herself grandly on a brocade chair with a rustle of skirts and refusing to move until the tea was brought. "You're a sweet girl at heart, and I'll do my best, but I can never feel the way you do about India. It will always be foreign to me."

But Maud had never had a dream of India, nor the magic of finding true love even before she set foot on its

135

shores. Seeing Fraser being kind and chivalrous to her aunt now, handing her the tea Jaya brought while Alex escaped to wander through the bungalow, she was even more downcast, and she could no more explain her reasons than fly.

She had India, and she had Fraser's love, and in terms of importance, she knew she had put them in reverse order. It didn't really matter where in the world you found love. It was love itself that was the essence of existence. There was piquancy in discovering the simple truth of it here in her mother's house.

She moved about, touching things that Constance would have touched: a half-finished painting, the brushes still dipped in the container of cleaning fluid; first rough sketches in pencil and charcoal, stacked against a wall. Alex went from room to room, swiftly in and out of her parents' chamber and into the one that had been destined for herself. It was prettily decorated, the mosquito net in position above the bed, dainty trinkets that Constance would have chosen on the dressing table.

Tears suddenly choked her, and she had to get out of there fast. Was it deliberate or coincidence, that everyone seemed to be leaving her strictly alone? She was filled with a grief she hadn't known since the day she had heard of her mother's death. She stumbled towards the long french windows of her room and onto the verandah to gulp in fresh air as though she were drowning. The horizon spun for a moment, and she leaned back in a corner of the verandah, where cool green vines cascaded over a trelliswork to give shade in the hottest part of the day.

She leaned back even more when she heard the mutter of voices below, not wanting anyone to see her distress. And then she drew in her breath as she recognized her father's voice, speaking to the Indian retainer. It was harsh and tense.

"Don't underestimate them, Chohban. If all seems lost, then fire the place yourself. Don't be caught like rats in a trap, for God's sake."

"My duty is to you, Sahib Truscott," the man protested. "I pledged myself to defend you always—"

"You'll do as I say, man! Don't be a hero. Think of yourself and your wife. You've been good and faithful servants to me and mine, but if a choice has to be made, then save yourselves. Do I have your promise?"

"Until the stars fall, Sahib—"

Alex heard her father give a grim laugh that sent a chill through her.

"They say there is blood in the stars lately, Chohban. Do you believe all the portents of evil? No, don't bother to answer, old friend. Why should you deny your beliefs, any more than we do? That's one of the damnable follies . . ."

The voices faded and she realized the men were moving away. She seemed frozen, unable to move, hardly able to breathe, and then she heard movements from inside the bungalow.

"Alex, where are you?"

At Fraser's voice, she seemed to come to life and slipped back inside the room. He moved towards her, and to Alex it seemed as though he moved in slow motion. She was still caught up in the terrible nightmare that was becoming clear to her at last. All the whispers she had heard of late; the sudden silences between her father and David Gould when she was around; the doubled guard at the palace, and yet the forced sense of almost desperate gaiety inside the palace walls; Ellen Forbes' Monday Club, where the ladies had been unaccountably anxious lately and had spoken of some trouble over cartridges . . .

Alex hadn't understood much of it, and it had seemed they hadn't wanted to worry her with it all and insisted that it would all blow over, talking instead of frivolous matters, of women's fripperies and the next ball . . . but now, everything seemed to crystallize in her own father's words: "If all seems lost, then fire the place yourself . . . there is blood in the stars . . . all the portents of evil . . . why deny your beliefs . . . ?"

"Fraser, what's happening?" Her lips felt wooden, her voice cracked. "To us—to India. Are we in danger? I'm not a child, though everyone seems to treat me so! What's *happening?*"

She suddenly raged at him, and as he went swiftly towards her, to catch at her trembling arms, she beat against him, hating him and everyone else for protecting her when she didn't need protection. She was a woman, capable of thinking for herself, and if he didn't believe it to be so, then his love for her was no more than the love for a pretty child, and it was worthless.

Humiliation swept through her so quickly it made her gasp with the pain of it. It had been a day of pain and realization. The anguish of being here, where she had thought she wanted to be, and now knew she didn't; the eavesdropping that had made her feel betrayed by her own father, by Fraser and everyone she knew.

He didn't insult her by pretending not to know what she was talking about. "What have you heard, Alex?" He spoke in the same harsh tones as her father. They might never have held each other close, never been on the brink of intimacy, never loved.

He gripped her arms cruelly, as if he thought she

knew something of vital importance. Of course, he was an army scout. Or was it a spy? Did he now expect her to spy for him too? Thoughts danced in and out of her head like the clawing of some beautiful poisonous spider, each jab hurting more than the last. She felt betrayed, hurt, as if all the ugliness of India was suddenly revealed to her. And yet, what had she heard, today and in past weeks? Only scattered fragments of conversation.

"Tell me the truth." She shook with mingled fury and tears. "Are we all in danger? Even my father speaks of blood in the stars, and he's no longer the most poetic of men."

"Is that all?" Fraser attempted to lighten the charged atmosphere between them. "You heard a piece of Indian folklore and let your imagination do the rest? It's this place, dearest, and thoughts of your mother. Come away—"

She shook herself free of him, standing rigid and ashen-faced. She was beautiful in her fear, her eyes dark and haunted. Against the cool cotton of her day dress, her nipples stood out sharply, twin points of tension. She was more desirable than the sun and moon, but Fraser felt less desire than anger as she railed at him. Anger at himself and her parents, for not trusting her to learn the truth gradually. She had to learn it brutally now, and he knew he would be clumsy in the telling because of his own guilt.

"It's more than folklore, isn't it? What of these cartridges? Why should Father instruct Chohban to fire this beautiful bungalow if he had to, rather than be caught like rats in a trap? I have a right to know. My mother—"

She choked on the word. Would Constance have told

her or made things seem beautiful as always? At last, Alex knew what her Aunt Maud had always known, that where there was lightness, there were also dark shadows.

Fraser told her quickly all there was to know, sparing nothing. Small incidents that seemed little enough on their own assumed gigantic proportions when put together to mean the suppression of a people's identity. Alex listened intently, the beads of perspiration on her forehead and around her mouth the only indication of her horror.

"Why did you tell me none of this on the ship? Was it because you thought me as flighty as Miss Hilary Delmont and unable to think intelligently?"

"Dammit, I didn't know any more than you until I reached my garrison!"

He didn't like her accusing voice. He wasn't on trial, for God's sake, but Alexandra Truscott made him feel as though he was. He snapped at her, and she thought him as arrogant as at their first meeting, when he'd hauled her back from the edge of the dock at Tilbury.

"You knew the country wasn't as serene as I believed it to be—"

"Would you have listened if I'd tried to tell you? Would you have wanted to hear? Your parents should have told you. It's taken more than a few months to bring everything to the boil."

Her heart beat sickeningly. "Tell me what you mean. I'm sick of listening to riddles. Blood in the stars, indeed!" She ridiculed the words that she might once have thought eerily charming, the way that children enjoyed fairy tales involving demons and devils.

"We've tried to smother these people by fair means and foul, forgetting their own deep traditions. We've tried to make them all equal, when the caste system is so important to them. We've forbidden them the right to suttee—"

"Don't blind me with words I don't understand," Alex snapped at him. Fraser stared at her with narrowed eyes. They stood a foot apart and it might have been an ocean.

"Did your parents tell you so little of India after all, lassie? Suttee is officially forbidden, but it's known that it still occurs in remote areas. It's the right of an Indian wife to throw herself on the funeral pyre of her husband and perish in the flames with him—"

"Stop it!" Her pale face suddenly flooded with color at the crisp, graphic words. "Are you deliberately trying to frighten and shock me? If what you say is true, is it so bad to want to end such a vile custom?"

"It is, when outsiders try to cut out the heart of a nation's traditions," he said grimly. Alex fought back the tears she wouldn't show. They made her throat ache. Everything was changing, and she couldn't stop it . . .

"Alexandra, what are you doing? Is Fraser there with you? There's tea waiting for you here, and your father wants to leave soon—" Aunt Maud's voice broke through the tension-filled atmosphere in Alex's room. She pushed past this stranger, her love, and called to Aunt Maud that she was coming at once.

"Alex—"

She ignored Fraser's sudden low plea and rejoined her aunt. The tear-stained eyes and flushed cheeks told their own tale, and Maud tut-tutted at once.

"There now! I knew all along that it was a mistake to make so much of coming here, my love. Your mother wouldn't have wanted your tears. Come and let your old aunt dry them!"

141

Alex was suddenly in her arms, sobs wrenching out of her. For the moment, let Aunt Maud think it was sorrow for her mother that was tearing her apart. There would be time enough, when she was calmer, to reveal all that she knew, unwittingly from her father and now from Fraser Mackinnon.

She made no fuss about leaving when her father was ready. She was quiet on the journey back, and Fraser sat unsmiling, his face hard and set. If Maud suspected the two of them had had a tiff while they were alone, she privately thought it not such a bad thing. Alex was so intense and so young. It was easy enough for her to fall into the arms of the first handsome man she met, and there were plenty of others in the sea. Perhaps at the prince's birthday ball she would meet other young officers and realize that Fraser Mackinnon, charming though he was, was only one man among many eligible suitors. Thus Maud cheered herself.

As soon as Fraser had left them at the palace, Alex sought out her father in his office. He had had enough socializing for one day and wanted the peace of his sanctuary. He barked at her to enter, scowling when she appeared. David Gould had been dispatched to Delhi for the day, and all Felix wanted was to be left alone.

"What is it, my dear? I have work to do—"

She was always direct when she wanted to know something. "Why didn't you tell me about the troubles, Father? About the cartridges and the soldiers being reluctant to use them, and all the burnings and the blood in the stars—"

"Now just hold on a moment, young lady!" He held up his hand as her voice became impassioned. "Who's been filling your head with such nonsense?"

"You have, Father! I heard you talking with Choh-

142

ban at the bungalow, and I demanded that Fraser tell me more—"

"Mackinnon!" Felix said bitterly. "I thought I could trust the man not to alarm my womenfolk."

"We *should* be alarmed if we're in danger!" Alex cried. "Can't you see how foolish it is to keep us in ignorance? And if you think of me as a woman, then treat me like one. I'm not a child any longer!"

"No, you're not," he said grudgingly. "All right. So you know there's been some trouble. It will pass. It always does."

"Does it? Is that why you've instructed Chohban to fire the bungalow if need be? Father, don't play with me. How serious is it?"

Felix glared at her across his desk. She was so like her mother, and yet there was something more in her. He found himself resenting the fact that she had a strength Constance hadn't possessed. She had all the sensual beauty of a woman but the logic of a man, and it was a combination he wasn't sure he liked. His generation liked their women to be decorative but content to remain in the background. It was irritating to find a woman who probed and questioned, especially when it was his own daughter.

"All right. It could be serious, and it pays to take every possible precaution," he admitted at last. "But we need have no worries here. Prince Shunimar's palace is a fortress, and his chowkidars will be loyal if need be."

He hoped his words were true. It was only a few months ago when some palace guards had been involved in a minor skirmish. Sir Peter Wallace had already called Felix to account on that score. The offending chowkidars had been dealt with and the new guard doubled. But Felix knew only too well how flames could be fanned by a mass revolt, and he chose not to admit that although a doubled guard meant twice the protection, it also meant twice the number to mutiny.

He came round the desk to his daughter and ruffled her hair with an unusual show of affection. He cursed Mackinnon for upsetting her so. With his next words he buried his head in the sand, like so many of his countrymen.

"Do you think I'd have brought you here if there'd been any real risk, my love?"

"You couldn't have stopped me. You and Mother made a promise, remember?" She leaned up and kissed him. "Anyway, thank you for showing me the bungalow. I don't think I shall want to go there again."

"That's all right then." His relief was enormous. If Alex had been adamant about wanting to live there, he couldn't have borne it. And Alex had a way of wheedling what she wanted out of anyone.

Calmly, she explained everything she knew to Aunt Maud, who listened with horrified eyes.

"I shall have words with your father over this," she said indignantly. "He had no right to keep it from us."

"He did it for the best, Aunt Maud." Alex found herself defending him. She went on as her aunt said nothing. "I was determined to come, and even if I'd known, it wouldn't have stopped me." She realized that too.

"Why didn't Fraser say anything?" Maud said suddenly.

"I don't know. He says that the cartridge incident was unknown to him. It happened while we were coming from England. We can't blame Fraser!"

But Alex did, and she didn't know why. She still felt

that sense of betrayal, of hurt, of loss of innocence somehow.

She didn't altogether mind when he sent a message to say that business prevented him from escorting the ladies for the next two weeks. She needed time apart from him. But she missed him, and her temper suffered because of it.

"I'm not sure this environment suits you, Alexandra," Aunt Maud said crossly, when Alex had complained a dozen times about the needlework she was doing. They both sat on the verandah of the Residency, enjoying the sunshine, having observed the daily ritual of Prince Shunimar's chowkidars on parade.

It was about the only time they ever saw the prince, when he stood on his balcony, as wide as he was tall, looking even larger in the elaborate and richly embroidered garments he wore as proof of his position. Surrounding him were always the two astrologers, whom Alex privately called the evil duo.

"You think I prefer the rainy shores of England?" Alex asked as she threw the needlework down in annoyance. Who wouldn't prefer the climate here, with its warmth and color? And yet, and yet . . . For an instant, Alex was swamped with a sudden nostalgia for England, for its special greenery, the smells of London that were dear and familiar and not strange and exotic. She brushed the thought aside. How absurd, after all the years of longing for India!

"I think you need some activity, dear," Maud said briskly. "Why not ask your father if Mr. Gould can take us to the Monday Club, since Fraser is not available? I'm sure the young man will be only too pleased to act as escort. It's too annoying to be confined here like prisoners, just because it's not the done thing for a woman to travel about alone!"

Alex brightened. Why not, indeed? She had enjoyed the meetings so far. Ellen was a good hostess, and it was like a breath of home to sit with the other ladies and talk about places they all knew well. She caught her breath. This was home, she reminded herself.

Besides, it wouldn't hurt Fraser Mackinnon to know she didn't depend on his company entirely! She gathered up her skirts.

"I'll put it to Father at once. He's always sending David to Delhi for something or other. It can be no trouble to him to take us to Ellen Forbes' house!"

It was soon accomplished, and if David went pinker than usual at being given such a pleasant task, he undertook it with his usual seriousness. He was a sweet boy, Alex thought with a sigh, but so dreary. So sweet and so obliging, and with about as much vitality as a dead leaf.

But it helped to lighten the two weeks before the prince's birthday ball, when they saw nothing of Fraser Mackinnon and Alex tried to tell herself she didn't care. It was obvious to Ellen Forbes that she did. On the second Monday, Ellen asked Alex if she could help her to pass around the dainty cakes she had baked that morning.

"What's happened between you and Fraser, darling?" Ellen said as soon as they were alone.

Alex intended to be breezy, to pass it off as if there was nothing wrong, but it proved impossible. A lump stuck in her throat, and she was overwhelmed with sudden misery.

"Nothing's happened. That's what's wrong! I haven't seen him since we went to the bungalow."

Quickly, she told Ellen what had occurred there. Ellen smiled ruefully. "Perhaps we're all to blame for pretending things are as calm as we'd like, Alex. I worry too. I worry for John and for the children, but I try not to show it. There are times when women have to be stronger than men. I'm sure his absence is for a genuine reason. He loves you, Alex—"

"Does he?"

"Now, that's a silly question! You don't need me to tell you the answer. Didn't he buy you the love tokens from Chandni Chowk? I'll bet you have them where you can see them every day."

Alex gave a watery smile. "They're all beside my bed, so that they're the first things I see when I awake each morning."

"You *see?*" Ellen said in triumph.

Alex wasn't quite sure what she was supposed to see, but she followed Ellen into the drawing room with the plate of madeira cakes, feeling considerably better.

The ladies exclaimed on the excellence of Ellen's baking.

"Have you heard the latest?" the wife of a captain in the Queen's 60th Rifles at Meerut trilled as she bit delicately into a piece of cake. "There are rumors circulating that there is bone dust mixed with the flour, and now the natives refuse to buy government flour! Did you ever hear anything so ludicrous? They'll believe anything!"

Everyone laughed, though Ellen wished the lady had refrained from mentioning the fact until all her madeira cake had been distributed. And Alex thought she could detect a hint of desperation in the laughter. They were superficially bright and cheerful, but beneath it all . . . she tried not to notice the sidelong glances from one to another at the Monday Club.

And whether Fraser's absence from her side recently

was for a genuine reason or not, she would see him soon, at the prince's ball. The thought of it was like an oasis in the desert. Whatever else was happening, Prince Shunimar's birthday ball would take place, and his splendidly bedecked elephants would go proudly on parade to show the world . . . Alex knew not what.

Chapter Nine

ALEX HAD ATTENDED MANY BIG PARTIES AND DANCES IN London, but never one like Prince Shunimar's birthday ball. Felix had tried to prepare her and Maud for the splendor to come, but description could never do justice to the dazzle of the prince's regalia, the brilliance of the British officers' dress uniforms, the glitter of diamonds and emeralds and rubies on their ladies.

Alex herself wore a gleaming gown of autumn-bronze silk, layers and layers of softly falling fabric, hooped and ruched, the low neckline revealing the creamy curves of her breasts, her hair becomingly arranged in ringlets that caressed her shoulders, Constance's gleaming pearls around her neck catching every facet of light from the brilliant chandeliers and wall lights. Maud had sighed briefly, seeing the vision before her, wishing that Alex's mother could see her lovely daughter on such an occasion as this.

But the only person Alex wanted to see was Fraser. Was it an accident that he was so late in arriving, or was it done to pique her? Her heart plummeted when she saw two familiar figures bearing down on her and Aunt Maud, and she forced a pleased smile to her lips as she made the introductions to Felix, returning with some iced lemonade for them.

"Father, may I introduce Lady Delmont and Miss Hilary Delmont, whom we met on the ship. It's good to see you again, Lady Delmont—" She hoped no one would notice she had not included Hilary in the words.

"And you too, dear girl," the older woman gushed. "How splendid you look this evening. India obviously suits you, Alex, but do be careful to keep that lovely skin out of the sun, won't you? It's so tiresome to relinquish our English rose complexions."

To Alex, already a pale golden hue from her walks around the prince's palace grounds, the comment was not so much advice as a comparison with her dear Hilary's ghostlike skin. Hilary did not bloom under the Indian sun, and after a preliminary few words with the Truscott ladies, continued to let her eyes roam about the sumptuous audience room for the most eligible males.

Who had invited them, Alex seethed. Was it Fraser? Had he somehow organized this without telling her? Obviously, not all the invitations had come through Felix Truscott's office, and it had shaken her to see the cool and lovely Hilary Delmont, dressed in a sea-green crinoline that flattered her dark beauty.

Alex was seized with an acute burst of jealous misery, and not until she saw several dashing British officers, resplendent in their red braided jackets and elegant trousers, congregate at Hilary's side to sign her dance card, did she begin to call herself a fool and to breathe more easily.

She turned to make some light, breezy comment to her aunt, only to find her deep in conversation with Lady Delmont. It was ridiculous to feel momentarily alone in this great company of people, the colors of the room as brilliant as in a kaleidoscope, the chatter as bright and exuberant as in an aviary, and yet that was exactly how she felt.

Prince Shunimar himself sat apart from the rest, heavily laden with attire of cloth of gold, his astrologers about him, and one by one selected groups were presented to him as though he were a fabled god. It was all unreal, a charade they all played.

Her eyes stopped their seeking and her heart leaped. Fraser Mackinnon was walking towards her, as beautiful a man as ever lived.

He walked straight towards her, his eyes as dark and inscrutable as any Oriental's, and only when he reached her did Alex realize she had been standing as though mesmerized, the throbbing pulse in her neck betraying all her emotions more endearingly to Fraser than any words.

He reached her side and took both her hands in his, raising each palm to his lips in a brief greeting. In the crush of people, the gesture was mostly unnoticed, but Maud noted it and knew at once why her niece had been so out of sorts lately and why she suddenly seemed to blossom like a rose in the warmth of the sun.

"This is my dance, I believe, Miss Truscott," Fraser murmured, as the strains of a waltz filled the room. He held out his arms to her and she moved into them as though in a dream. Whose name was on her dance card she neither knew nor cared. All she wanted was to be in Fraser's arms. The power of her own feelings was overwhelming.

He held her as close as decorum allowed, although with so many other dancers whirling around, it wasn't difficult to snatch a moment of extra closeness now and then.

"You look stunning, my dearest." He breathed the words against the softness of her hair, and the rough timbre of his voice made her fall in love with him all over again. The flippant reply she intended to make died on her lips, and she could only look at him wordlessly for a moment before he twirled her close once more.

"Oh, Fraser, why have you been neglecting me?" she asked huskily. "Did I anger you so much with my foolishness at the bungalow? Did I seem such a child to you?"

They spun around the room, and the colors merged like the glorious twilight. When they steadied again, she saw that Fraser's eyes were gentle.

"I would never neglect you through choice, my lassie, and if you angered me, believe me I understood so well all the frustration and pain you felt that day. And no, you didn't seem a child to me, Alex. That's not the way I think of you."

Happiness brought back the teasing words to her lips, and she laughed up into his face coquettishly.

"How do you think of me then?"

He grazed his thumb softly against her bare arm, and a shiver of excitement ran through her. He only had to touch her flesh and she was aflame. She was weak at the knowledge. Such feelings had never been part of her experience before, such powerful sensations that grew and flowered, spreading out from the very core of her.

"I think of you as my woman," he said thickly. "And well ye know it, ye little witch!"

The music ended, almost like an intrusion into the magical world they had conjured up for themselves. Reluctantly, they broke apart, and Fraser led her back to the corner where her father and aunt sat. With them were the Delmont ladies, a red-faced David Gould and Sir Peter Wallace. The jealousy soared back as Alex saw Hilary's delighted face as she and Fraser approached.

"Fraser! We did so hope you would be here this evening. Mother knows Sir Peter well, and when he added our names to his invitation list, we wondered if we would see you. I hope you're going to mark my card!"

She thrust it under his nose, and he smilingly scrawled his name several times. There was hardly room for more, Alex saw with childish satisfaction, for Hilary was clearly much in demand by the young officers. And she was relieved to know that it hadn't been Fraser's idea for the Delmonts to be here!

She was increasingly surprised at the depth of her own feelings. Not only about her beloved, but the attendant emotions that went with the discovery of love. The jealousy, the possessiveness, the strange loneliness whenever they were apart, the isolation in a crowd until she found him—these were all as new to her as love, and she realized that her education at Lady Margaret's Academy had been far from complete.

"What are you smiling about so enigmatically, Alex?" Aunt Maud remarked, causing her niece's face to scorch with color.

"I was just admiring the wonderful ball gowns, Aunt Maud," she invented hastily, quite sure that her aunt didn't believe her for a minute.

She hardly cared. It was enough for her that Fraser was here and that he loved her. She would never doubt it again. His eyes spoke of love every time he looked at her. Whenever he touched her, his hands spoke a language only they understood. Miraculously, she no longer felt so jealous when he danced dutifully with Hilary and several other ladies. Nothing could touch what they shared. It was as though love threw a protective shield around both of them. It was a strange realization.

At midnight, a huge gong resounded through the palace, and the prince clapped his hands in the sudden silence in the audience room. He took little part in the proceedings, merely sitting on his princely throne and observing the merriment, but Felix had told his ladies that Shunimar himself always led the guests to watch his elephants.

"We will now watch the elephants parade," he announced. "My chowkidars will lead you to the viewing places. Be so kind as to follow them."

The ladies in their shimmering gowns moved excitedly through the maze of corridors, an endless procession following the prince and guided by his guards. Finally, they all emerged on a great balcony overlooking a courtyard. The palace was so vast, Alex was sure she had never been anywhere near this part before. Below them, the darkness of the night was lit by the flare of torches, held by chowkidars standing motionless in a huge square. The guests crowded onto the balcony, crushed together to get a better view. Shunimar himself, protected by his astrologers and guards, was seated in the midst of them. At his nod, a strange signal was given from a reed instrument, and a sudden blare of trumpets made them all gasp.

What happened next was like something out of the Arabian Nights. Squeezed between her aunt and her father, with Fraser standing directly behind her, Alex caught her breath at the spectacle of the elephants moving majestically into the square below. Dressed now in the raiments she and Fraser had been shown, they glittered and gleamed, as each one followed the one in front. On their backs, the howdahs rocked, their riders dressed identically in pure red silk, with gold turbans blazing on their heads.

The ladies gasped, the gentlemen cleared their throats to hide their own emotion at seeing such a display, as the elephants slowly turned and wove about the courtyard in formations that were obviously well rehearsed. Again and again they were applauded and cheered, and Shunimar was clearly well satisfied with the response.

And as Alex clapped with the rest of them, she became aware that Fraser's hands were moving sensuously against her back, as though he were unable to resist this chance to be close to her. Perhaps other young men were also seizing the chance to fondle their ladies . . .

Alex didn't stop to consider the fact. All she knew was how deliciously wicked it was, in the midst of all these people, to feel the warm pressure of strong, sensitive fingers caressing her spine and the curve of her hips and buttocks, and to feel those lovely new sensations begin again.

Unconsciously, she leaned back even more against Fraser, turning her head swiftly to smile and exclaim to him about the performance of the elephants, but really to see the warmth of his eyes and feel the hot blood race in her veins at the desire she saw there. It was a desire she shared, knowing instinctively that this wasn't a purely male prerogative. Knowing now that a woman could need and want, with all the passion of a man.

Alex felt that need in him as a sudden surge of the guests behind him pushed him nearer to her. She felt his maleness with a start of surprise and awe. Her mouth went dry, because truly this was the first time she had discovered the strength of a man's body, that could change a tender root to a pulsating shaft of power. It should frighten her, but it didn't.

She felt him move against her a little, and the soft hoops of her crinoline seemed to envelop him. She felt a searing excitement in her veins, a sudden urge to know more, to know all there was to know of the completeness between a man and a woman, and the primitive longing to turn swiftly into Fraser's arms and be one with him was enough to make her gasp anew.

"Isn't it just fabulous, Alex?" Aunt Maud's voice said in her ear, and Alex gave a high-pitched laugh, because what she was finding so fabulous was far and away more intimate and more beautiful than any parade of elephants!

Her voice was slightly cracked. "I've never known anything so stupendous in my life."

She glanced back at Fraser as she spoke, and the sexual awareness between them spoke more than mere words ever could. In one brief meeting of darkened eyes and flushed cheeks and parted mouths, all that was needed was questioned and answered.

By the time the ball was ended, Alex felt as though she had come through a lifetime of emotions. It was near dawn before the last of the guests left the palace, and by that time, Fraser Mackinnon had begged for a short time alone with Felix.

Thinking the man wanted to speak on business, Felix took him into his office for a last drink of brandy before Fraser went back to his garrison.

They sat companionably on the wide leather chairs, sprawled out in the aftermath of an incredible evening, the like of which only Eastern royalty could provide. Through the office windows, a pale dawn sky streaked the heavens with gold and silver tints and the delicate watercolors of pink and blue.

"Speak up, man," Felix said genially. "If there's trouble brewing, I'm not sure I really want to hear it when I'm dog-tired, but I suppose I had better."

Fraser gripped his brandy glass more tightly, suddenly nervous, and it wasn't a feeling he often knew.

"It's not business, Truscott," he said abruptly. "It's —there's only one way to say this, and that's to come right out with it. I love your daughter, Felix, and I want your permission to court her. More than that—I want as short an engagement as possible, for 'tis my belief that the more secure we all feel in this country at the present, the better for all of us!"

Felix sat openmouthed. This wasn't what he had expected to hear. He wasn't fool enough not to have seen some attachment on his daughter's account, but he'd put it down to adolescence. The girl was still a child. He reminded himself that only recently he had agreed that she was no longer a child . . . but in the ways of men, she certainly was. He looked suspicious.

"This is a surprise and no mistake, Mackinnon." He spoke gruffly. "You and my daughter—"

Fraser bridled at once, guiltily pushing away the fact that if he had his way, he would make Alex his, body and soul, at the first opportunity!

"I assure you, sir, my intentions are strictly honorable, and if it seems I speak with undue haste, 'tis because I believe it's what Alexandra and I both want. We want to be together, Felix."

"You've spoken to my daughter?" Felix said keenly.

Fraser held the smile of remembering in check. He had spoken to her, in words and actions, and he still had the burning sensation of that special look she had given him on the balcony. It was love and desire and sheer wondrous womanhood aching to be fulfilled, and he had never loved her more than when he had seen that naked look of love on her face.

"I have, sir," he said gravely.

"She's very young. Too young to be married. Dammit, man, she's not eighteen for several months yet! Yet in many ways, she's already more mature than I expected. That could be on your account, of course." For the first time he viewed the Highlander as though through the eyes of a young and vulnerable young woman and gave in to the inevitable.

"You have my permission to court her, Mackinnon," Felix went on. "An engagement, if you like, but I want no hasty wedding to set tongues wagging, you hear? I'll have your word on that before you leave here."

"All right." Fraser spoke slowly, but he could see the other was adamant. And an engagement gave a couple more intimacy than mere walking-out. And God forgive him, but he wanted intimacy with Alexandra Truscott more than life!

"In a way, it simplifies things when we travel to Krubah Tea," Felix went on, half to himself. "As my daughter's fiancé, you'll be a fitting escort. I take it the arrangements still stand for that?"

"Of course. I look forward to it. Now I think we had both better get some sleep or we'll be fit for nothing tomorrow. I'm sure Alex will be already in bed by now. May I call and ask her formally tomorrow?"

"Do you have to return to your garrison? It's near daylight already. There are rooms to spare here, man. We're rattling in empty rooms. You're welcome to stay, since you're to be my son-in-law!"

Felix smiled for the first time, suddenly liking the sound and the notion of it. Fraser welcomed the offer of a room, and the two men parted on the best of terms. And in the morning, Alex was astonished and delighted to see Fraser entering the dining room to join her family for breakfast. And when she found out the reason for his prolonged visit, she was ecstatic.

Now, at last, he could give her a discreet kiss in front of them all, and she could hug his arm and smile into his face without trying to hide her feelings. And Maud could only be pleased for her niece's obvious happiness and try to ignore the poignant stab of regret that such happiness had been denied to herself all those years ago.

Plans could now be made with more gusto than before about the visit to Krubah Tea. In two weeks' time, they would leave for the hills, where it would be cool and refreshing, as the temperature in the plains began to soar. It would be the end of April when they returned, and with every week that passed, Alex hoped her father would agree that her marriage to Fraser should not be too long delayed. Her own nature demanded that it must be soon. She loved him so much. She wanted him so much . . .

Now, when Alex didn't see Fraser too often, she was reassured by the knowledge that it was army business that kept them apart. They went into Delhi the day after the prince's ball, and he bought her an engagement ring at Delhi's finest jeweler's, a huge sapphire surrounded by a circlet of diamonds that glittered on her finger and later drew gasps of admiration from Maud and Felix.

An announcement in all the Delhi newspapers was all the celebration they wanted, for Alex truly felt that the prince's ball had been party enough. All their friends and acquaintances had been there, and there was too much to do to prepare for the visit to the hills to think of anything else.

Many British ladies went to the hills during the summer months, some to hill stations of the Company with their menfolk, others to spend the time there with their children, while their husbands sweltered it out in the cities.

Alex had looked forward to seeing the tea estate of which she had heard so much. She looked forward to it doubly now, with Fraser officially affianced to her. Aunt Maud could hardly forbid her to spend a little time alone with him now . . . but she discovered that Aunt Maud had her own ideas on that. On the day before their departure, Maud broached the subject.

"Alex, dear, you remember that little talk we had on the ship?" At sight of her rosy cheeks, Alex knew immediately which talk was referred to but pretended that she didn't.

"Which talk was that, Aunt Maud?" she asked innocently.

Suddenly realizing by the twitch of Alex's mouth that she knew very well, Maud gave her familiar snort.

"Now, Alex, since you and dear Fraser have become engaged, you must realize it's even more necessary for the two of you to be—restrained—in your—your association—"

She stumbled on, until finally Alex could bear it no

longer. She put her arms around her aunt and spoke softly and lovingly to her.

"Dear Aunt Maud, I do know what you mean, and please rest easy. Both Fraser and I love and respect you and Father and would never do anything to bring shame to you. Does that answer your question?"

If it did, it also said nothing about refusing to admit to feelings that ran stronger in both of them than any they had known before. It said nothing about keeping apart when they so wanted to be together. It said nothing about making sure they would be alone whenever possible . . .

Aunt Maud smiled happily, reassured by Alex's words. "It does, my love. And you'll forgive me for bringing up such a delicate matter."

"Of course. Now let's continue our packing and let our faces cool down, shall we?"

It was strange that there were times now when she felt so much older and wiser than Aunt Maud.

The carriage took the four of them away from the palace grounds on the morning of April 15th. The morning sparkled with fresh, earthy scents after the early dews had dried on the trees and shrubs. Birds sang joyously, and Alex felt that this must be close to perfection, riding across the plains alongside Fraser, her father and aunt seated opposite, the Indian driver more a friend than a servant, and ahead of them the distant, smoky blue hills, where it would be cool and sweetly fragrant and she would see at last the tea estate of which she had heard so much.

Finally, Felix had told his daughter just how important this place was to all of them. In a rare moment of revelation, he had told her briefly last night that should she ever need sanctuary, she was to go to Krubah Tea, where the estate manager would see to her every need. If the time should ever come when she needed such assistance, Alex's future would be assured in the dividends from Krubah Tea, and her father's partner, Miles Thompson, would do all that was necessary for her.

"Please don't speak as though you were about to die, Father!" Alex had exclaimed. "You're not ill, are you? You're still a vigorous man."

"I'm not ill, my love, just taking precautions. There are only two things dear to my heart now. One is you, and the other is my interest in Krubah Tea. Both mean much to me, because of your mother, Alex, so indulge me in my moment of sentimentality."

Her throat had thickened, hearing the sadness in his voice, and she had asked no more questions, thinking it merely a whim on his part, though it was a surprise to know that Felix was a major shareholder in Krubah Tea, that it had made him a wealthy man and that this wealth would be Alex's legacy.

She wasn't thinking of such things as the carriage took them deeper and deeper into gradually rising ground, the slopes of which were forested with thickets of rhododendron trees, alive with color. There were other carriages on the road, and occasionally they stopped for refreshment at a small hostelry.

They stopped for the night at a hotel in a clearing and were so tired that all they wanted to do was sleep. There were few facilities for bathing, and the ladies had to make do as best they could. It was hardly the journey Alex had envisaged, with herself and Fraser taking a moonlight stroll and spending a little time alone.

Such a pleasant occurrence wasn't possible until they finally reached the tea estate. Until then, Felix advised them not to wander far from the hotel because of the dangers of marauding animals, of snakes and spiders and other unmentionable hazards. One hint was enough to keep Alex strictly indoors at all times.

But they finally reached the estate, and the wide, white building with its cool verandah spoke of opulence and good living. Miles Thompson greeted Felix like a brother and was more than welcoming to the other guests. Miles was white-haired but bronzed by the sun. He had married late in life and had no children, but his wife, Louisa, was a handsome, comfortably proportioned woman who showed them all to their rooms herself.

"Your father has his permanent quarters, even though he doesn't come here as much as we would all like," Louisa smiled at Alex. "But when he can get away from his business, this is his home, and we'd like you to think of it that way too, Alexandra."

Alex warmed to her at once, and when the older woman heard that Alex and Fraser had recently become engaged, she said that they must have a special celebration that evening. It was truly like being part of one large family, Alex thought with gratitude and with an odd lump in her throat. It was almost like having a mother taking charge of everything.

And at last, she and Fraser could take those moonlight strolls, safe in the estate surroundings, with the evening scents of the tea bushes captured on the summer breeze. The sky had never looked more beautiful to Alex as on those idyllic nights, when the moon rode high and full among a million stars and the hills all around them were softened and rounded by the darkness.

Here, there was no hint of sepoys revolting, of skirmishes in the night, of thatched roofs suddenly blazing from a rebel's torch. There was no thought of the insult of greased cartridges, of caste dignity being crushed by Company rules, of the nonsense of bone dust being mixed with government flour.

If the two older men discussed such matters at grave length, while the matrons chattered together in Louisa's lady's room of London and needlework and the new season's fashions and discovered an empathy in each other's company that was a bonus in itself, then the two younger people felt as though the world was theirs.

They walked to the foot of the tiered slopes of tea bushes, shadowed by the night. Nearby was a small thatched hut, several of which were dotted about the estate, the purpose of which they didn't know.

When they stopped, Fraser drew her immediately into his arms, imprisoning her in his embrace, and her heart began to beat erratically. They had walked some distance from the house, which stood in startling white beauty in the moonlight. But she saw none of it now. All she saw was Fraser's nearness, and she melted against him as though her limbs had turned to water.

"Do you know how long it is since we've been properly alone together, my lassie?" She heard the tension in his voice, the suppressed desire. "I've had to keep my feelings in check all the while, and it gets more difficult every day."

"We went into Delhi to buy an engagement ring alone, Fraser—" she said faintly.

"Alone with a million other people milling in the city!" he commented. "That's not what I mean, and ye know it, don't ye, Alexandra?"

The way he spoke her name and the way his accent became more pronounced when he was deeply moved made her shiver. She felt his hands slide down from her waist to caress the silkiness of her dress over her hips. She felt the pressure of his thumbs against her groin, and she felt that familiar dryness of her mouth again.

His lips brushed her mouth, tantalizing her, his tongue moving softly over her lips and leaving them cool in the night with the moistness of his touch.

"We're alone now, my love," she whispered, knowing that with the words she was giving him what he wanted, what she wanted, without thought of the proprieties or thought of yesterday or tomorrow. None of it mattered, because there was only today, tonight, here and now, and the passion that blazed between them like molten fire.

They stood so close, they were almost part of each other already . . . almost. But without that final, beautiful submission and possession that given in love was as mystical as the scriptures.

"Do you know what you're saying, my lassie?"

"I know. I do know, Fraser."

They moved together towards the little hut. There was no door. It was just an enclosure with some rough matting on the floor. It didn't matter. They gave no thought to insects or worse that might be lurking inside. It was warm and musty, as though the thatch held the warmth of the day, and very slowly, Fraser began to unfasten her bodice, taking his time so as not to alarm her with his desire but drinking in every bit of her pale beauty as it was revealed to him.

Her breasts were full and firm, the peaks ready for his touch and his lips. The first contact sent warm shafts of desire shooting through Alex, so that she gasped out with the wonder of it. His fingers moved downwards over the soft silk of her gown, caressing the soft belly and finding what he sought, and it was his turn to be stunned by her loveliness and the sensations she awoke in him.

He knew he must go slowly, that she had not been with any man before, but the ache in him was becoming almost painful now.

"There's no need to be frightened, my sweet one," he murmured.

"I'm not afraid," she whispered, knowing it was not entirely true.

"Touch me, Alex."

She looked into the shadowed darkness of his face uncomprehendingly for a moment and was glad that he couldn't see the wild color in her cheeks that she knew must be there. They burned as if with a fever.

She had no idea what to do, how to behave, but Fraser's hand and her own instincts guided her, and after the first timid moments, it seemed as though she was instructed by his own reactions to her tender strokings, and she became less tentative. It was, after all, one of life's secrets she had so longed to know.

As for him . . . she was as beautiful for him as a pure mountain stream in his beloved Highlands. She was fresh and pure and loving . . . and even as he thought the words, Fraser knew he must not take this too far. Desirable as she was, and so ready for love, the times they were living through made him more cautious than he might otherwise have been. There was blood in the stars, and Fraser, as well as Felix Truscott, was not so naive as to disregard the ancient sayings.

Somewhere in the night, a flock of birds rose noisily from the treetops, their cries an anguished sound, and Alex jumped, clinging to Fraser in sudden fright.

"What was that?" she stuttered.

"It is time to go, my love, before our absence is noticed and misconstrued."

He still breathed heavily, and they both knew that this night was ending differently from the way they had both imagined. A little chill of sadness swept over Alex. She didn't know why, but it seemed as though a small ghost of a premonition was seeping into her bones tonight. She had wanted to cling to Fraser as a woman and also as a child, to be reassured that they would always be as close as this, that nothing could part them.

As if he read her mind, he kissed her with a swift, rough passion. "There'll be other times, lassie. We have all our lives ahead of us."

But there seemed a restraint in him from that night on, as though he was almost unwilling to commit himself to the final act of belonging he craved. As though he had to be quite certain that they both had a world in which to share their love.

The old Alex might have been affronted, thinking he didn't really love her. Yet from somewhere deep in her soul, she sensed a greater crisis on the horizon than that presented here. And it didn't spoil their time at the tea estate. In some strange way, it melded them more securely together, and it was with regret and many lovely memories that they finally reached the Pearl of the Plain once more, two weeks later.

Chapter Ten

"I'LL SEE YOU WHEN I CAN," FRASER PROMISED AS THEY
said good-bye. "But don't fret if 'tis a few days, Alex."

"I won't," she said, knowing she must make the best
of it.

And she mustn't be sad in their lovely palace home.
Aunt Maud was exhausted and wanted to sleep for a
week. Her father went immediately to resume his
regular audience with Prince Shunimar and came back
to his office a while later.

Alex was talking there with David Gould, and both
saw at once that the audience hadn't gone well. Her
father looked as black as thunder.

"Bloody astrologers, begging your pardon, my dear!
Stirring up trouble even when it doesn't exist. We all
know there's plenty of unrest among the sepoys, but

these bastards would see fire and flames in the bloody teacups, and their omens have really put the frights up Shunimar this time."

Alex could see the lines of tension puckering David Gould's normally sunny face as he agreed.

"It's been uneasy here for a week, sir. I'm no more gullible than the next man, but everyone's been affected by the warnings. They say the new moon has an aura of death around it, and Prince Shunimar refuses to move from his sleeping chamber—"

"So I noticed," Felix said savagely. "The place stinks like a cross between a Calcutta brothel and an incense den!"

"It's the protective oils the astrologers suggest—"

"I know what it is! Bloody heathen devils!"

The fact that her father swore without even noticing it alarmed Alex more than his actual words. He was clearly acutely worried. She remembered the old retainer's words at the bungalow about blood in the stars . . . and now this.

She glanced through the window. It was brilliant daylight, the sky the color of English cornflowers, the sun dazzling. If she searched for it, she could see the thin slice of the moon, fluffy white now. Only last night, she and Fraser had admired its beauty, a slim crescent of silver against a backcloth of blue velvet. What did those others see in it that normal people did not?

"What are they saying, Father?" she said quickly, angry at half beginning to believe in charms and portents herself.

He looked her way, as if only just realizing that she was there. His mouth tightened.

"You've just heard most of it! There's talk of death and destruction and brother fighting brother. The astrologers say all their charts point to it, and there's no

169

avoiding it. That is, if you care to believe the bloody nonsense, of course, and since Shunimar does, he's even talking of moving the whole court to an old territory in the south that he once controlled. Such a move is impossible and not within Company policy. There's too much red tape involved to allow things to change that quickly!"

"Is the danger right here then?" Alex felt her heart leap sickeningly.

"God knows!" Felix was too furious to think properly. He should have been here, he kept telling himself. He shouldn't have gone off to Krubah Tea, knowing of all the unrest. And yet, it may have had its uses. Alex would know which way to run, if running was needed . . . God, but he was thinking like a bloody native now, he thought, even angrier.

"Should I tell Aunt Maud?"

"She'll find out for herself if the palace goes up in smoke," he said brutally.

"I say, sir, steady on!" David muttered with British upper lip. "No need to alarm the ladies unduly."

Felix rounded on him. "Am I surrounded by lunatics? If we burn, there'll be no sparing of ladies' feelings then! We've the best army in the world, man, but most of 'em are native platoons. It only needs one leaf in the wind to shake up a whole tree. I shouldn't need to tell you that! And this cartridge question's not done with yet. My bet is it'll all come down to that. And if just one regiment mutinies, God help the rest of us."

There was silence in the room, but a silence so brittle it almost crackled with tension. Alex turned quickly and left the office, and no one called her back. She leaned against the door, breathing so heavily that stars danced in front of her eyes. For a moment, she panicked totally.

Had all her life led up to this? Had the dream of India, lovingly nurtured by her parents and so longed for by herself, been destined to end as cruelly as her father now suggested?

She shook off the panic. It would all blow over. Everyone said so. It was the phrase on everyone's lips. Whether they believed it or not, it was the only way to keep sane. And how could disaster be so imminent, when on the surface all seemed as serene as usual? The chowkidars were as enigmatic as always, guarding their prince with no hint of mutiny. The servants went about their business, as silent and attentive as ever.

The only thing that seemed strange on such a day as this was the absence of birdsong. Normally, the air was filled with their sweet singing, but today there was none. And, no doubt, the astrologers would see that as yet another omen.

When she mentioned the strange silence to Aunt Maud, Alex tried to make light of it. What was the point of worrying her aunt when it might be quite unfounded? And to Alex's surprise, her aunt was philosophical.

"We're all in God's hands. If we were meant to perish in this dangerous paradise, then so be it."

"What odd words to use!"

"But rather apt, I think. Even paradise had its serpents." If it hadn't been for the slight tremble in Maud's voice, Alex might have thought her aunt was being extraordinarily shortsighted about the whole thing. But she heard the tremble and suddenly held her aunt close for a moment. Her own voice shook a little.

"In case I ever forgot to say it properly, Aunt Maud, thank you for coming to India with me and for taking Mother's place so wonderfully over the years."

"Well, since we're being so frank, darling, I could say

171

thank you for being the daughter I never had." Maud went pink at the words, but it seemed to be a moment for speaking from the heart. The two of them hugged each other and then broke apart.

"It may be that we go back to Krubah Tea for another visit sometime," Alex said carefully. "Would you mind?"

"Not at all! I enjoyed Louisa Thompson's company, and it was certainly less cloying than here in the plains."

They smiled at one another, both knowing what a return to the tea estate would mean. Both agreeing by silent consent to make no more of it. Unless danger became imminent . . .

And in the next week, Alex began to wonder what all the fuss was about. Certainly, the palace guards seemed to gather in small groups rather more than usual, their faces sullen rather than bland, and Prince Shunimar steadfastly refused to leave his sleeping chamber, having all his meals taken to him there. Felix spent much of his time traveling between the palace and Delhi, and when he was in his office, his voice was often raised as he swore at the incompetence of those he had to deal with.

"As if Father were the only sane one amongst them," Alex confided with a smile to Fraser on one of the rare evenings he came to visit. Only to herself did she admit her nervousness and that the tension, inside the palace and out, was affecting everyone, including herself.

"Perhaps he is." Fraser took her seriously. "It's as we all feared, Alex. One of the Indian regiments has refused to use the greased cartridges. I got news of it only today. The regiment has been disarmed, and this will undoubtedly whip up ill feeling. They felt insulted at being asked to use the cartridges. Now they'll feel

172

doubly insulted at being dismissed from a regiment in which they had much pride."

Her mouth felt dry. They walked together in the perfect twilight of the Pearl of the Plain, the air heavy with blossoms and the heat of the day still sultry. Yet it was as if the chill of winter struck at Alex's heart.

"I don't want to think of the consequences." Her lips felt wooden as she spoke. Fraser's arm wrapped around her like a protective cloak.

"Then don't think of it," he said roughly. "For tonight, let's think of nothing but ourselves, my darling."

But for both of them, the joy of being together was suddenly tarnished, the thought uppermost in their minds of how long this idyll could last. Felix had already suggested she and Aunt Maud go back to the tea estate for a few weeks, just in case, but Alex had flatly refused. It was pointless to anticipate trouble. It might never happen. And she would be so far away from Fraser.

She hugged his arm to her side as they walked in the seclusion of the palace shrubberies, the ever-present peacocks forming a brilliant procession behind them.

"Fraser, it will be all right, won't it? *We'll* be all right—"

He pulled her into his arms, his voice fierce with passion. "Aye, sweet lassie, you and I are indestructible! We've a legend to live up to, Alex, one that's been handed down in my family, and I've still to tell you of it. But not until we're wed. 'Tis a Mackinnon tradition. Do ye think I'd let these blood-seeking fools deprive me of that?"

"Won't you tell me now?" She was charmed by the thought.

Fraser gave a short laugh. "I will not! Don't you see,

Alexandra, it's our talisman? Something for us to cling to, come what may. We can survive anything, like my ancestors, Jamie and Katrina, and when 'tis all over, 'twill be time for the telling."

"You speak so strangely at times. Almost like one of Prince Shunimar's astrologers!" She felt slightly piqued at not hearing this legend of which he'd hinted before, but comforted also at the thought of it being a talisman. If Fraser believed it to be so, then so would she.

He kissed her soft lips, gently at first, and then with a passion that made her blood sing in her veins.

"Trust me, dearest. I've no intention of losing you now that I've found you. Remember that. I'll always find you, Alex."

The words were so beautiful that the tears threatened to blur her eyes. She blinked them away. The peacocks cried out in a sudden chorus, and they both laughed, shooing them away.

"Ellen Forbes has invited Aunt Maud and me for tea on Sunday," she remembered to tell him as they continued their walk, arms entwined. "The Monday Club is canceled this week, as some of the ladies have bad colds, but May the 10th is little Victor's birthday, and Ellen wanted a tea party for him. Captain Forbes is away with his regiment at present, so he'll miss it. I think Ellen feels lonely at times."

"I'm sure you'll have a lovely time gossiping the day away," Fraser grinned. "Would you like me to take you there and bring you back?"

"Oh, if you could, it would be wonderful!"

"I'll force myself to spend an hour or two in your company! I'll collect you both whenever you wish."

"About two o'clock in the afternoon then," she said. It was something to look forward to, and she must think of a suitable present for Victor. Her normal optimism

174

returned. There was a child's birthday to be celebrated on the 10th of May, and she would be in the company of English friends. How could there be any bad omens on the horizon?

Aunt Maud took to her bed on Saturday evening with a heavy cold and refused to get up on Sunday, being waited on by Pandira and asking Alex to make abject apologies to Ellen and to young Victor. But she was sure Ellen would much prefer her to stay away rather than spread infection to the Forbes household! So Fraser and Alex set off together for Delhi.

"I'm sure your aunt is right, and she'll recover much quicker by staying in bed," he commented.

"Especially with Pandira fetching and carrying," Alex smiled. "Aunt Maud has the woman eating out of her hand. It's so funny, but they seem to have an odd affection for each other, despite the way Aunt Maud orders her about."

"Servants are the same the world over. Some resent taking orders, others thrive on it!"

"That's quite an observation! But a true one, of course. The two old retainers at the bungalow were like that, weren't they? I'm sure they'd die for Father if they had to."

Now why had she said that? Why spoil a lovely afternoon, still and hot, with thoughts of dying? If Fraser noticed it, he ignored it, pointing out instead a flock of exotic birds that suddenly soared into the sky as if from nowhere. India was full of surprises. You never knew what was around the next corner. It was what made it so exciting.

"Will you come to the birthday party, Fraser? I'm sure Ellen will ask you. It will hardly be like Prince Shunimar's extravagance, of course!"

He shook his head. "I've some people to see, darling, but I'll come back for you whenever you say."

But he came into the Forbes' house and swung the birthday boy around his head, making him squeal with laughter, and gave Victor a box of candies. Alex gave the child a toy model of an elephant that waggled its ears when wound up with a key in its back and amused him and his brother all afternoon.

"When is Fraser coming for you, Alex? Not too early, I hope," Ellen said later, when they had feasted on cream cakes and jelly and crawled about on their knees to play with the boys, to the raised eyebrows of the Indian houseboy, unused to seeing two English ladies in crinoline dresses behaving like children.

"About seven o'clock."

"That's wonderful. We can sit down and recover when these two angels have gone to bed—"

Her voice was drowned in the howls of protest, but the boys would be tired out long before then. The heat and the excitement sapped their strength before they knew it, and there would be a welcome blissful hour of peace for the two women to sit and drink tea together.

Sita, the ayah, collected the children for their baths once the formal tea was over, and Ellen was about to speak to Alex when they both heard galloping hoof-beats, as if someone was in a desperate hurry. They both turned to the window curiously, but before they could even comment, the door burst open and Fraser rushed in, his face white.

Fear leaped to Alex's heart in a moment. He shouldn't be here yet. It was too early. Something had happened. Something terrible. Crazy thoughts spun around in her head, and she saw Ellen start to rise. Before she had moved one step, Alex was across the room and Fraser's

176

hands were gripping hers very tightly. They were both as cold as ice.

"What is it?" she gasped out.

"Shunimar's palace has been burned to the ground," he said savagely. "The chowkidars went mad shortly after we left there. God knows the reason, but the prince and his entourage have been hacked to pieces—"

Alex felt great dry sobs tearing at her throat. She shook from head to foot, wanting to know, afraid to know . . .

"What of my father and Aunt Maud?" Her voice was hoarse with dread. "Did they get away? Oh, God, tell me they got away—"

He slapped her face as her voice became shriller. A thick, red weal began to appear in the pallor of her skin.

"I can't tell you, Alex." He hated to be the one to bring her such news. "I saw a pall of smoke in the sky soon after I left here and thought nothing of it until the rumors began to circulate. Then I rode there immediately, but there was nothing anyone could do. The heat was so intense that everyone inside that inferno must have perished—"

He didn't tell her of the awful stench of burning human flesh and elephant hide, or of the terrifying screams, human and animal, that would stay in his memory forever. She swayed on her feet, and Ellen's arm slipped around her too, her face as white as Alex's.

"I can't bear it. I can't! Father, and Aunt Maud—"

Fraser slapped her again. She would be beaten to a pulp at this rate, and it meant nothing to her. Her head was filled with wool. She couldn't think properly, couldn't feel . . .

177

"Listen to me, Alex. There's a chance they got away. I'm not trying to build false hopes, but there are all kinds of garbled stories. Two British people were supposedly hustled out by a servant woman. It's possible. You said yourself that Pandira was fond of your aunt. Let's hope to God that's what happened."

He didn't tell her that another Englishman, presumably David Gould, was seen fleeing in agony before he fell, ablaze from head to toe, while the black devils jeered around him. He felt Alex's violent shaking and spoke rapidly to Ellen Forbes.

"Have you got some brandy? I think you should both take some to steady your nerves. You'll keep her here tonight, won't you, Ellen?"

"Of course she must stay here—"

"No! I must find Father and Aunt Maud! If they got away, I must be with them!"

"You can't search the country by yourself," Fraser said harshly. "Stay here and let others look for them, which they undoubtedly will. Your father was Resident at Shunimar's palace and an important man."

Alex looked at him wildly as the glass of brandy was thrust into her hand. A prince was killed by his own men, and Fraser thought to fob her off by telling her that her father was important. Felix Truscott was of no importance, no more than any of them were, if all India rose up against the British. The thought unnerved her again, and she could hardly put the glass to her lips and swallow the stinging liquid.

"There's more to tell ye." Fraser had to go on, knowing that the women should be aware of what was happening. "There's bad trouble at Meerut with the 3rd Light Cavalry."

Ellen drew in her breath. Captain Forbes was not at

Meerut, but he was near to it. Fraser went on grimly, and she forced herself to listen.

"Yesterday they refused to use the new Enfield cartridges." His voice was clipped. "Eighty-five sowars were sentenced to ten years penal servitude for the refusal, in the mistaken hope of stamping out the unrest. They were paraded in the oppressive heat, fettered like animals, and had their medals and uniforms stripped off their backs. The shame of it makes me want to vomit, and General Hewitt will be reckonable to God for such a move at such a volatile time. He's old and senile and should be locked away himself—"

"Fraser, that's terrible!" Ellen's voice was a whisper now, her face white. Alex could hardly take in the enormity of it, compared with the shock of her father's fate. But she knew by Fraser's set face, and by Ellen's reaction, that the situation had become explosive.

Burning the Pearl of the Plain had been one more gesture of hatred against the power of John Company and those who catered to its every command, like Prince Shunimar. His astrologers had been right, Alex thought shiveringly. Every word had been right . . . and she was suddenly very frightened. She tried to listen sensibly to Fraser's urgent voice, but the words seemed to swirl about in her head.

"Listen to me, Alex. You're to stay here with Ellen until you hear from me again, or until the situation worsens. And pray to God that it doesn't."

She looked up into his face.

"You think that it will, don't you?"

"Unfortunately, I see nothing else for it. The Company has grown complacent over the years, and the British regiments have been sent far and wide. If the

179

mutiny erupts and spreads, Delhi could be a holocaust. There's no way I can lessen the seriousness of it. At the first hint of trouble, you and Ellen and the children make for the tea estate. You'll be safe there."

But he wouldn't be safe. He would be in the thick of any fighting. Alex didn't need to be a clairvoyant to know that. Her fear for herself and her anguish over her father and Aunt Maud shifted to fear on Fraser's account. She swallowed hard, knowing better than to beg him to come with them, for them all to go now. He wouldn't want her to beg, and he wouldn't desert his cause for a woman, not even for Alex.

He was speaking rapidly to Ellen now. "Can you trust your servants? The children's ayah?"

"I believe so. They've been with us for years."

Fraser nodded. "Then trust me. If I can get word to your husband, I will, but I prefer not to send messages that may get into the wrong hands. Lock your doors tonight, and send a reliable servant to bring back any reports of trouble. If you're in the slightest doubt, then *go*. Rest assured that if Alex's father and her aunt are able, they too will make for the tea estate."

They all knew the implications if they were not able.

"We'll do exactly as you say, Fraser." Alex prayed that she sounded stronger than she felt. Her mind was in a turmoil. So much had happened so fast. A few hours ago she had thought she had everything. Now, she had nothing. Except Fraser. Uncaring that Ellen was in the room, she clung to him.

"Come back safe," she whispered. His face was warm against hers, the roughness of his moustache scratching her soft skin. She felt his tension as he tried to boost her confidence.

"Remember what I once told you. I'll always find you, Alex, no matter where you are. Now I must go."

He hugged her close, the sweet familiarity of him a poignant farewell. Minutes later, the two women were alone. They stared at one another and then involuntarily clasped each other tightly for support.

"We must be strong, Ellen," Alex said. "You for the children and me for Father and Aunt Maud. I refuse to believe they're dead—"

Her voice broke, and Ellen gave her a little shake. "I refuse to believe it too. But let's think sensibly. I'll send Netuh into the city. He's trustworthy and will be loyal to John's family. If we must leave here, then we should prepare, Alex. We'll need clothes for ourselves and the children. Let's keep ourselves occupied and not think too deeply about what may be happening."

She bit her lip, and Alex knew she must be tormented with fear for her husband. Alex felt guilty that until now she hadn't thought what this must all mean to Ellen. She had been too concerned with her own grief.

"I wonder if we should wait," she said slowly. "Why not go now, Ellen? Let's take the children now."

"Not yet. I refuse to panic like rats caught in a trap! And I don't want to alarm the boys." She stopped speaking as Sita brought them back to say good-night, bathed and shining in their cotton nightshirts.

It was almost impossible to believe that when they had gone laughingly upstairs, none of this had happened. Fraser hadn't arrived to tell her she might now be without a living relative in the world. She hugged the little boys, and the thought uppermost in her own mind was a prayer that they would all survive whatever came.

When they had been put to bed, Ellen called the servants into the drawing room and spoke calmly and concisely to them, telling them of Fraser Mackinnon's visit and asking for their support. But Alex noted that she made no mention of any possible escape to the hills.

That alone made her realize that from now on, no one could be sure who was the enemy.

Fraser rode with all speed through the Delhi suburbs to the home of Sir Peter Wallace. The news he brought was enough to make Sir Peter leap up from his late siesta, dismissing the punkah-wallah with an impatient gesture, his whole body bristling with agitation. He was alarmed and furious about the Meerut situation, but it was the burning of one of his Residencies that was almost treasonable in his eyes.

"Shunimar's palace, by all that's holy! The bastards! What news of Truscott and his family, man?"

Fraser related all he knew. Thank God, Alex was safe. Over and over, he had blessed the Forbes child's birthday for getting her away from the palace on this day.

"Personally, I doubt that there's much hope for Truscott and his sister," he said. "Though the report I told his daughter was true. Two white people were seen being helped away by a native woman. It must have been the Truscotts, but how far they got with the natives in a murderous mood, God only knows, sir."

Sir Peter drummed his fingers on the bamboo table on his verandah. "Not far, I'd guess," he grunted. "Pity. Good man, Truscott. And a tragedy for the daughter too. Good thing you and she are engaged, Mackinnon. She'll have someone."

He spoke in short, terse little sentences, trying to think. There were no rules for this situation. And it wasn't over yet. Dear God, it was only just beginning.

"What of David Gould?"

"Dead. Burned alive, while the bastards watched, jabbing him with sabers all the while, I was told. Poor devil. I was only near enough to hear the screams and smell the smells, and that was enough for me, I can tell ye! The heat made the whole countryside shimmer like a mirage and intensified everything."

Sir Peter snorted to cover his emotion. The boy had been a good worker, and he regretted sending him to work for Truscott. If he'd remained here in Delhi, he'd have been safe. As safe as any of them were.

From somewhere in his house came the sound of women's chatter and a high little laugh Fraser knew. Sir Peter came to a decision and spoke quickly.

"Look here, m'boy, this is a terrible dilemma for us all, but the army will have to make the first move to the palace, to see if it's safe for Company officials to investigate. You know as well as I do that we have to follow procedure."

Fraser wished procedure to kingdom come, but there would be no moving this obstinate man.

"Fact is, Mackinnon, I've got two ladies visiting here at present, and I don't want to alarm them. You know them, I believe. Lady Delmont and her daughter, doing the Grand Tour, though they seem particularly charmed with Delhi and are in no hurry to move on for the present."

"I'd question the wisdom of that idea, Sir Peter."

"Short of telling 'em the city's about to burn about their ears, I'll say nothing, and I'd ask you to do the same," he said sharply. "Now, if you'd like to stay for some tea, I'll call a servant—"

"I think not. I must report back to my regiment. I expect orders to go to Meerut—"

Before Fraser could make a move, the Delmont ladies appeared on the verandah, and Lady Delmont went a dull red when she saw Sir Peter's visitor.

"So, Fraser! I believe congratulations are in order for you and the little Truscott gel."

She spoke with all the warmth of a winter's day, and it was Hilary who seemed less perturbed than her mama at the news. Remembering the flock of officers around her at Prince Shunimar's birthday ball, Fraser could only guess at the reason.

"I hope you and Alex will be very happy, Fraser," she said sincerely.

"Thank you." He smiled briefly. "I'd like to stay and take tea with you, but I'm afraid I must take my leave. Enjoy the rest of your stay in Delhi, ladies."

He dearly wanted to tell them to get out while they still could. Already, he was wishing he'd told Alex and Ellen to leave the city now, before any trouble started. But he presumed that Ellen wouldn't want to leave her home until absolutely necessary. She'd want to be where Captain Forbes could find his family.

Sir Peter Wallace's words were uppermost in his mind as he left the house. Alex would be glad she had Fraser, and it was reciprocal. If her father and aunt were dead, she would have no one in the world but himself. And he, too, had no one but her.

He discounted all the second cousins and members of his clan in Scotland. They were as distant in spirit as they were in body, though he knew full well that clan fealty was too deep in his veins to be ignored. It was still strong and would be again if he ever went home, but Alex was his heartbeat.

But now was not the time to dream of home, or of Alex. He rode to his garrison with his latest report, already knowing what his orders would be. Barely taking time to snatch a quick meal and change his horse for a fresher one, he set out on the forty-mile ride to Meerut.

Chapter Eleven

IT HAD GROWN DARK LONG BEFORE FRASER REACHED
Meerut, but he could see the smoke and flames rising
over buildings that shimmered in the heat like the ruins
of the Pearl of the Plain. He'd been in the army's
service for long enough to become toughened and
steely-nerved, but fear twisted his stomach as the
stench of death met his nostrils.

The nearer he rode, the more the road out of Meerut
swarmed with panic-stricken residents, natives and
British alike, on foot, on horseback, in dog-traps and
carriages. He heard an English voice shouting at him to
get away while he could.

"They've freed the mutineers, man! The jail's on
fire!" the voice shrieked at him from a careening

vehicle. "The whole city's gone mad. They're burning everything in sight, and foreigners don't stand a chance. The bastards are murdering every British man, woman and child! Get away while you can, and don't be a bloody hero!"

Fraser didn't wait a moment longer, and the man's voice faded into the distance as the Scotsman urged his horse on. The uproar coming from the city was terrifying. Bloodcurdling screams, followed by horrific gurglings that told their own tale; splintering glass, deafening shots, shouting and weeping. The dust rose in a great cloud from the road, and even in the darkness it was colored misty red.

Fraser whipped out his rain cloak from his saddle pack. He would swelter inside it, but it would give some disguise to his bright plaid. For once, he cursed its distinctive hues. He dug his heels in his horse and flung himself forward over the nag's back. It was his duty to see what was happening and to report back to his garrison in the hope of staving off further bloodshed by having reinforcements sent. A hope that faded with every yard he galloped.

Somehow he got inside the town through the twisting streets and alleyways. There was so much confusion everywhere, it was easier than he had thought to mingle with the crush of people. The native sowars and sepoys were an evil black horde, intent on murder, slashing and killing and blaspheming in their own tongue, no longer servile to their British masters. The town had erupted into violence in a single night.

Bodies were strewn everywhere, hacked to pieces, bleeding, mutilated beyond recognition. He saw a white woman stagger from a house, holding the remnants of one arm to her side, surprise almost more than horror in her eyes as she looked vacantly about her before falling in a heap of crinoline skirts, and it was only then that Fraser saw the sabre deep in her back.

A horse suddenly reared up in front of him. A British soldier in tatters, whose face was vaguely familiar to him, peered desperately into his eyes.

"Mackinnon, ain't it? Get the bloody hell out of here and get us a commander who knows what he's doing, man! There's nothing else you can do for us. We're all doomed. The black buggers have turned turtle and sworn to murder every one of us, and the bloody general's like a frozen fish and don't know which way to turn. Bring us help, for God's sake!"

Fraser clutched at the other's bridle. "Give me more information, damn it. What d'you know? Where are they heading?"

"I ain't got a bloody crystal ball, but my guess is Delhi. They've been screaming about making the old Shah Bahadur the new emperor. But I'm not planning to go there to find out—"

Even as the soldier pulled furiously away from Fraser's grasping hand, there was a sudden gigantic surge of horses from the garrison quarter of the town. Panic-stricken people hampered Fraser's every move. He swore furiously.

Wherever the mutineers were going, they were going now. Fraser tried desperately to turn his horse about to follow them. A young Indian boy appeared from nowhere, clawing at his bridle.

For a split second, Fraser felt more outrage than any other emotion, wondering if he was to be murdered by this chit . . . and then he saw the wild-eyed fear in the boy's eyes. This was no mutineer, but a child caught in the middle of a war.

"Take me with you, Sahib. They will kill me! Take me to Delhi, for the love of Allah! I have many uncles there—"

"Get away," Fraser said savagely. "You'll be safe enough here, but not if you're seen with me!"

In an instant the boy had produced a knife from his clothing and slashed at Fraser's bare leg above the glimpse of his plaid hose. As the blood spurted, Fraser kicked out instinctively at the ragamuffin. From now on, no one was to be trusted, not even children.

"Bloody feringhi!" the boy shrieked. "May the dogs piss on you! May Allah fill your belly with camel turds!"

His voice was swallowed up in the melee, and now Fraser knew he must be on his guard every minute. He thought swiftly, his thoughts so confused it was like trying to make sense of a nightmare. This *was* a nightmare . . .

He had two choices. To go to his regiment and report. To go to Delhi and warn Alex and Ellen to flee.

He cursed the sense of duty that made no choice of it at all. Fear for Alex gripped his gut as he turned his horse away from the Delhi road and headed in the direction of his garrison, merging with the terrified masses trying to get out of Meerut, most of them being cut down without mercy.

Head down, leaning heavily over his horse's back and needing all the cunning of his scout's training now, somehow he managed to get away from the appalling massacre behind him. The sights were gone, but not the sounds. They were still in his head and would stay with him for a very long time.

His leg stung from the slash of the boy's knife; his chest was so tight it felt as if it would burst. He rode as if demented, expecting at any minute to encounter a fresh band of mutineers, eager for his blood. It was almost a surprise when at last he saw the thin spirals of smoke from his garrison, where everything appeared to be as normal. Except that nothing now would be normal ever again.

Netuh, the Forbes' aging servant, came bursting into the house without formality. His eyes were bulged and rolling, and he fought to catch his breath from his exertion. He was unused to running, but the urgency with which some of his cousins had spoken had sent him running through many of Delhi's dark, twisting alleyways.

"'Tis true, Mem'sahib! The stars weep with blood tonight! My cousins say the sky will be filled with it by morning—"

"Talk sense, Netuh!" Ellen said sharply, refusing to let the old man's terror seep into her bones. She had enough fear of her own without absorbing his.

"Tell me quietly what you've heard," she commanded, trying to stop the hammering of her heart. Both she and Alex sat on the edge of their chairs, hands tightly clasped together, and each knew of the other's fear.

Netuh glowered at his Mem'sahib. It was foolish to pay no heed to the warnings in the sky. Foolish, and calamitous.

"The city is waiting, Mem'sahib. The moon is in mourning. The mosques cannot hold all the prayers of the needy tonight. Tomorrow they too will weep, and their tears will fill a river, and the river will run with blood—"

"For God's sake, stop that!" Ellen jumped to her feet, her face blazing with anger. "I asked you for a sensible report, not the mumblings of a street fakir! If you've nothing better to tell me, then get to your bed, you old fool!"

Netuh's eyes flashed dangerously, and then he salaamed deeply, backing away from the two women to disappear through the split cane curtain that parted with a hiss like that of a snake.

Ellen ran a trembling hand across her forehead. "I've never spoken to any servant like that before," she said shakily. "John would never forgive me—"

That she could even think of such mundane matters when their very lives might be in peril told Alex that it was time she took control of the situation here. Ellen was under a great strain. Worry for her husband and her children was splitting her thoughts, and she seemed unable to make any real decisions. She should have wrung the truth out of old Netuh, not sent him off to bed in disgrace. It would make an enemy out of him, when they might need every friend they had.

It was past midnight, and yet the entire city seemed alive and awake. It was as Netuh had said. The city was waiting. *The stars weep with blood . . . the sky will be filled with it by morning . . .*

"Ellen, I think we should wake the children," she said urgently. "You say you can trust Sita. Has she any relatives?"

It was certain that she would have. There were always many relatives. Ellen nodded, her eyes still dazed.

"Send her to ask one of them to bring an ekka," Alex went on rapidly. "If she wants to come with us, then let her, but you and I and the children must leave now, tonight, Ellen. Do you understand? I'm very afraid that if we wait until morning, it may be too late."

"I can't! John won't know where to find me—" Ellen

stammered, seeming to lose control of her thoughts, and Alex seized her cold hands.

"Yes, he will! Fraser will get a message to him, and even if that's not possible, Captain Forbes heard us talk often enough about Krubah Tea while we were on the ship. He'll guess that's where we've gone for safety. It will probably only be for a short while, Ellen. Just until the trouble blows over."

She bit her lip as she repeated the familiar phrase. Her own thoughts were in turmoil. They didn't even know what was coming, but Alex was filled with a dread certainty that they must flee and flee now, before it was too late.

And at least Ellen could save herself and the children, and Captain Forbes must take his chances. Ellen still had his children, while if anything happened to Fraser, Alex would have no one. In the hours since Fraser had gone, she had been forced to accept that her father and aunt were almost certainly dead.

She couldn't conceivably think of them as surviving the holocaust at the Pearl of the Plain. She grieved to her soul, but if they were dead, there was nothing anyone could do for them, but she could help the Forbes family. And help them she would, even if she had to do it against Ellen's will.

She swallowed down the lump blocking her throat whenever she thought of her father and Aunt Maud and put her hands on Ellen's trembling shoulders.

"Shall I find Sita, or will you?" She spoke in a voice that allowed no argument.

"I'll do it," Ellen said quickly. "You rouse the boys, Alex. It's probably best if we tell none of the other servants what's happening. We'll just leave as soon as the ekka arrives."

"Now you're talking sense," Alex said. "When Sita's gone, get a few clothes together for us all. Myself included, if you will. I've nothing but the clothes I stand up in—"

She stopped, suddenly realizing the truth of it. She had nothing at all, not even the small love tokens Fraser had bought her so long ago on a lovely day in Delhi. Involuntarily, she fingered her mother's pearls, and the tears started in her eyes. Constance had never prepared her for this. She swallowed again, and Ellen gave her a quick hug.

"We'll survive, Alex. We have to. There has to be someone for our men to come home to."

"I thought I was supporting you." Alex smiled weakly, knowing they both needed each other. And then, aware of the emotional strain they were under, each turned away and attended to the allotted tasks without another word.

The small boys grumbled sleepily as Alex woke them quickly, trying not to alarm them. She spoke quietly, yet there was a desperate feeling of urgency inside her, almost as if she had that sixth sense so many of the street soothsayers professed.

Something drove her on, making her determined to get this little family away from here as fast as possible to the safety of the tea estate. A sanctuary, her father had once called it. She wondered if he had realized then how prophetic his words had been.

It dawned on her that she began to feel older than her seventeen years. As if, with the assumed deaths of Felix and Maud Truscott, Alex had somehow donned the mantle of maturity their passing had left.

And there was an instinctive knowledge inside her. If they all survived this night, they would survive anything. She and Fraser would be together again, and he would relate the legend of his ancestors that was their talisman. Even through all that had happened and was yet to happen, she rejoiced that he had kept the legend from her. It was their talisman . . .

"Why must I wake up, Alex?" Victor complained. "Is it still my birthday?"

"More or less," she said. "I've got an extra surprise for you, darling. We're going to stay with some friends of mine in the hills. It will be cooler there, and you won't have to go to lessons for a while."

"Nor me?" Edward was awake at once, jumping up and down beneath his mosquito net. "Is it my surprise as well?"

"Of course. I'll help you both to dress."

"Why are we going in the middle of the night? Daddy says we must stay indoors when it's dark."

Alex hadn't anticipated this. Edward's small face became stubborn. She thought quickly.

"We have his permission. It's cooler for traveling at night, and we're going in an ekka, like the Indian ladies use. It'll be fun. Sita may be coming with us."

Before she had finished, Edward obviously decided it was all right if they had his father's permission, and Alex sighed with relief as he began scrabbling for the clothes he'd worn last night. She couldn't bother with looking for fresh ones. She helped the two of them to dress, and by then, Ellen was throwing things into traveling bags and wondering how they would carry everything they needed.

"We should just take essentials," Alex suggested. "It will help us to squeeze in if we take off our hooped petticoats, Ellen. We'll be squashed enough inside the vehicle."

Ellen nodded. What did it matter if their skirts

weren't as widely fashionable for a few days? Fashion was the least important thing on either of their minds right now.

"Sita's coming with us," she told Alex quietly. "She's afraid for her own safety. It's well known that she's the ayah of a British family."

The implications were unspoken.

In less than half an hour, Sita was back, moving silently into the house. Outside the rear of the Forbes house, an ekka waited with a trusted cousin of Sita's to drive it. The curtains would be an added security measure to conceal the women and children in case danger threatened.

A thrill of fear ran through Alex. Life had changed so quickly and dramatically, there was no time to wonder if they did the right thing. All her instincts told her it was right, and she had never needed to follow them more. And if by a miracle, Felix and Maud were still alive, they too would surely endeavor to reach the tea estate. The thought gave her strength.

Netuh would be in his quarters by now, and a good thing, Ellen said swiftly. The other servants would be sleeping. The fewer people who knew they were slipping out into the night, the better for all of them. Without a backward glance at the home she had known for so long, Ellen ushered the children out to the waiting ekka and climbed in behind them. Once inside, she and Alex each took a boy on her lap, while Sita passed on Alex's directions to her cousin, who spoke little English.

They were on their way. Alex breathed a long sigh of relief, anxious to be away from the beautiful city with its dreamlike quality in the faint red light of dawn. Her heart jolted against her ribs. It could not be dawn yet.

The sky was still dark, the stars still glittering. She jerked the curtain aside a little more, peering back.

Above the rooftops of Delhi, the towering minarets and gleaming mosques and the gigantic wall of the Red Fort, there was definitely a dull red glow in the sky. Far away across the plains to the north, in the direction of Meerut. Her heart thudded uncontrollably. She pulled the curtains across once more. Captain Forbes was somewhere in the Meerut area, she knew not where. And Fraser had gone there to get a firsthand report for his regiment. If anything happened to him, to either of them.

"What is it, Alex?" Ellen spoke in a cracked voice. "You're breathing so quickly. Did you see something? Is anyone following us?"

"It's nothing," she lied. "I thought I heard shouting, but it was only some late-night revelers. They startled me."

She prayed Ellen would believe her. Whether she did or not, Alex couldn't say, but the other girl's hand reached across and held hers tightly until they were well away from the lovely city of Delhi and plunging upwards into the safer reaches of the hills, where the forests would hide them on their journey.

And in each of their minds was the heartbreaking worry of whether they would ever see their loved ones again.

The little donkey-drawn ekka couldn't travel at the same speed with which the Truscott carriage had taken Fraser and Alex's family on the first visit to Krubah Tea. There had to be frequent stops, both on the animal's lazy account and for Sita's cousin to stretch his legs and go wandering off into the forest.

"I make apology for my cousin, Mem'sahib," Sita said sorrowfully to Ellen. "He has an ailment and cannot sit still for long at one time. But he is trustworthy and will return. Please be patient."

They had no choice, though Alex fumed with frustration and could have screamed at the time-wasting. Reason told her that if the mutineers wanted a prime victory, they would try to capture Delhi. They wouldn't search the country round about for stray British women and children. There were hundreds still there in the British section of the city, in garrison houses and Company mansions, probably quite ignorant of imminent danger. More than enough feringhis to satisfy any native bloodlust. She shuddered at the visual pictures her mind produced. The more thoughts that bombarded her, the more appalled Alex became at the endless possibilities for atrocities, and the more sure she was that they had done the right thing.

"We can't go on like this all night, Alex," Ellen murmured wearily, when they had stopped for the sixth time for the donkey to rest and the cousin to make his sojourn into the forest. "We should stop at the nearest hotel and make a fresh start in the morning. We're far enough from Delhi now."

"I've no idea where to find a hotel," Alex muttered. "I know the general direction of the tea estate, but my father knew the route, and it wasn't necessary for me to follow a map!"

She felt angry and alarmed as she said the words. It was madness to rush out into the night without knowing where they were going. They may be following completely the wrong direction. In her haste, she hadn't thought to consult a map. They could be heading for wild country where tigers and other animals roamed freely, and they would merely be exchanging one danger for another. She felt total panic for a moment.

"The missy Sahib need have no fears," Sita's calm voice said quietly. "My cousin Langhi knows these forests and hills. He will take us safely to the Krubah Tea estate of which he has heard tell. He will know of a resting-place for a few hours. It may be better that we rest by day and travel by night. We will ask when he returns."

Clearly, they were now in the hands of Langhi and Sita. It was almost a relief to realize it. They could do nothing but be taken on this strange journey that seemed as if it would never end. The fretful children began to waken from their first sleep just as the dawn really was lightening the sky in a spectacular display of pinks and golds and blues.

Soon, the sun would be rising, and the heat of the day would be as oppressive as ever. It would be stifling within the curtained ekka. Sita's words were wise ones. As soon as Langhi came back, she spoke to him quickly in their native tongue, and he nodded, pointing vaguely westwards and holding up all his fingers.

"Langhi says there is a resting-place about ten miles from here. We will stay there until nightfall if it pleases you, Mem'sahib and missy Sahib."

She spoke respectfully, but Alex had the uncanny feeling that the Indians would do as they pleased and that the British women were mere pawns. She nodded as Ellen said quickly that they would do whatever Langhi suggested. She just hoped that they could be trusted. If not, she and Ellen and the little boys were already as good as dead.

"Trust her, Alex," Ellen murmured under her breath, as Sita continued to speak with her cousin.

"She's been with us since the boys were born. She wouldn't let harm come to them. She would kill first."

But not her cousin. Alex decided not to pursue the gnawing thought. And at last, the resting-house came into view, a modest little place, half-hidden by trees and surely not on the road Alex had taken before. But Langhi was taking them through a denser part of the forest, through roads that were no more than tracks, but no doubt there was wisdom in that too.

It was brilliant daylight when they stopped and climbed stiffly down from the ekka. It wasn't designed for long journeys, and the discomfort was even more intensified when they alighted. The children were hungry and thirsty, and Langhi went inside the place first, to check on accommodations and meals.

They were welcomed, to Alex's enormous relief. The resting-house was clean enough, though primitive. But the manager was respectful, and at least the place was hidden from the road. Alex knew that she wouldn't feel entirely safe until they had reached the tea estate.

They were given a simple meal of pulao, spiced rice and chicken, with unleavened bread called nan that was fairly unpalatable, but by now they were hungry enough to eat anything. The children were used enough to Indian food to eat it without comment, the excitement of the flight followed by the monotonous trundling of the ekka making them nearly drop with sleep again.

Ellen asked to be shown to their rooms. There was only one, she was told apologetically. A large family room, in which they could all stay, with cots for the children and palliasses for her and Alex. Sita could sleep on the verandah. Langhi would stay outside with the donkey.

It was the best they could do. It was so different from

Prince Shunimar's fabulous palace, Alex could have wept, but if she did, she knew it would border on hysteria, and she pushed the feeling down with a great effort.

And after all, it didn't matter. The boys fell asleep as soon as they were settled in their cots, and after talking quietly for some minutes, Ellen slept quickly too. Alex lay staring at the ceiling above her mosquito net for a while, imagining she could hear the sounds of screaming, smell the burning, feel the flames engulfing her and see the tortured faces of her beloved father and dear Aunt Maud, who had braved a foreign land to be with her.

She cried out mutely in the rush of sleep that overcame her, willing the images away, and the gauze net stirred softly in a small breeze from the punkah screen outside on the verandah where Sita dozed.

Inevitably, her thoughts turned to Fraser. Where was he now? What was he doing? Was he safe? Did the worry for her own safety jeopardize his own in any way? She prayed for him as she had never prayed before. She prayed for them all, for her father and Aunt Maud, for Captain Forbes and all the thousands of British civilians, the army and Company personnel who might be in so much danger, but most of all, she prayed for Fraser.

And she longed for him. She was lost without him. This night that had begun so sweetly, with a ride into Delhi for Victor's birthday, had ended so terribly, and still she didn't know what was happening in Delhi. Fraser could be in the midst of it all, and she would never know. A sob escaped her lips.

Had they found each other so briefly, only to be parted forever by an enemy they had once thought so loyal a friend? She tried to cling to their talisman, to

Fraser's own belief that they would always be together, indestructible, but all she could see was the blood in the stars . . .

He had once told her of the beauties of Scotland that they would one day see together. He had told her how they would soar together down a mountainside, and it had all seemed so beautiful, and as impossible now as catching one of those distant stars. But she wouldn't want to do that anyway. Not a star that was tainted with blood . . .

Alex awoke with a start, cold to the bone, even though the day grew hotter and more sultry by the hour. She moved restlessly beneath the thin cotton sheet, curled up as tightly as a child in the womb. She made herself relax and drifted off to sleep again to the shrill, sweet call of the hummingbirds and the fragrance of the rhododendron trees.

And at last, her dreams became less fraught. She was so exhausted that her mind completely closed off the terrors of the past day and night. Instead, she dreamed of a lover's arms holding her, in a world filled with beauty and passion and with no hint of violence. She floated into Fraser's waiting embrace, wanting to give herself to him, to taste the pleasures of love, to be part of him.

"Didn't I tell you I would always find you, my Alex?" His sensual, dreaming voice spoke in her ear. "Didn't I promise you that nothing could come between us now?"

"Oh, yes," she breathed, not wanting to break the spell of his body claiming hers, wanting hers so gloriously, so perfectly.

In her sleep, her own hands touched her body, and it was Fraser's hands that caressed her. His hands that cupped her breasts and circled their rosy peaks and followed the touch with his lips. It was Fraser's hands that made their downward trail to the warmth of her thighs, which reacted to his touch like a flower opening in the warmth of the sun.

Fraser . . . who whispered the words of love and made tender explorations into the soft sweetness of her, that led her to realms of sensation she had never known. His whispered words of love only added to the joy between them, making each new sensation more deeply pleasurable.

And then at last, the union for which they both yearned was exquisitely fulfilled. As he lay with her, her body warmed and cherished by his, it was as though these were the only moments left to them, and yet there was no haste, no clumsiness, only the matchless joining of a man and a woman in perfect love.

In her dream, Alex lived the moments of which she had no real knowledge, and yet knowing and loving the man so well was enough to furnish her imagination beyond anything she had yet experienced. In sleep, her body reacted as though she was brought to the ultimate brink of ecstasy. She floated, weightless, in the arms of her beloved.

Somewhere nearby, in the dense green forest that separated the cool hills from the vast, shimmering heat-haze below, in which Delhi was the center, an animal made a sudden, sharp warning sound, and Alex was rudely awakened.

Her mind refused to relinquish the past minutes so abruptly. She wanted to hold on to the dream, to hold on to Fraser's image. She closed her eyes tightly, her hand straying to the warm flush of passion still on her cheeks, as if to shut out the harsh daylight and every intrusive sound. She heard the low murmur of voices on the verandah.

"What does it mean, Sita? Does your cousin have thoughts on it? It's like a huge dust storm in the plain."

"Not a dust storm, Mem'sahib. Langhi thinks it is the dust disturbed by many horses. It sits over Delhi like a cloud. I fear it may not lift for many days, and we did right to depart."

Alex caught her breath, hearing the ominous words from the old ayah. She moved her fingers from her face, but she had already felt the dampness beneath them. The dream she had just shared with Fraser . . . the dream of India . . . was finally over.

Chapter Twelve

THE JOURNEY TO THE KRUBAH TEA ESTATE SEEMED interminable. Langhi took them through little-used roads which were supposedly quicker but which added days to the traveling. They were all exhausted when they reached the white building at last, and to Alex it was little short of the sanctuary her father had called it, as if some sixth sense had told him she would need its protective walls.

She nearly fell into the arms of Louisa and Miles Thompson, and when they had all spilled out their story to the startled couple, grief finally overcame Alex. They were safe at last. She and Ellen and the children and Sita . . . but what of her father and Aunt Maud? In her heart, she knew she would never see them again.

And what was happening now, in the burning streets of Delhi, to Fraser, to Captain Forbes, and hundreds like them . . . ?

Later, when she was talking alone with Miles Thompson, she cried uncontrollably in his arms. "I can't bear it, Mr. Thompson! First Mother, and now this! Nothing's the way I expected. I've got nothing left—"

"Hush, my dear." He was visibly affected by her distress, his own eyes filling. Felix Truscott had been part of his life for many years too. "It pains me to see you like this, but I don't know how to comfort you. I'm a practical man, and I can only tell you that if your father truly is dead, then you become my partner, my dear. This is your home as long as you wish to stay. I have a copy of your father's will, Alex. The original is safely with our solicitors."

"I don't want to talk of wills," she began hysterically. "It makes it sound so—so definite—"

"We must talk of it, Alex," Miles said roughly to hide his emotion. He led her to an armchair in the airy sitting room. They might be a million miles from the holocaust that had been Meerut, and might even now be Delhi, but thoughts of it were uppermost in both their minds.

"Your father left everything to you." Miles was deliberately brusque. "All his shares in Krubah Tea, and all the dividends as they become due. If we assume for the moment that Felix is dead, then you're a wealthy young woman, Alex. If that means nothing to you, remember that you have even more riches. You have the love of a good man in Fraser Mackinnon. I wouldn't say that you had nothing, my dear."

She swallowed. Perhaps, after all, she was luckier than most. And if both Felix and Constance were gone, she had the legacy they had left her. Not the material one, but the love for India they had given her and Constance's wish that she should know every experience to the full. That was something she and Fraser shared. Unconsciously, she squared her slender shoulders.

"You're right, of course," she mumbled. "I'm sorry I wept over you, Mr. Thompson—"

He kissed the top of her bright head in a fatherly way. "I'd have been surprised if you hadn't. These days can't have been easy. When did you last eat? The resting-houses don't cater to refined tastes. I'm sure we can find something to suit your palate."

There had been a time when she'd thought she'd be unable to eat again. Grief and worry had taken away her appetite. But she was too young to mourn forever. And she was too resilient to resist the good cooking along with the sympathy she knew she could expect in Louisa Thompson's household.

In this tranquil environment, there would be a chance to come to terms with her new situation. And there were Ellen and the boys too. Miles was right. She wasn't alone. She had so much. She held on to the thought, even in the long, lonely hours of each night, when the only thing she wanted was Fraser. When would she ever hold him again? When would she ever know the joy of being in his arms?

Scouts from all regiments in the area were reporting back to their barracks, and the reports became more garbled by the hour. Some units simply couldn't or wouldn't believe that the 3rd Light Cavalry in Meerut had mutinied.

"You must believe it!" Fraser blazed to some of the disbelievers in his own garrison. "They're making for

Delhi, I tell ye! There won't be a British civilian alive there if we don't do something, and fast!"

He prayed to God that Alex had got out. He'd seen murder in the eyes of those black devils. There would be murder on both sides. He knew well enough that in a struggle for survival, war made savages of everybody.

"The mutiny was premature," another man shouted. "The plotting's been going on for months, but nobody heeded the warnings. If they took Meerut, with British troops in abundance, what hope do we have if they try to take Delhi, with all-native garrisons in the city? We've no chance!"

General opinion was the same. British forces in the vicinity were seriously lacking in numbers, compared with the strength of the native garrisons. The many grudges against the East India Company had finally turned into something of a religious war, with every sect affronted by the cartridge question. Those who hated the British and saw the chance to turn the situation to their advantage seized it greedily.

"Chance or no, there are hundreds of British citizens in Delhi. We can't abandon them." The generals were all agreed on that. "We must ask Government House for reinforcements."

But while the arguments went on, the mutineers had reached Delhi and begun an orgy of savage killings, routing British homes, burning and raping and proving their first-class training as soldiers under British leadership. Only now, they were intent on slaughtering the men who had trained them.

In the Red Fort where he lived, the tottering eighty-year-old Shah Bahadur, the last of the Mogul rulers, was proclaimed Emperor of India. Now, the massacre could begin in full spate. The full horror of it quickly spread through the whole city, and confusion and chaos added to the terror of British citizens trying vainly to escape.

Scouts and messengers were dispatched with all haste to outlying areas, in the hope of bringing fresh British regiments in to relieve Delhi from the victorious native rebels.

The arsenal in the city couldn't be reached for supplies of guns and ammunition, and the lack of transport hampered all movement, since this was generally dependent on hired civilian contractors, most of whom had gone into hiding or had already perished at the hands of the mutineers. The sick and wounded had little help, and many died where they fell.

"We have regiments in plenty!" the Company officials screamed. "Why don't they come? What are the imbecile generals playing at?"

Sir Peter Wallace held a hastily called meeting at his house on the outskirts of Delhi late on the evening of May 10th. He and half a dozen colleagues had been brought word of the Meerut uprising and were discussing what was to be done about the many British citizens at risk.

"I don't think we need feel too threatened," Brian Morgan, the oldest of the group, remarked. "Should danger become imminent, the Governor-General will act quickly to bring in more troops."

"I'd say the danger is right upon us, man, when British citizens are being slaughtered in their beds," Sir Peter snapped.

"There's no reason to think they'll take any more action," another argued stubbornly. "We've had these cloudbursts before. They always blow over."

Sir Peter banged his hand on the table. "The next person to say those words can get out right now!" he roared. "Here we are with my best man killed—you've

all heard the news of Felix Truscott, I take it—his
Residency burned along with the whole of Shunimar's
palace, and God knows what's happened to his pretty
daughter—and you talk about cloudbursts blowing
over. I tell you, we've seen nothing yet—"

"There's no need to shout, Sir Peter!" The Company
official went puce with anger at being spoken to like this
in front of his colleagues.

Sir Peter's gray whiskers bristled with fury. "Are you
all deaf or blind? We're in mortal peril, man, and
there'll be precious little respect shown for you if a
native sabre slits through your guts!"

The native Bahru glared at them all beneath lowered
brows. He was here to take notes, and his pencil jabbed
viciously at the pad on his lap. None of them noticed or
cared.

"Can we at least cool our tempers?" Brian Morgan
tried to placate the two of them. "This is getting us
nowhere. What's your suggestion, Sir Peter?"

"I say we get our people away from here tonight, if
possible," Sir Peter said forcefully. "All British civilians will be in danger, and so will Indian sympathizers.
Like this one, for instance." He jerked his head towards Bahru, still scribbling.

"I won't be driven out of my home. I've lived there
for twenty years," Brian Morgan said stubbornly.

Sir Peter sighed, sensing the same feeling in the rest
of them. It was madness to stay. Men like himself
would stay, of course. But they had a responsibility to
others, to get them out while they still could.

"I'm not telling you to run, Morgan. But it's your
duty to warn as many people as possible. I'm ordering
you all to do it. As you know, there are two English
ladies staying here at present, but I've every intention

of sending Lady Delmont and her daughter to Agra as soon as this meeting's over."

He stopped speaking, his head swiveling sideways. A dull, distant thudding noise seemed to be gathering momentum. The entire earth seemed to vibrate with it. The noise was accompanied by a murmuring in the air that gradually became a roar, a murderous roar, from the direction of the Meerut road.

Sir Peter knocked over a chair as he rushed to the window and then staggered back at the sight beyond his garden fence. It seemed to him at that moment that the entire Bengal army was advancing towards the house.

"My God, we're too late," he said hoarsely through dry lips. "We're all done for—"

He turned as he spoke, in time to catch the gleam of a blade aimed straight at his heart. Bahru finally rid himself of his hated Company boss, before the rest of the Britishers could even think to haul him away. But it hardly mattered.

Seconds later, the place swarmed with the Meerut mutineers, the slashing sabres finishing off what Bahru had begun, the rebels ignoring all his screaming protestations of loyalty as they coldly decapitated him.

The Delmont ladies, awakened by all the noise, came out onto the landing to see what was wrong and were cut to ribbons where they stood, their faces still showing curiosity until there was nothing left to show.

Once the mutineers reached Delhi, the entire city was in chaos, and new military units were unavoidably slow in arriving to ease the situation. It was weeks before Fraser Mackinnon was able to volunteer to take word to British garrisons to the west of Delhi in the urgent search for reinforcements.

Fraser had a dual motive in volunteering to go so far afield. Apart from his duty, the army garrisons were within reasonable reach of the Krubah Tea estate. He was desperate to know if Alex had reached there safely.

Under cover of night, he had already ridden to the Forbes' house and found it empty. Furniture was wrecked, curtains slashed. But there was no one there nor any sign of blood, to his wild relief, but he was constantly tortured by the thought of Alex falling into the murderers' hands.

Local regiments could only put up a token resistance to the might of the native force now in control of Delhi. They needed guns, and they needed them quickly. Telegraph messages passed from Lord Canning in Calcutta to the Commander-in-Chief of British forces, General Anson, but the lack of transport was hampering every move in the efforts to get guns and ammunition, provisions and medical supplies, to the beleaguered city.

"I don't care who's in charge," Fraser snapped, when he reached one of the western garrisons and found the soldiers less than anxious to join in against a mutiny. "I'm just bringing the message that we must have more men."

"Tell it to the Company! They sent too many overseas and forgot to bring them back!"

Fraser had no patience to argue with them, but he had pity for them too. He'd delivered his message to the garrison commander, and for all he knew these poor devils might be the next to be massacred by the mutineers controlling Delhi. He held his sharp retorts in check and set out to ride the distance between the tented garrison and Krubah Tea.

He was feverishly impatient to hold Alex close to him again. Only when he held her in his arms and felt her softness against him would he really believe that she was safe.

Alex was sitting in the garden drawing pictures for the two little Forbes boys. She and Ellen and Louisa did the best they could, feeling that a proper routine would give the children some stability. The garden was fragrant with oleanders and the English flowers Louisa had brought with her and guarded so jealously. Wallflowers and lupins and pale tea roses that flourished in the June sunshine of the hills.

People constantly came and went during the everyday business of the tea estate, and it was nothing to hear horses' hoofbeats pounding along the road. Alex merely glanced up as they sounded that morning, but then she glanced again.

There was something about this rider, something in the proud stance and the set of his head, reminding Alex in a swift moment of nostalgia of the beautiful and elegant Prince Albert, the Queen's husband.

The drawing materials slid off her lap as she leaped to her feet, her heart beating with a wild, soaring hope. Within minutes then, she was being held in Fraser's arms, feeling the roughness of his unshaven chin against hers, laughing and crying at the same time and holding him as though she would never let him go, locked in his embrace.

His kiss was sweet on her lips, the release of tension inside her almost unbearable, as she acknowledged now how desperately afraid she had been that she might never see him again. Neither of them noticed the small boys running towards the house to tell their mother that there was a visitor.

All they saw was each other. All they wanted was the miracle of being together again.

"Oh Fraser, Fraser, I can hardly believe it's you."
She wept against his face. "I've dreamed of this moment so often, I think I must be still dreaming."

"'Tis no dream, my lassie," he said thickly, as emotional as she. "If 'tis, then I pray that we never wake up."

Alex swallowed painfully, looking up into his beloved face, searching for answers she had to know.

"Have you heard any news of my father?" The question trembled on her lips. He shook his head. He was tempted to fill her with false hope, but in his heart he knew it was hopeless.

"No news at all, dearest. All Delhi is aflame now. Thank God you and Ellen got away. The Delmonts weren't so lucky—"

He saw her lovely face whiten. Any jealousy she might have felt on Hilary Delmont's account disappeared as Fraser told her of the murders at Sir Peter Wallace's home.

"How terrible! Sir Peter was always asking Father to take me there for tea, but we never went."

"Well, ye'll never go now," Fraser said harshly. "The house is a burned-out shell, and everyone in it that night was slaughtered. The devils have finally turned against us, Alex."

Shock rippled through her. They would probably be all people that she knew. Guests at the Residency of the Pearl of the Plain, on her father's guest list at Prince Shunimar's birthday ball. How long ago it all seemed now. How distant, those lovely, glorious days when she too had felt part of a prince's life.

She found it suddenly painful to breathe as faintness threatened to overcome her. She clung to Fraser, fighting off the nausea, and then running footsteps came from the house, as Ellen and Louisa and Miles rushed out to join them, all eager for news. And for Ellen, the longing to know if her husband was safe.

"I wish I could tell you something definite," Fraser said. "But I cannot. Everything's in such confusion. There are terrible rumors of massacres and of fresh mutinies by native regiments at Cawnpore and Lucknow."

"We're so isolated here, man," Miles commented. "It's like something from another world to hear of such atrocities—"

Fraser smiled grimly. "Be thankful that ye are, Thompson. There are sights in Delhi that are beyond belief."

Alex shuddered, and the young Forbes boys looked at Fraser curiously.

"What's atrocities?" Victor mouthed the word carefully. Ellen gathered him up in her arms.

"Nothing for you to worry your head about, sweetheart," she said quickly. "We'll go inside, shall we? I daresay Alex has finished drawing for today. Will you boys pick up everything and bring it to the house, please?"

"We'll all go inside." Louisa followed her lead. "Fraser must be hungry and thirsty, and we're fine hosts to stand out here instead of offering him hospitality."

"How long can you stay, darling?" Alex asked him quietly, as hand in hand they went towards the house, a servant taking his horse for stabling and feeding.

"No more than a day or two." He said what she already guessed, the squeeze of his fingers telling her how much longer he would choose to be with her if he could.

A day or two. It was so little out of a lifetime when no one knew the extent of a lifetime anymore. One never did, but now it was all the more precarious. He might leave this idyllic place, and she would never see him again. The thought overwhelmed Alex, drumming through her mind all the while they drank tea and later ate the evening meal and pretended a gaiety neither of them really felt. This could be the last time . . .

When the children had gone to bed, Ellen retired to sit and talk with Louisa and Miles, leaving Alex and Fraser discreetly alone. But even sitting in the circle of his arms, she was restless, as if the very air was pressing down on her. He seemed to read her mind and suggested a walk outside.

They left the confines of the house and gardens behind and walked to where it was balmy and sweet in the moonlight. The scent of the tea bushes intensified by night dews, the rustling of the gray-green leaves a warm whisper of sound in the night.

They neared the small thatched hut where they had been once before as though it were a trysting-place, and desire flamed between them as they kissed and clung and sank to the soft, rushy floor still entwined in each other's arms.

"God, but I've missed ye, my Alex!" Fraser said thickly against her mouth. "I've been out of my mind with worry for ye these past weeks, not knowing if ye were alive or dead."

"It's been the same for me! Not knowing was the worst of it, dearest. Wondering if I'd ever see you again. I almost lost faith in our talisman, Fraser—"

He tipped her chin up towards his face, his long, sensitive fingers making her flesh tingle, making the warmth fill her veins and her pulse race.

"But only almost, Alex. Ye knew we'd be together again, didn't ye? Ye must always have faith."

"Somehow I did know, deep down. But I don't feel

the same about Father and Aunt Maud, Fraser. I know I'll never see them again. It's been too long. If they'd still been alive, surely they'd have found a way here by now. You don't have to pretend with me anymore."

The soft, weak tears ran down her cheeks, and he kissed them away, wishing he could tell her differently.

"Your father wouldn't want you to mourn him, darling," he said gently. "He'd want you to live a full life."

"So would my mother. She was a warm and generous person, and she gave me so much. She said once that if she had one thing to give me, it would be that all my senses were alive to every God-given pleasure on this earth."

She didn't know if she had ever told him Constance's words before. She could think of nothing at that moment but the sudden charged atmosphere between them as the words were spoken. The night was soft and beautiful, and they might never meet again. And they were so very much in love. Alex trembled as Fraser ran his hands over her body as if to imprint every touch of her into his brain. He pulled her close to him, and she could feel the hardening of him against her.

"I could make you mine in this special place of ours, my love, and right now I think ye'd offer no resistance. But 'tis not the place for our loving. I want no hasty joining, but a lingering memory to warm my cold nights. Do ye want it as badly as I do, Alex?"

"Yes," she whispered. "Oh, yes, my love—"

"Then if ye're still of the same mind when ye've had time to think and consider it, leave your bedroom door unbolted tonight. I'll not think harshly of ye if I find ye've changed your mind, lassie. I want ye to be very sure."

His lips found hers again, and he wondered how in

God's name he was able to restrain himself like this, when he ached for her so badly it was as if fire burned through his every pore. But she was so young and vulnerable, and some devil of conscience in him knew that she must make the decision alone, without the temptation of his presence.

Her arms clung to him, her eyes lustrous in the moonlight, her mouth full and sensual.

"I won't change my mind. Can we go back to the house now? I'm suddenly tired and wanting my bed. They go to bed early here, Fraser."

They rose together, both knowing her words were an invitation and a need. His arm was tight around her waist as they walked back to the lovely white moonlit house.

As if to confirm what she had said, the house was quiet now, and they kissed good-night as though they would not meet again until morning.

Alex undressed quickly, finding that her fingers were all thumbs as they trembled with buttons and laces. She trembled all over, wanting him so much and yet still afraid of giving herself to a man.

The ghosts of the girlish secrets told in the darkness at Lady Margaret's Academy came back to taunt her. She knew nothing, only that she loved Fraser Mackinnon more than life, and it was that fact that calmed her taut nerves, so that by the time she heard the soft turning of her door handle, she lay between the sheets in her virginal nightgown, the gossamer mosquito net no more than a gauzy veil between them, and longed for the fulfillment of her dreams.

He slipped off the robe that Miles had put at his disposal and lifted the net. Between half-closed lids, Alex glimpsed his magnificent torso, spare and muscular, the generous sprinkling of dark hair on his chest echoing downwards in a fine line over his flat belly to the luxuriance below. She caught her breath, her heartbeats erratic, the strange feeling of starting on a fantastic voyage of discovery never quite leaving her.

Fraser took her in his arms, and she was warmed by his body. He aroused her slowly, knowing that this was the first time and wanting it to be as beautiful as he could make it.

She held him close, finding the texture of his skin an excitement in itself and wanting to touch her body to his, to feel unfettered by even the thin fabric of her nightgown. She hardly knew when it was tossed aside, or when the delights of touching and kissing and exploring one another was over.

Somehow she knew that the moment was right, and she felt the welcome weight of him cover her body, and it was natural to open up to him and to breathe more shallowly as he entered her, as if she knew instinctively that the small discomfort was a small price to pay for the joy of belonging.

"Oh, Fraser, I never knew it would be like this!" she whispered against his shoulder as his slow and sensual movements sent shafts of pleasure through her, radiating out from the core of her. "I never knew I could feel so—so complete. I feel as if I didn't exist until now."

"Our life together begins now," he whispered back. "Nothing else before tonight matters, darling. You're as much my wife now as if a dozen preachers had said the words over us."

She felt the heat in her cheeks. She could feel the throb of his heartbeats against hers. They felt like one heart, one beat. Her voice was a thread of sound when she spoke.

"Then you won't feel badly of me tomorrow, Fraser? For not insisting that we wait?"

His answer was a kiss of such passion that it made her weak. His tongue parted the softness of her lips, complementing the ecstasy his manhood gave her. She felt truly one with him and was humbled and exalted by the knowledge.

"I'll never think badly of ye, Alex," he said huskily. "Ye've a spirit in ye that fires my blood and warms my heart, and I make no apology for the Gaelic poetry ye bring out in me!"

She felt the rhythmic movements quicken and rose to meet him. Together they soared to the skies and reached the summit. The moment was so exquisite, the tears started to Alex's eyes, and she heard Fraser give a small, wrenched sound in his throat as he held her tight to him, rocking her in his arms as he held himself excruciatingly in check lest his seed surge into her.

Alex lay back exhausted, not fully understanding, as he slowly moved away from her. He couldn't risk leaving her with a child, although the thought of it was infinitely desirable to him. Alex with his bairn . . . but that must wait until the true marriage, spoken over by preachers.

"Fraser—"

He leaned over her again, pulling the soft cotton sheet over her lower limbs protectively.

"Hush, darling. I'll stay a wee while, but then I had best get back to my own room before I fall asleep here and shock the household."

"I wish you could stay forever," she said passionately. "I don't ever want us to part again—not now."

He put his fingers on her lips. "Especially not now," he agreed tenderly. "But we both know I have to leave here soon."

He watched the soft rise and fall of her breasts, full and white in the light from the window, as she lay with

her arms above her head in an unconsciously abandoned gesture. His sweet, innocent Alex, whom he
would defend to the death, he thought fiercely, and
with the thought came the return of the ugliness in the
city he had left.

"Dearest, I shall have to leave tomorrow evening,"
he said quietly.

"So soon?" She was aghast. Not even one more
night?

She wanted to cling to him, to beg him not to go, not
to leave her, but somehow she resisted the urge. She
thrust her arms into her nightgown again, suddenly
cold, and snuggled down in the bed with Fraser's arms
holding her close.

"We'll be together again, my love. Our talisman will
keep us safe." He hesitated. "I would tell ye the story
of Jamie and Katrina and the Bonnie Prince now, my
love, but I've a superstitious nature, and the tale is best
kept in my own head for the present. I'll tell ye one
thing. Katrina would have found a kindred spirit in ye.
She was a fiery, passionate one, too, and as much loved
by my ancestor, Jamie Mackinnon, as I love ye, my
Alexandra."

"Then I'll wait to hear it," she said huskily, moved
by the simple words of this powerful man who was not
too big to heed a family legend and to be charmed by it.

"We'll not anticipate our marriage again until it's
made legal," Fraser then said to her surprise. "I'm not
sure I could hold back all my passion again, Alex. It
shortens my life!"

She saw the lights dancing in his eyes and fell into a
teasing mood, demanding that he explain what he
meant! When he did, she blushed and giggled and felt
that her education was finally complete. They were
reluctant to part, but at last Fraser said he must go, or

the servants would be about the house, and her reputation would be in shreds.

She hardly cared. She stretched luxuriously in the warm bed after he had gone, suddenly feeling deliciously tired and lethargic. She reached out her hand to where Fraser had lain beside her and rested her head in the dent that his head had made in the pillow and felt a strange certainty that whatever else happened in this vast, beautiful, barbaric country, they would survive.

Chapter Thirteen

AFTER FRASER LEFT, THE DAYS BECAME TEDIOUS AND fraught with anxiety. Reports and rumors of the massacres, the cruelties of Indians and British alike, seeped into the most remote areas, brought by travelers and tradesmen or by the occasional escaping soldier, unable to stand any more of the fighting and nearly driven mad by it.

Alex found the tension as oppressive as the burning plains of Delhi had been before they left. It must be ten times worse there now, waiting for the rains to begin. Ellen said they were late this year, and waiting for the hot weather to break always made tempers brittle.

The rains always came later in the hills, and it was uncomfortable even there by now. It was nearing July, and still there was no news of peace in the cities. A traveler arrived at Krubah Tea with hysterical reports of the violence continuing in Delhi and no British reinforcements arriving yet.

There was even graver news of a massive betrayal in Cawnpore, when one of the Indian leaders, Nana Sahib, allowed the British out of the city he had captured and let them take to the thatched boats for Allahabad. Once on the river, the boats were fired, the tinder-dry thatch instantly bursting into flames. Men, women and children were slaughtered, burned or shot or drowned, and the river ran red with blood for days.

Such tales chilled the women at the tea estate, and Ellen grew thinner and more withdrawn as there was still no news of Captain Forbes. Time and again she begged any traveler for news of her husband's regiment, always to be met with blank faces.

If it hadn't been for the innocent chatter of the children, Alex thought that Ellen would go completely out of her mind. As it was, she forced herself to keep sane for their sakes. Much of their time was spent in sewing garments, with bales of fabric Louisa had acquired for them. Both Alex and Ellen were adequate seamstresses, and having brought so little clothing of their own, were glad of the occupation.

Alex's birthday came and went, and she was disinclined to celebrate. Again, for the children's sake, they had a cake and a semblance of a party, and Alex wept inside that Fraser couldn't be sharing this day with her. Fate was so cruel to keep them apart. They had had part of one ecstatic night together, and ever since then, each morning when Alex awoke, her hands unconsciously reached out to where Fraser should be.

She ached to awaken with him beside her, to fall asleep in his arms. She tried to cling to a dream, but she wondered desperately if they would ever meet again. She was eighteen years old and felt more like a hundred.

One hazy morning in July, before the sun rose too mercilessly in the sky, the clatter of a cart was heard approaching the house. The British women looked up idly from their chairs on the verandah. Carts came and went quite regularly, and sometimes there was a constant stream of people, from the tea estate workers to casual callers. A visitor was nothing to be curious about.

But suddenly, Sita, who had been amusing the little boys, gave an exclamation as she recognized the native driver, who was bellowing at the donkey to be still.

"It is my cousin Guttran! He is Langhi's brother! What does he mean in coming here? Why should he be so far from home? Have the stars led him? It does not bode well—"

She began a low moaning and wringing of her hands, and Alex was filled with exasperation. There were times when the omens and prophesies of India became more irritating than charming.

The man climbed stiffly down from the cart, gesticulating with his arms, speaking rapidly to Sita in their own dialect.

A foul smell came from the direction of the cart, and the ladies quickly tipped eau de cologne from the tiny bottles hanging at their waists onto their handkerchiefs and pressed them to their noses.

Sita suddenly spun around towards Ellen, rattling out the gist of her cousin's words. "Mem'sahib, my cousin says he found a British officer lying near the river. He thought he was dead—and my dog of a relative admits he was trying to relieve the officer of his boots—when the man groaned and frightened Guttran out of his wits. The officer seemed to waken from the dead, and Guttran is calling it a miracle! He was always a fool. But the man kept moaning and calling the name of Krubah, promising Guttran a reward to take him there. Guttran spent days finding out what 'Krubah' meant, but now he is here, and the Britisher is in the cart, and my cousin thinks he may be dead after all, with all the jolting and the loss of blood—"

Ellen rushed past them both and gingerly lifted the corner of the rough piece of matting thrown over the object in the cart. Her scream was pure anguish. Alex ran towards her, shouting at Sita to take the children indoors.

She reached the cart and had to force down the nausea as she looked at the broken shell of Captain Forbes. He was barely recognizable. His left arm was shattered but looked as though it had been hastily attended to, or he would surely have bled to death.

The wound still looked grisly and unwholesome. His once well-groomed hair was lank and plastered to his head with grime and sweat. His face was gray and gaunt, a long slash down one cheek, his eyes wild and staring. He barely breathed . . . but at least he did breathe. He was alive!

For the moment, Ellen seemed incapable of movement. She stood as if frozen, yet Alex could see she was near to collapse at seeing her handsome husband so diminished.

"Sita, find Mr. Thompson at once and ask him to send for a doctor immediately!" Alex took charge as the ayah returned with the other cousin. "Ellen, ask Louisa to prepare a room for your husband, and

Guttran and Langhi can carry him indoors. He must get out of this hot sun at once. He has a burning fever."

The women scuttled around at Alex's orders. She called to a round-eyed servant girl hovering nearby. "You there. Find a punkah-wallah and send him to the room Mrs. Thompson is preparing. Then fill some jugs with cool water and bring them to the room. Quick-quick!"

The girl jumped at her sharp tone and did as she was bidden. Alex's heart was thudding. All the time she was thinking that this poor wreck of a man could be Fraser . . . helped by some caring Indian or surviving British family.

She prayed that the doctor would come to Captain Forbes soon. She prayed that he would survive the ordeal of his wound and the long journey here. In some strange way, she felt that if John survived, so would Fraser . . . she made herself believe it. So she could still believe in omens, she thought wryly, even now.

It was more than a week before Captain Forbes became lucid. In that time, the Indian doctor rarely left him except to snatch a few hours' sleep. Ellen discovered a total aversion to the sick room and was ashamed and humiliated that she swooned each time the smell of the room washed over her.

Alex gritted her teeth and offered to help the doctor and the unswerving Sita in Ellen's place, still with that intuitive feeling that she was helping Fraser. She bathed the wound, she administered medicine to the cracked lips, she sponged the feverish body with no more emotion than a great sadness and compassion.

Through all the delirium, she listened in sick horror to tales of murder and mutilation and was unable to close her ears to any of it. It was a million miles removed from the gentle life at Lady Margaret's or the richness of a prince's palace . . .

She was finally awakened one morning by Sita telling her the crisis had passed, the officer's eyes were clear and he was asking for food. And Ellen and the children were by his bedside at last. Alex felt the tears start to her own eyes. John was restored to his wife and family, even though his army days must be over. No man could fight with only one arm, and eventually they must consider what to do with their lives.

Ellen appeared in her room without warning, and Alex began to say how glad she was, when she was struck by the odd expression in Ellen's eyes.

"What is it?" she said at once, heart pounding.

"Alex, John has been telling me a weird tale. But I'm not sure if it's right to raise your hopes about your father—"

"My father?" she croaked.

"John's regiment was at Cawnpore these past weeks, and there was talk of a deranged Englishman. No one knew him, and his speech was incoherent. He was tall and completely white-haired as though from shock. The natives found him a figure of fun, and John thinks they didn't kill him for that reason. Alex, John says that people heard him calling crazily for Constance, and he remembered—"

"Constance was my mother's name," Alex whispered, her heart drumming. "And the man was my father, I know it!"

She was as tense as a spring, wanting to rush into Captain Forbes' bedroom and shake more information out of him. As if guessing her intentions, Ellen put her hands on the younger girl's shoulders and stopped her.

"Don't be certain, my love. A crazy man says

anything. It's not an unusual name among British ladies—"

"Do you expect me to forget what you've just told me?" Alex blazed at her. "I have to know for certain. I have to go back—"

"Alex, no!" Ellen cried out. "It would be suicide to go back. You're safe here!"

"What else did John say? Tell me everything. I may piece it together." She didn't heed Ellen's words.

"Bits of words. Names that didn't mean anything. The man didn't mention your name, or your aunt's. That's why I think it's probably all a mistake. I didn't want to tell you—"

"What other names? I'll ask John myself if you don't tell me!" Alex was near crazed herself with the surging hope that Felix might still be alive after all.

"Please be still, darling," Ellen pleaded. "You fright en me with that wild look in your eyes. John spoke of something like 'chop.' I didn't understand it—"

"Chohban." Alex was suddenly icily calm. "Father's gone to the bungalow. I must go there. Perhaps I can help him to return here. He'll need help—"

Sudden grief overcame her as she remembered Ellen's vivid words about the deranged Englishman whose hair had probably turned white with shock. Her beloved father . . .

Ellen was aghast. "Alex, you can't do this! How can you go there? You know what's happening to British civilians. A young girl alone will stand no chance! Fraser would forbid it—"

"Fraser would help me," Alex retorted. "The bunga-low is between Cawnpore and Delhi, but well away from the cities. I'll go back the way we came, in the ekka, Ellen. I'll wear Indian clothes, and I'll have Langhi and Guttran to protect me. They've both proved themselves loyal, and one of them can look for Fraser. They have an uncanny way of finding people. Fraser will help me to bring Father here."

Even to herself, the idea sounded risky and Ellen tried vainly to make her think again. But there was no dissuading her. Finally, Ellen begged her not to leave without proper thought and consultation with Miles Thompson and his wife. Alex was forced to agree, since Miles had assumed the role of guardian since her father's presumed death.

But Miles was away from the tea estate and wouldn't return until the next evening. She burned with frustration at the waiting, and she insisted on speaking with John Forbes about the strange Englishman. He could tell her little more.

"I wasn't sure whether to say anything at all," he said flatly. "I guessed you'd feel this way, but I fear for a young woman alone, Alex, and it may be a wild goose chase—"

"I'm strong," she said quietly. "And I have to go."

He studied her, taut and brave and beautiful, and gave a slow nod. She saw the exhaustion on his face and felt guilty for having tired him.

"You and your family must stay here as long as you wish," she said suddenly. "You mustn't hurry away."

She bit her lip, realizing that they had nothing to leave for. They had no home, and John had no more career. To her surprise, his voice held no bitterness.

"I might ask if we can stay for good." He spoke as though he had given it some thought. "I'm thankful to be alive, and there's little I can do with only one good arm. But I've a good brain, and Miles says the administration work here is getting too much for him. Would he accept my services, Alex? We'd have to have a tutor for the boys, but we could advertise for someone—"

"You seem to have thought of everything!"

"I've had little else to do."

She leaned forward and kissed him lightly on the forehead. They had gone through too much together in the past week for her to be modest.

"Then stay. Miles will agree, I know it."

She would see to it that he did. If her father were dead, then Alex could insist on a place being available for the Forbes family. Even if he were alive, from the sound of his condition, Alex would still be virtually in control of the Truscott share of Krubah Tea. It was a sobering, poignant thought.

It was three days before Miles Thompson returned to Krubah Tea. In that time, he had become aware of the extent of the violence in the cities to the east. And his reaction to Alex's news was an explosive one.

"I forbid it, Alexandra!" he bellowed, like the ghost of Felix Truscott. "In your father's absence, I absolutely forbid it! It would be sheer madness to go back—"

"It's because of Father that I must!" She leaped to her feet. "Short of locking me up, you cannot stop me. I *will* go and try to find him!"

They glared at one another. Miles put up all the sensible arguments, and she always came back to one vital point.

"John says no one recognizes the man. But I'd know him, however he had changed. And he's at the bungalow. I know where that is. Don't try and stop me anymore. Sita's cousins have promised to take me. I trust them—"

Miles scowled. "I trust them too—just as far as I can throw them. You're your father's daughter, all right, Alex. Stubborn and self-willed. If you were a man, I might not try to block you, but a young woman—"

She ran and kissed him, knowing she had won.

"Just help me, Mr. Thompson. Give us some provisions for the journey and some money, please. I want to go as quickly as possible. One of the servants has given me some clothes with which I can disguise myself. Won't you let me model one of the saris for you so you can see what a splendid Indian girl I make?"

She began wheedling him, the way she used to do with Felix, and she saw the grudging smile on his lips at her sweet persuasion. He sighed, still dead against the notion, but Louisa had already told him to let Alex go. She must have the chance to do as her heart dictated, and he asked himself now how he had ever hoped to stop her!

"Go on, my love," Louisa said gently now. "We'll have a little fashion parade."

Alex laughed, though her stomach suddenly churned. It was all arranged. She would leave in the morning, and suddenly she too felt the fear. But she dismissed it from her mind as she went to her room and changed quickly out of the cumbersome crinoline into the softly swirling garment that transformed her.

Silk against her skin . . . As she wound the sari about her body and swathed it over her head and across her face, so that only her beautiful eyes were revealed, Alex caught her breath. Seeing herself in the mirror, it was like seeing someone else. A sensual woman that no outer garments could disguise, young and slender, with the fire of adventure smoldering in her blue eyes. This journey would be an adventure, after all. For a few seconds, she wished passionately that Fraser could see her now, like this . . .

But her coloring was undoubtedly European, she thought with a shiver of unease, and the silken folds of the sari must cover her fair hair at all times. She refused to think any more of the danger, turned and rejoined the others downstairs.

"You look marvelous, Alex!" Ellen exclaimed. "And so different!"

"Not different enough," Miles grunted. "But as long as you keep inside the curtains of the vehicle and travel mostly by night you may do all right."

"I think you look beautiful, Alex," Louisa added softly.

"That's not really the idea. The last thing I want is to be conspicuous!"

The plan was to leave the next morning. It was safe to travel in daylight while they were still so far from the plains. Sita had stern words with her cousins that night.

"Defend the missy Sahib at all times, and do not shame the honor of our family by letting your gaze dwell on her too often. Do not shame it even more by forgetting your loyalty to the British. We swore to serve them, and a turncoat is as despicable as a thief. Pay heed to the words of your elder, my cousins. If ill befalls the missy Sahib at your hands, it will be shown in the stars—"

"We hear you, Sita," Guttran said irritably. "Would I have brought the Englishman all this way if I had not been loyal? I could have stabbed him where he lay and had his fine pair of boots."

"And I would have refused to leave Delhi if my loyalty was in doubt," Langhi snapped. "Show your trust in us, cousin!"

She nodded, having little choice, but satisfied at having had her say.

When it was time to leave, Alex made a quick farewell, not wanting to prolong these moments. Whether she ever saw any of these people again was in the hands of God or the stars, or whatever faith was guiding her now. The thought uppermost in her mind was that something was guiding her to the Englishman Captain Forbes had spoken of and guiding her also to Fraser Mackinnon.

The journey was very different from the one Alex had taken with Ellen and the children. Fear had driven them away from Delhi, but every turn of the wheels now took her nearer to the violence. She told herself a hundred times that it was foolhardy . . . but she was driven on by something akin to desperation.

And despite the fear, there was a strange kind of exhilaration inside her too. If fate was kind, she might find her father alive, when she had given him up for dead. She had long given up hope of ever seeing poor Aunt Maud again. But above all was the searing certainty that she would find Fraser, and they would be together again.

Sita's cousins were courteous and protective of the young missy Sahib. Even without their cousin's warning, they would have defended her, admiring her foolish bravery and hoping she would find her heart's desire at the end of the journey. Alex soon realized it was to be a long and wearisome one.

During the descent to the plains, where the heat struck an acute lethargy into Alex, it rained with a sudden fury that drenched the parched earth and turned it into sodden quagmires. The ekka wheels were often stuck fast in mud, and the two Indians screamed and swore at the donkey as they strained and tugged to free the vehicle. The delays were frequent. The rain chilled Alex through, yet often within minutes of its arrival it had stopped, the sun blazed out, and everything steamed uncomfortably again.

Many times she longed guiltily for the cool, green meadows of England, instead of this unending country with its strange animal calls in the night, the bellowing of distant elephants, the screeching of monkeys, the slithering into the darkness of things that scuttled and crawled and had her taut with terror.

"How much farther?" she asked Langhi wearily when it seemed they had been traveling forever, and she had lost count of the nights after nearly two weeks.

It must be the end of July by now, she calculated, trying to keep some sense of continuity in her mind. She had been cheered to hear from a traveler a few nights ago that Nana Sahib had been defeated at Cawnpore. It must be a good omen, she had thought hopefully. Cawnpore might be safe by now . . .

Langhi pointed distantly ahead in answer to her question. She could see nothing but a faint blur of dust on the horizon and slightly to the north of them.

"There is Delhi, missy Sahib," he grunted. "We have been keeping well away from it, because of the trouble. Now we begin to go northwards again in the direction Sahib Thompson gave us for your father's bungalow."

"How much longer will it take!" She couldn't believe they hadn't even reached Delhi yet. She had assumed they were long past it. She could have wept. Each day they delayed, the greater the possible danger to the unfortunate Englishman she sought.

Guttran shrugged. "There's no hurrying fate and the Indian donkey, missy Sahib," he said enigmatically.

Alex could have hit him.

"Couldn't you *try?*" She was heavily sarcastic.

Days ago she had begun to feel like a leaf blown by the wind. The two men muttered together in their own language for much of the time, glancing at her with guarded looks. She trusted them, but there were times when she longed to hear an English voice, to be with her own kind, to be home . . .

The breath caught in her throat with a kind of sweet pain. Home . . . home was England, fresh and green. Not here, not India. She longed for the calm order of English days . . . and for Fraser to share them with her. She longed for normality again.

They had almost reached the vicinity of the bungalow. They traveled more cautiously now, and always by night. Sometimes it seemed as though they used the only vehicle in the world, the noise of its wheels clattering in the darkness, putting new fear into Alex that it must draw attention to them.

At other times, the tracks and roads seemed populated by an endless crush of carriages, carts, elephants and camels, the red dust swirling into the sky from many feet, as British and natives hurried away from the cities or rushed towards them. There was either utter confusion or an eerie silence.

Alex's nerve almost broke, but always she held onto the fact that every mile brought her nearer to Fraser and to finding out the truth about the deranged Englishman. She prayed that it was Felix and that his condition wasn't beyond help.

By now, she traveled alone with Guttran. Langhi had left two days ago to look for the scout, Fraser Mackinnon. He knew him by sight, from his visits to the Forbes' house in Delhi, and promised to bring him to the bungalow with all speed.

At the last resting-house before they reached it, Alex looked at herself in the cracked mirror in her room. She was supposed to be a wealthy Indian lady traveling with a servant, but once the travel-stained sari was removed, she looked gaunt and thin, the once-lovely cheekbones prominently visible.

Her eyes were haunted, and she longed for this journey to be over. All her strength seemed to be ebbing away, and she longed to sleep and sleep . . .

For a moment, utter panic overcame her. How could Langhi hope to find Fraser? There was no way of knowing that he had come to Cawnpore, only the inconsistent reports of deserters or traveling-men, often at second or third hand. Was she completely mad and doomed to become as deranged as the unknown Englishman?

Perhaps so. But she couldn't rest until her mission was done. Her chin tilted in the old, unconsciously arrogant fashion, and her blue eyes lost their glazed look and flashed back at her.

"I won't be beaten now," she muttered. "I'll do what I came to do, and then I'll rest."

Next night, the ekka moved more silently through wooded areas, made temporarily lush by the frequent rains. Alex might have been in a wilderness. The curtained vehicle stifled her. She began to feel unable to breathe, as if some awful weight was pressing down on her. Then she felt the ekka stop, and Guttran came running back to her. She thrust the curtain aside.

"Look away, missy Sahib," he said in a harsh voice. "There is nothing for you here—"

She looked, and would have screamed if she dared. But screams might alert an unseen enemy, and the scene in front of her told her that an enemy had already been here. To the bungalow, that her mother had loved so much . . .

Her heart pounded sickeningly. The blackened ruins of a much-loved home reared up into a dawn-pink sky. A faint wisp of smoke still hung on the acrid air, suggesting that the attack had not long been over. Sobs tore at Alex's throat as she clambered down from the vehicle. The air was cool, but the breeze carried the stench of death.

"My father—" she said brokenly. Guttran's hand pulled at her arm as she began to move nearer to the ruin.

"We must leave here, missy Sahib. If the man was your father, he will have perished. We must go quickly. I will find a house of a relative—"

"*No!*" For once, the mention of another relative couldn't make her smile. "I won't leave. Langhi will bring my fiancé here. I must stay! Go if you wish, but leave me alone, please!"

She wrenched away from him, the sari billowing in the breeze as she stumbled towards the shell of the building, aching with tears and sorrow. She clambered over broken timbers and slashed, smoldering furniture and wept for all that was gone.

Suddenly, she heard a faint sound that made her heart stop and then race crazily. A human sound among the carnage . . . Guttran was right behind her and heard it too. His fingers dug into her arm again, his other hand motioning her to be quiet. He crept forward, straining to see through the half-light. Then he crouched down, and Alex saw the crumpled heap at the same moment. The figure of a grizzled old man, but his skin was dark, his features Indian.

"Chohban!"

She croaked his name, kneeling down beside him, and then saw to her horror that there was only half of him remaining. The lower half of his body was hacked to pieces, and how he still drew breath, she couldn't imagine. There was nothing anyone could do for him. She forced down the nausea.

"Missy Sahib, get away!" The thin, reedy voice

wavered. "They killed my Jaya and the Englishman. They played with him, taunting him, and then they—" His eyes rolled as Guttran swore at him to spare the woman's feelings.

"Chohban, was it my father?" she begged. The man was dead, that was certain, but she had to know . . .

"No," he grated with the pain. "Sahib Truscott and his sister died in the fire at the Pearl of the Plain, missy. So sorry—"

His mouth gushed blood, and he was dead.

Somehow Alex got to her feet. She wanted to run. She wanted to hide, to bury herself away from the truth. She had known it all along, and yet she had refused to believe it. Now it felt as though she mourned her father twice over. She rocked with the pain of it, wishing she could keen and weep like the Indian women did. Needing to cry her heart out and not be afraid that unseen enemies would swoop down in the midst of her grief.

Strong arms suddenly hauled her to her feet. The fear was smothered in her throat before she had a chance to scream. There was a voice murmuring words of comfort in her ears, and she was so near demented, she could hardly register its tone. She didn't know it . . . how could she?

As if sanity returned like a thunderbolt, the voice assumed familiarity. There were other voices gabbling quietly in the background—Guttran and his cousin Langhi, just returned from Cawnpore. And the arms that held Alex close were the arms she had longed for and dreamed about, a million times and more . . .

"Fraser!" His name was a trembling whisper on her lips. "Are you real? Is it really you, my darling?"

"Aye, it's me, my foolish, beautiful lassie. What in God's name are ye doing here, when I thought ye were safely away at the tea estate? Were they mad to let ye come here?"

"They couldn't stop me!" She sobbed in his arms. "I heard about the Englishman, and I thought—I thought—"

His brief anger died away, and he held her tight.

"I know, lassie. I know what ye thought. I thought so myself for a while, which is why I was following the Englishman's trail myself. Your fellow found me on the Cawnpore road, and it's a wonder he didn't get his throat slit for his trouble, for jumping out at me the way he did!"

She shivered at the mock seriousness in his voice. All this journey was for nothing . . . yet not for nothing, while she was safe in Fraser's arms. She looked up into his eyes, the silk sari whispering softly about her face and body. She was filthy and disheveled, but to Fraser she was still beautiful and would always be so.

"What do we do now?" she said in a gulping voice. It was suddenly all too much. The ordeal of the journey, finding the bungalow burned, Chohban dying in front of her. . . . She felt Fraser's arms tighten.

"We go east of Lucknow. I'd take you to the Residency, but the city's under siege. The Residency is surrounded, despite its acres of land. But God knows when the city will be relieved. We're still hopelessly outnumbered. I know of a British family to the east who will take you in—"

"Where will you be?" she stammered, all this becoming too much to absorb all at once.

"Back to Lucknow," he said briefly.

"Take me there too. I don't ever want to be parted from you again, Fraser! I'm afraid!" She clung to him.

He gave a wry smile, curving her cheek with his finger and seeing the shadows there.

"How can a lassie who's just done what you have be afraid of anything?"

"I'm afraid of losing you, my love."

He didn't speak for a few moments. Then he sighed. "God knows I'd rather have you near me, where I can keep an eye on you! If these fellows will follow me to Lucknow with the ekka, there may be a chance. Do ye risk it, Alex?"

"I'd risk anything. Haven't I proved that?"

His answer was to kiss her soft lips and to treasure this moment of sweetness in the midst of hell. And to pray that he was doing the right thing in taking her into it with him.

Chapter Fourteen

ONCE AGREED ON IT, THEY MOVED AWAY FROM THE
remains of the bungalow and into the woods. Already
the vultures were gathering, scenting blood in the ruins
behind them. Fraser spoke rapidly to the two natives,
telling them to keep watch, and he and Alex climbed
into the ekka together. And at last, she felt as though
all her tight knots of tension began to unravel.

She was overjoyed at their being together again, but
it was too soon to forget the horrors at the bungalow or
her grief at losing her father twice over.

"I should never have believed for a moment that it
was Father!" She wept in Fraser's arms. "No one could
have survived the fire at Prince Shunimar's palace. I
acted like a child."

"Perhaps you were a child then, but not anymore, darling." He spoke gently. "To make this journey alone, for whatever reason, took a lot of courage. Don't belittle yourself, Alexandra."

She gave a tremulous smile. "Father used to call me that. It always meant he was cross with me. I'd give the world to hear him say it now!"

He held her until her shuddering sobs eased. Gradually, she became aware of the warmth of his hands through the thin silk of her sari, of Fraser being the man she loved and of herself as a woman. The pain of the last hours receded, and she felt the remembered caress of his palm on her breast, sweet and warm.

"I wish I could be with ye every hour of the day, dearest, if only to ensure that ye wouldn't go running off on a fool's errand at the slightest provocation," he said huskily.

"Am I a fool as well?" She whispered the words, knowing he was teasing her and so unused of late to the lovely sound of it.

"Maybe we're all fools, for thinking we can conquer a land that's not ours." He was suddenly serious.

Alex twisted in his arms to look into his face in the dim interior of the ekka. Outside, it was daylight now, but they remained enclosed in their own private world. Chinks of light through the partly opened curtains showed the surprise in her face. She heard the bitterness in his voice, the sense of disillusion she herself felt.

"Has India lost its charm for you too, Fraser?" she said quietly.

"Me *too?*" He gave a brief laugh. "I can't believe what I'm hearing, lassie! Is this the girl who dreamed of a burnished land across the sea, ablaze with gold and silver and fabulous palaces—?"

"But not with fire and violence and death!" The words tumbled out. "I once thought this land held everything for me. All my life I dreamed of living here with my parents, in peace and beauty. Instead, I've got nothing."

He could feel the thudding of her heart against his. "You've got me. You'll always have me."

Tears started to her eyes again, and she leaned her cheek to his rough one.

"And I thank God for it, my love. But you understand what I'm trying to say, don't you?"

"Aye, I understand only too well. India holds precious little for me anymore. Sometimes I too get a hunger to see my own folks again. My own hearth, my own glens. We all get those feelings occasionally, Alex."

"And if they become more than occasional feelings?"

He looked deep into her eyes. "What are you telling me? That you want to go home?"

"Don't you? Be honest with me! You and I must always be honest, Fraser."

He shrugged his shoulders. "I canna go yet," he said abruptly, and she knew by his lapse into dialect that he was disturbed. "I canna desert, and nor would ye have me do so, lassie."

"Of course not!" Alex said quickly, though for one wild, sweet moment, she wanted to beg him to take her home, to flee to a port, any port, and find the first available ship for England. But she couldn't ask it of him. Not now. Not yet.

"Maybe when all this is over, we should go home," he said slowly. "I always wanted to show you my mountains."

"And to soar down them with me."

He touched her mouth with his, softly at first, and then the kiss deepened and became a pledge without words. One day, when all this was over, they would go home.

Alex clung to the thought as she had once clung to the dream of India.

They were alone, yet not alone. The ekka was cramped, but neither of them noticed. They had food bought at the last resting-house and the comfort of each other's arms. The Indians kept guard outside until the shadows grew long and the sun began its magnificent descent towards the horizon.

"We'll leave now," Fraser said quietly. "Lucknow has a tortuous maze of streets and little alleyways to rival Delhi's. I know a route that should keep us safe."

It would need more luck than knowledge, Fraser thought grimly, but he didn't worry Alex with the thought. By now, he too was garbed in loose native garments, his skin already dark enough by his years in the Indian sun to fool anyone at night. He had considered it the safest way of traveling. If challenged, they were an Indian couple traveling with servants to Lucknow.

As they rode, he told her rapidly of events since she had fled Delhi with Ellen Forbes and the children, and she told him quickly of Captain Forbes' safe arrival at Krubah Tea.

"He'll be an asset to the business," Fraser nodded, when Alex told him of John's suggestion. "As for the luckless British remaining in Delhi, it's difficult to get in and out of the city to see what's happening. But new regiments are expected imminently now, and we have every hope that victory will soon be ours. It has to be," he said with sudden passion. "We can't let the mutinous bastards undo everything we've fought for all these years. We have to fight back. War makes animals of us all."

She didn't comment on his choice of words. Unladylike or not, she agreed with them all.

"Have there been many killings, Fraser? Has it been very terrible?"

He glanced at her and remembered her words. There must be honesty between them.

"A massacre," he said simply. "Most of the people you met at Prince Shunimar's birthday ball are gone. We've lost fine military men. Sir Henry Lawrence at Lucknow, General Barnard—I won't reel off a list of names that mean little to you, dearest. But our losses have been near to disastrous—"

"But still you hold out."

He smiled grimly. "When did the British army ever give in to an enemy? Will ye answer me that?"

"I can't. I know nothing of battles."

"Did your education at that fancy school of yours tell you nothing of history, lassie?" he teased her.

He wanted to keep her in a light mood while they traveled. The nearer to the once beautiful city of Lucknow they got, the more she would need to be calm. There would be time enough for hysteria . . . he wavered at the thought. It would be easy enough to tell the Indians to head east and to take Alex to safety. But she would never forgive him, and he didn't have the stomach to be parted from her again.

If fate chose to let them die, then let them die together. Fraser simply didn't believe their time had come yet. And nor would it while he still had his family's legend to relate to Alex. When the time was right. When he made her his bride.

It took several days to reach the outskirts of Lucknow. They arrived by moonlight, and the beautiful mosques and minarets gleamed like silver in its glow. Alex had pushed the curtain aside until they neared the city, and then she began to see the destruction. They were suddenly stopped by a sepoy patrol, and her heart beat crazily in her chest. Two of the sepoys went to pull the curtains apart, then paused as Guttran prattled. They laughed coarsely at the Indian's words.

"He's told them we're newlyweds," Fraser whispered. "He's a good fellow. He makes a joke of it to the men to distract their attention from us. If anyone looks inside, we must act like lovers, Alex. Will it be any hardship?"

The teasing grew thin as she shook her head. Her mouth was dry with fear. She wished desperately that they were indeed newlyweds and on their way to some secret destination in England, instead of heading straight into danger.

Her first glimpse of the city before they were stopped had been horrific enough, and the nearer they got to the Residency through the twisting alleyways, the more a hum of noise seemed to fill her ears. A noise like perpetual moaning, weeping . . . Battle debris was strewn over the roads, and there was a terrible stench she couldn't identify. She put her hand over her nose, and Fraser answered her unspoken question.

"There's no time to bury the bodies. They lie where they fall, until the vultures pick them clean. You get used to such sights, Alex." She would have to, he thought grimly.

"Are there many Europeans at the Residency?" she asked through chattering lips, wishing dearly that she was already safely inside. Fraser could only answer vaguely, since the numbers were constantly changing like a shifting tide, whether due to deaths or escapes or entrants seeking a haven.

"Oh, plenty enough," he said to reassure her. "We're defended by nearly two thousand British soldiers, including officers and surgeons. There are civilian volunteers and near to a thousand native troops, still loyal to the Company."

John Company . . . it was a long while since Alex had thought of the East India Company in those affectionate terms. A long time since she had thought of it at all, now that her father was no longer part of it. She strained to see through the chinks in the ekka's curtain, and then the ekka was halted abruptly.

This time, the curtains were thrust apart without warning. Fraser had pulled Alex into his arms, so that she was half-hidden against him. He waved an imperious arm to the sepoy peering suspiciously inside, rattling words at him in his own dialect and calling him the son of a dog for disturbing a man with his bride.

Outside the vehicle, their two Indian protectors made similar appeals to the sepoys, and at last, they were told to get through if they must, if they preferred to be shot with the feringhis.

Alex flinched. That term had never been applied to her before. Feringhis . . . the derogatory native word for "foreigners."

The ekka clattered through the gates, and they were challenged again, this time by an English voice, and Fraser quickly made himself known. By now, Alex was almost petrified by the din all around her. The moaning had gathered strength, until it was like a constant dull animal howl. It was no more than the combined voices on either side of the Residency defenses, but it was the most unnerving sound she had ever heard.

"Go to the house of Mrs. Arbuthnot," the soldier grunted to Fraser. "She'll probably take the young lady in, though there will be precious little to eat. The devils are effectively cutting off our food supplies now."

Alex could hear the swift resentment in the man's voice, as if her own presence was putting one more burden on an already dwindling food supply. Things were indeed bad if they could resent their own people.

"Are there many women here?" she asked Fraser as the ekka continued on its way, skirting heaps of rubble and missiles of all kinds, thrown over the walls and left to rot. Stinking vegetation, iron bars, stones and bits of dead animals all littered the streets and sickened Alex's stomach.

"Some hundreds. Ladies and their children and the usual camp followers," Fraser assured her. "You'll be safe with Mrs. Arbuthnot, dearest. She's a good woman, and the wife of an officer."

It was foolish to think that they could have stayed together. They were in the middle of a battleground, yet Alex knew that British etiquette must be followed at all costs.

"I can stay awhile," he went on, as if reading her thoughts. "And then I must report back to the barracks for orders. Ye'll find that some days seem almost normal, Alex. And others—well, since ye're here, ye must find out for yourself. At least I'll always know where to find ye now. Ye'll promise me ye'll stay put this time?"

She nodded quickly. For the moment she was safe. There was no sound of guns. No burning thatch. No dreadful sights of wounded in the streets. If it was the calm before the storm, then at least she thanked God fervently for this small respite. She was safe and alive, and Fraser was beside her.

Mrs. Arbuthnot was a round, bustling woman who welcomed Alex with tears in her eyes when Fraser introduced her.

"I met your mother once, my dear, a charming and lovely woman. And your father was so tall and distinguished. They were a handsome couple."

"Yes, they were." Alex was suddenly choked. She didn't want to speak of them, nor to think that in other circumstances, her parents might have been hosts to this woman and her husband at some sparkling ball.

"You'll be wanting a bath," Mrs. Arbuthnot said briskly. "We have reasonable ablutions here, Alex. If you would like to take advantage of them too, Mr. Mackinnon, you're very welcome. I can offer you some supper if you're hungry."

"I'm ravenous—" Alex said without thinking.

"Perhaps just a morsel, until Alex has her own rations allocated here," Fraser commented.

Until that moment, Alex hadn't realized that food was in short supply, nor how desperate those defending this corner of British India were for food and clothing. There was little bread, butter or milk in the city, Fraser informed her briefly. What there was fetched extortionate prices.

Those who still had animals, goats for milking or chickens for meat and eggs, guarded them jealously. More often, they were either stolen by starving British or native sepoys, or requisitioned by the butchers, who insisted that everyone should have fair rations.

"I'm not all that hungry," Alex murmured. After hearing the tales, she had little stomach for food but accepted a piece of hard, coarse bread and some questionable soup made by Mrs. Arbuthnot's cook. In normal times, it would be totally unpalatable, but these were not normal times.

She wondered how the two Indians who had brought her here would fare. On arrival here, they had gone silently away into the night, without waiting to be properly thanked. There was little she could give them but her undying gratitude anyway.

But once Alex sank into a hot hip bath, some of the tension left her. Scrubbing herself with proper soap, and with a few drops of Mrs. Arbuthnot's eau de cologne sprinkled into the water, she could pretend for a little while that this wasn't some nightmare they lived through.

Her innate optimism gradually returned. She wouldn't think of the past, only the future. What it held was still in the hands of fate, but they were together. She rose from the bath, drying herself quickly on the soft towel Mrs. Arbuthnot had placed ready for her. She had already been shown the little room where she would sleep.

She was thinner, but her body was still young and supple and ready for love. The feelings so long suppressed came surging back again, as she donned the borrowed dress, which had belonged to one of Mrs. Arbuthnot's daughters. She still had the gleam of Constance's perfect pearls to lie against her throat, complementing her delicate complexion. And Alex began to feel human again.

While Alex bathed, Captain Arbuthnot had returned. He and Fraser discussed the present situation. General Henry Havelock's troops had won several major victories and countless minor ones, but there were still not enough men to defeat the rebels in the

cities where the main trouble now existed, namely
Delhi and Lucknow.

"I pray that Delhi will be relieved soon," Captain
Arbuthnot said roughly. "Our daughters are the wives
of officers there, and we've heard nothing from them
for weeks. The last official news is that our regiments
are holding the Delhi Ridge, and they seem to be
beating the bastards. More of our troops were arriving
there at last. God knows where they've been held up all
this time."

"And what of here? All seems quiet tonight."

The other shrugged, offering Fraser the brandy
bottle and being refused. Fraser wasn't in the mood for
drinking. "You've seen it all before, Mackinnon. A
night or two of quiet, and then all hell breaks loose. I
swear they breed new bastards overnight! As one falls,
two more take his place, slashing and murdering. We're
devilishly short of ammunition and medical supplies.
Many of the women have taken up nursing duties in the
old banqueting hall that's now a hospital. But you know
all that, don't you? By God, how quickly the old order
changeth!"

There was nothing Fraser could say in reply to such
gloom. He wondered how any of them kept as cheerful
as they did. He especially admired the ladies for their
fortitude. Several months of privations had put new
spirit in them rather than crushing them.

Despite the lack of proper food and the shabbiness of
their dress, they still retained their dignity, their sense
of Britishness that was echoed in the patched and
tattered remnants of the flag still fluttering from the
Residency flagpole in defiance of the rebels.

"The bath is ready for you, Mr. Mackinnon." Mrs.
Arbuthnot appeared in the room, and Fraser was glad
to get away from the hard-drinking officer. He was

probably one who still had illicit supplies, and Fraser couldn't blame him for drinking to forget, as long as it didn't impair his usefulness behind a gun.

"Alex and I will take some tea in the drawing room," Mrs. Arbuthnot said pointedly. "Perhaps you would care to join us there later, Mr. Mackinnon."

She spoke with all the poise one might expect to find in a London drawing room, instead of in this small house forming one of the defenses within the Residency, its walls showing distinct bullet holes.

Tomorrow, Alex would see the full extent of the damage to this lovely old city and how several months under siege could turn the greedy into animals, the weak to jibbering wrecks. For tonight, she was cushioned by warmth and friendship.

When Fraser had bathed, he joined the ladies and saw that for all her worry and anguish, Alex was as beautiful as ever. As dear to him, and as desirable. Still his lassie, his woman.

As if Mrs. Arbuthnot suddenly recognized the glances passing between these two, she stopped her chattering about people and places Alex didn't know and got to her feet.

"You two will want to be alone for a while before Mr. Mackinnon has to leave," she announced, firmly determined to take care of this beautiful and fragile-looking girl as if she was her own daughter. It may help to smother her fear for her own two.

"I have some things to see to, so I'll leave you for half an hour. If the room is too hot for you, call for the punkah-wallah—"

They hardly heard her. They went through the motions of thanking her and assuring her that they were quite comfortable, and all the time they were wishing her gone. All they wanted was to be alone, to look and touch, to be together again. All immediate danger was past, and for half an hour they could be lovers again . . .

"The lady does not give us much time," Fraser murmured against the softness of Alex's newly washed hair, still fragrantly damp.

"Are you surprised?" she said teasingly. "She only had to see your expression each time you looked at me to know what you were thinking!"

"And what was I thinking?" He spoke softly, his arms around her on the long sofa, his body warm against hers, his hands caressing her curves beneath the bombazine gown she wore. She shivered deliciously, as all the sleeping feelings began to awaken at his touch.

"That you would like to rid me of this dress and lie with me, as we did once before," she whispered.

"Alexandra, where is your girlish modesty?" His eyes laughed at her, loving her daring. His finger circled one peaked nipple, aroused by his nearness. She caught her breath at the darting sensation the contact sent through her.

"I don't know," she said faintly. "Somehow, I lose all sense of modesty when I'm with you, Fraser. Is it wicked, to have so little sense of shame?"

"No, lassie," he said softly. "It's beautiful. 'Tis the way a woman should feel with her man, with no foolish guilt to clutter up the emotions. A woman should be able to tell her man she loves him."

"I do love you, my darling. So much! I made this journey because of my foolish belief that I might find my father, but oh, Fraser, more than half of me really wanted to find you. If I feel any guilt, perhaps it should be because of that."

He put his fingers on her lips, pampering their softness.

"Hush, dearest. The past is gone forever, and we can never bring it back. Your father wouldn't wish you to mourn him forever. He'd be glad that you and I have a future."

Her blue eyes suddenly burned brightly into his. Her cheeks were flushed, her mouth parted.

"We do have a future, don't we? I just couldn't bear it, if after all this—"

"We do," Fraser said doggedly. "You and I are indestructible, Alexandra. Haven't I told you that before?"

She nodded. The love between them was as strong as ever, the needs as passionate, but they both knew that this was not the place or the time. Passion must wait, no matter how fervently each yearned for fulfillment of their love.

Fraser knew that if he persisted, she would allow him every intimacy, but he chose not to. A hasty fumbling and lifting of skirts would not do justice to Alex's loveliness. He subdued the fierce desire in his loins with a great effort.

"Maybe I should tell ye now about the legend of Jamie and Katrina," he said suddenly. "Ye've a lot in common with my spirited and beautiful ancestor—"

"No!" This time it was Alex who stopped him, suddenly afraid to know too much. The talisman must continue.

"You could tell me who they were, if you like," she went on. "That much wouldn't hurt, would it?"

"He was Jamie Mackinnon, and she was Katrina Fraser. They lived in the wild Highlands of Scotland, where my home is now, across the same glen. They were destined to marry from childhood, when their fathers promised them to each other—"

"Don't tell me anymore, my love, or I'll want to hear

it all!" She was charmed already. "Is that where your name comes from? A combination of his and hers?"

"That's right," Fraser nodded.

"And they were fortunate enough to love each other and fulfill their fathers' promise?" She couldn't resist asking for a little more after all. Fraser's arms tightened around her.

"They had the greatest love in the world, and it was second only to yours and mine, my sweet one. We already have the same great love, Alexandra, that lasts through time and beyond."

Her eyes felt damp at the simple, poetic words, spoken in that lilting Scots accent.

"That's the loveliest thing you ever said to me, Fraser. I'll remember it always."

"Maybe we should inscribe something of the sort over the lintel when we go home to Scotland," he said, and there was a definite question in his voice now.

Alex nodded slowly. "It would be fitting," she said. "It would be something for our children to ponder."

They broke apart reluctantly when they heard Mrs. Arbuthnot's obviously noisy return outside the drawing room door. Alex was sitting demurely on the sofa when the lady entered, with Fraser's arm still loosely around her.

"You'll forgive my husband for retiring early," their hostess said. "He has been on watch all day, and it puts such a strain on his eyes."

She might have been commenting on watching a game of cricket, Alex thought in amazement. Did one get used to living in such dire circumstances? Fraser guessed more correctly that the man had gone to bed roaring drunk and didn't blame him for that.

"Shall we be seeing you tomorrow, Mr. Mackinnon?" Mrs. Arbuthnot went on chattily. He avoided looking directly at Alex when he answered.

"Possibly, but I can't guarantee it. I am expecting to be sent further afield almost immediately. I go to meet General Havelock to find out when we can expect the large reinforcements we've been promised."

"Are we to be together for so short a time, Fraser?" Alex cried out.

He seized both her hands in his. "Dearest, trust in God and my canny scouting instincts! I may be away hours or days, I cannot tell. Just promise me ye'll not run off again, and I'll return to ye here."

"She'll stay with us, won't you, Alex, dear? Our lives have all changed, and we have to make the best of it."

Alex swallowed, knowing she was being uncharitable.

"Of course I'll be here. I won't give you any more cause for worry, Fraser!"

"And if you've the stomach for it, you can come with me and the other ladies to the hospital tomorrow and help tend the wounded. It's not always a pretty sight, but it keeps our hands busy and stops us thinking too much about things we can't change," Mrs. Arbuthnot went on with relentless cheerfulness. "At least we can tend the poor little children sick with the cholera and keep them happy. They'll be glad to see your pretty face."

Alex tried not to show her mounting horror. The hospital . . . wounded . . . children with cholera . . . She felt the hard clasp of Fraser's hand on hers, and the sudden faintness came and went. She remembered Ellen's distress at not being able to care for her own husband and vowed silently that she would be as strong as necessary. She was needed here. She had been sent for a purpose after all.

"I'll be glad to work at the hospital with you, Mrs. Arbuthnot," she said quietly.

She smothered her fear as she saw the satisfaction in the lady's eyes and sensed the reaction in Fraser. It was his approval she needed most. Fraser Mackinnon's . . . and all the ghosts of his ancestors, and hers, that she mustn't betray.

Chapter Fifteen

ALEX NOW LIVED IN A VERY DIFFERENT WORLD. LAST night, with the Arbuthnot house still warm from the day's heat and the soft shadows from the flickering oil lamps, it had seemed reasonably comfortable. In daylight, she could see the damage, the tattered curtains, the overlying dust everywhere that came not from bad housekeeping but from the constant rubble stirred up from outside by human and animal feet and the wheels of many vehicles, dust that was scattered inside every house through cracked or shattered windows.

Early that morning, she had looked through her bedroom window and drawn back in shock. The visible part of the city looked as though a hurricane had torn through it, uprooting trees and bushes and overturning carts, killing bullocks and donkeys that lay where they fell and were already being picked over by flies and birds.

Houses had crumbled as if made of cards, and bodies lay unattended in the dust or half-covered by hastily tossed matting. Alex still stood there numbly, when Mrs. Arbuthnot tapped on her door and came to where she was standing.

"The death-wallahs will try to collect them all up soon," Mrs. Arbuthnot said calmly. "It all depends on the day's activities whether they manage to dispose of them before they rot."

"It's appalling! I never dreamt it would be like this—" Alex's voice was dry as tinder.

"None of us did, my dear. Those of us who depended on servants for every little thing are now doing the most menial tasks. We see things at the hospital that no lady should ever see. If you've changed your mind, Alex, say so now. No one will know of it, and we can find you some other job. There is plenty of sewing and mending—"

"I've not changed my mind! Do I seem so feeble?"

Mrs. Arbuthnot smiled slightly. "That you do not! I just wanted to give you the option, that's all." She glanced at the sky. "It will probably rain today. I don't know which is worse, the dreadful heat that makes the smells intensify or the rains that drown us! Either way, it makes no difference to the attacks. We're due for one. They've left us alone for several days now. They think to trick us into thinking they've gone, so that we'll move out into the city, and then they'll pick us off like flies."

The calm way this genteel lady spoke of such things only made it more horrifying. Even as Mrs. Arbuthnot spoke, a distant noise of gunfire underlined her words.

"They'll start on the heavy guns soon," she went on

matter-of-factly. "They're better equipped than us, having captured much of the ammunition at Delhi. You'll soon get used to the noise, Alex. The high-pitched whine of the rifles, the deep thud of the Brown Bess muskets. You'll hear the musketballs ricochet and learn to dodge the grapeshot. The ladies have become amazingly proficient in identifying the different sounds! We'll get plenty more customers at the hospital today, so we'd best have some breakfast and be on our way, dear. Captain Arbuthnot has been gone this last hour."

"Breakfast?" Alex said faintly.

"'Twill do you no good to go without food. You need to line your stomach, meager though the meal will be."

Alex did as she was told, though it was hard to push the dry meal down her gullet after Mrs. Arbuthnot's graphic morning chat. The tea was weak, with a bare touch of milk to color it, since tea was now an extortionate price. Ironically so to Alex, whose life had revolved so much around the product. Then, after Mrs. Arbuthnot rammed her bonnet firmly on her head, they set out for the hospital that had once been a splendid banqueting hall.

Most of the British ladies had discarded their hoops by now, and their crinolines were less hot and cumbersome. Fashion hardly seemed to matter anymore. Alex's main thoughts as they walked carefully through the twisting, littered streets were to avoid treading on corpses, to try not to look at the gnawing scavengers and to keep her nostrils pressed tightly together to keep out the disgusting stench.

"You'll get used to it," Mrs. Arbuthnot said again.

"Will I?" Alex muttered. "I think Fraser should have warned me!"

"I understood you wanted to come."

So she did. She would never understand why. With

every step, it became a place beyond description. A place without hope. There was little jesting among the soldiers scanning the distance for the enemy that morning, but they could be behind the nearest door as easily as being miles away. Alex wondered if it was always like this or if, like Mrs. Arbuthnot, everyone expected a new and violent attack on that particular day. She had chosen a wonderful time to arrive in Lucknow . . . but was there ever a good time now?

Just as they reached the hospital, the drenching rain lashed down, sending them scuttling indoors. Alex looked back, and already the dust-thick streets were pools of stinking mud. Debris floated about, adding to the squalor.

Other ladies were arriving, seemingly unconcerned that their bonnets were dripping and their skirts filthy. How different from England . . . but Alex was given no time to consider it. A sudden bombardment of firing shook the hospital. Someone screamed and was quickly told to be quiet and get to work. There was no time for fear.

The hospital was crowded, makeshift beds lining every available space. The windows were barricaded, so that little air came inside, and the atmosphere was stifling and putrid.

"The devils don't stop fighting because it rains," someone snapped. "And our men don't stop dying either. Who've you got here, Mrs. Arbuthnot?"

Alex started, realizing that an elderly man in a once-white linen coat was staring at her. The coat was a stinking mess, and she suddenly realized it was covered in blood and slime, and she quickly averted her eyes.

"Alex, this is Surgeon Wade. You'll be working with him."

She felt utter shock. This disgusting-looking man was a surgeon? He looked her up and down, his eyes narrowed.

"What's this? Are you sending me hothouse flowers now?"

Alex felt her cheeks burn. She glared at the uncouth man. "I'm quite capable of tying a good bandage or sponging a wound—" she began, to be met with derisive laughter.

"Spare me your blushes, girl. Can you hold a man's hands tight while I'm taking the saw to his leg? Can you tie a tourniquet while a soldier screams at you to let him die?"

If her face had burned before, Alex felt it blanch now. She fought down the taste of bile in her mouth.

"I'll do whatever you ask of me," she snapped back. But dear God, don't let it be assisting at an amputation . . .

Surgeon Wade nodded, not giving her the chance to retreat. "Good. Follow me. We've a full house today, and there'll be more by the end of it. How's your sewing skill?"

He gave a raucous laugh as she realized what he meant. For a second, he squeezed her hand, and she hated the feel of him. She hated him.

"Don't worry, girl, I'll not ask you to sew up the stumps, but you can thread a needle, I hope?"

She followed him mutely, feeling as though she were going into a nightmare. The cries of the wounded were terrible, but when she reached the operating area, it was a hundred times worse. Many were waiting for amputations. Some could see and hear the previous ones. There was no chloroform, which had all run out. Laudanum was kept for the very sick, and those who needed it relied on rum or porter to dull the slice of the knife a fraction.

Amputations were done swiftly and cleanly, the injured or gangrenous limb tossed aside, penitrate of mercury applied to the raw flesh before the stump was stitched. There was no time for the surgeons to wash their hands or instruments between patients. Few amputees survived, since most wounds became infected and death followed. Surgeon Wade told Alex all this quite callously as he worked, unheeding of the screams. The patients already knew the probable outcome.

Alex was sickened, appalled, frightened and almost borne down with compassion. Somehow she reacted mechanically to the curt commands given to her. And by the end of the day she had a deep and abiding respect for this rough bear of a surgeon who knew that most of his work was doomed to failure and yet worked like a demon to keep every man alive just a little while longer.

If he worked, then so did she. She hardly realized how the time passed. Outside, the battle raged. At some time, the rain stopped, and the sun scorched the earth again. The black pall of battle smoke merged with the steaming buildings, and the air was choking. It was hard to breathe, and the sickly sweet smell of infected wounds was almost preferable to the cloying air of the city. Almost . . .

"I'm taking Alex home now."

She heard Mrs. Arbuthnot's voice as though through a haze. How long had she worked? An hour? Ten hours? She couldn't tell. The gunfire that had rocked their ears all through that terrible day had lessened to a spasmodic rumble in the distance. She looked down at the pretty dress she wore. It was bloodstained and filthy, and she stunk like a field hog. Tears ran down her cheeks from sheer exhaustion.

To her surprise, she felt a rough hand pat her shoulder. She no longer resented it.

"You're a good girl. You don't crumble. Same time tomorrow, Alex."

It was the first time Surgeon Wade had used her name. And she could only stand in horror at the thought that this day would be repeated again and again, and for God knew how long. She couldn't bear it . . . but she would have to bear it, the same as he did, the same as did all the poor wretches who depended on surgeons like him. And on women like her, to give them a little comfort while the orderlies held them down . . .

"Same time tomorrow," she echoed woodenly and then felt Mrs. Arbuthnot pull her away as Surgeon Wade gave all his attention to the next patient.

"Does he ever sleep?" she said, as her feet seemed to move without her noticing.

"Not much. He's coarse, but he's a marvel at his work. Patients wait for his services—"

They were outside in the cooler evening air, and the sound of hysterical laughter came from Alex's lips before she could stop it. It was so ludicrous for a man to wait to have his leg sawn off by the master . . . when in a few days he would probably be dead anyway . . .

"I'm sorry." She dissolved into silent weeping as they retraced their steps home. "It's just that it's all so—so hopeless."

"I know," Mrs. Arbuthnot said briefly. "But we have to give them what hope we can. The first day is always the worst."

"I can't go back there. I can't!" She was struck by the

most appalling attack of nerves. She shook violently, uncaring who saw her. "I thought I was to care for children with cholera!"

"I thought you were strong enough to help Surgeon Wade," Mrs. Arbuthnot commented quietly.

Alex said nothing, fighting back the tears and bitterly ashamed of herself for letting nerves get the better of her. She had worked with Surgeon Wade for just one day. Others must have spent weeks with him. And what of the man himself, who would be better suited to growing old with his grandchildren?

The panic left her, and she knew she must go back to the hospital the following day. Mrs. Arbuthnot nodded slightly, knowing it too. Mrs. Arbuthnot had thought her strong, and she would be strong.

The days merged into weeks. Alex would never grow accustomed to her hospital duties, but somehow she met each new day with enough courage to get through it, to fall into bed each night after a hasty bath to wash away the pain and anguish she felt she absorbed. And a word of praise from Surgeon Wade was a precious gem to treasure.

There was no news of Fraser. If he was dead, she didn't want to be told. She saw enough suffering. She didn't want to equate it with her love. She thought of him as whole and strong, not as one of the poor wrecks brought to the hospital. The attacks on the Residency and the city of Lucknow continued, and it was an endless ordeal. Sometimes she wondered if it would go on forever.

"Next!" Surgeon Wade barked out, when the latest patient had been carried away to recover from his surgery, his eyes haunting Alex as he let go of her hand.

He was no more than a boy, begging her to let his mother know when he died. She smothered the sobs in her throat and turned to take the hand of the next man to be placed on the table, while Surgeon Wade wiped his blade on his sleeve.

Her heart seemed to leap half out of her body as she looked down at the dirt-grimed face and the tortured expression as the man muttered half in delirium. A face she knew and dearly loved. She looked further in mounting horror. One leg was deeply torn beneath the remnants of a once-bright tartan, a leg surely destined for surgery . . .

"My God! Fraser! Fraser!" She screamed his name, feeling as though her heart would burst. Didn't he know her? Was he so far gone already?

"You know this man?" Surgeon Wade paused in his preparations.

"Yes, yes! He's my fiancé! Don't touch him! Please—not until I've had a chance to talk to him—"

"He needs attention now," Surgeon Wade said harshly. "That leg must come off if he's to survive—"

As if the realization of his fate and the sound of Alex's voice penetrated his mind at the same instant, Fraser's eyes opened wide, his hand clenched Alex's, and his voice became a lucid roar.

"Nobody's taking off my leg, man! I'll need it to walk the glens with my lassie! You hear me? If ye touch me with that bloody hacksaw of yours, I swear I'll throttle ye! I'll keep enough strength for that—"

Surgeon Wade scowled. The orderlies looked uncertain. "You've a poor chance if I don't—"

Sudden hope blazed in Alex. "But there is a chance?"

Surgeon Wade made a cold and brutal inspection of

the infected leg. Alex saw the way Fraser gritted his teeth, but he made no sound as the cruel examination went on.

"Do you have the stomach to wash the wound with spirits every few hours for a solid week and to watch him scream in agony while it bites into the flesh?" He whipped out the words to Alex. "That's what it means, girl. And more than that. It means finding the bloody spirits to do the job, and you know what they're charging for them these days—"

"I've got money. I'll do it."

She never hesitated. She held on tightly to Fraser's hand. He had lapsed into half-consciousness again, but she knew by the curl of his fingers around hers that he needed her to do this. And she would do it, whatever it cost.

Surgeon Wade grunted. "Take this one back," he said to the orderlies. "Find him a corner where he won't be too much of a nuisance with his bellowing. And you, girl, I'll give you an address where you can buy what you need. I'm relieving you from duties to get your requirements, but you'll have to pay for them yourself."

He scrawled down an address in the city. She would have to leave the safety of the Residency. She quaked inside, but she would do it. She did it for Fraser, and that made all the difference. She thought quickly. She would use the ekka once more. It was still at the Arbuthnot house. She would pay a servant to take her to the address. As she took the filthy piece of paper, Surgeon Wade put a hand on her arm, his voice harsh.

"If I had a girl like you willing to do this for me, Alexandra, I'd make damned sure I pulled through."

Next second, he was bawling for another patient, and

Alex forced down the rush of tears in her eyes. It was the greatest praise he could have given her.

Mrs. Arbuthnot was not at home to dissuade her. Alex knew she ran a terrible risk, but there was still the Indian sari she had used before . . . she put it on with shaking hands. If an enemy found an Englishwoman in disguise, her fate would be even worse, but she dared not even think of it. One of the few servants still loyal in the house agreed to take her through the alleyways to the house she sought, and she slipped inside the ekka and blessed the downpour of rain that might stop any inquiries.

Why should anyone inquire? The servant boy was a native of Lucknow and was apparently just taking his mistress from one point to another. All the same, it was a terrifying ride, and it seemed that all around her, Alex heard sounds of shattering glass, of rifle fire and the boom of heavy artillery. At last, they reached a narrow alley, and the boy said that this was the house of the merchant.

"Will you come with me?" she said tremblingly. "I may need your help."

He looked dubious until she promised him some rupees for his trouble. Far too many, but it was worth it for his aid, and she knew better than to pay him before her mission was done. They climbed a twisting staircase, gloomy and rank. For a second, Alex wondered if this was all a trap. Had the servant betrayed her after all? Could this be the house of a merchant who could supply all the needs of those with money to pay?

Her mouth dried, but at last they reached a narrow door, and the servant rapped on it and was told to enter. Alex didn't know what she had expected, but there was a small, wizened Indian inside, seated at an ornate desk. This was obviously some kind of office, though there was little else in the room. The servant, Niaz, motioned her to go forward.

"What can I do for you?" the man said in an oily voice.

Alex ignored her aversion to him and spoke quickly. "I'm told you can supply spirits for medical purposes. I need as much as you can spare. And if you have any laudanum too, that would be welcome," she added as an afterthought.

"Do you know the price for such things? You are British, I believe?"

"Does that make a difference?" Alex said passionately. "I was given this address. I assumed you to be sympathetic—"

He waved a bored hand. His fingers flashed with rings. "Did I say otherwise? The young lady is hasty in her judgment—"

"I don't have time for pretty speeches. A man may die—" Her voice suddenly broke.

"And this man is important to you?"

She detested being put on the rack like this. With every word, he twisted her heart. But pride didn't matter. If she had to beg, then she would beg.

"He is my life," she choked.

He leaned back in his chair, a gloating smile on his face. "Then his life is worth a great deal to you, Englishwoman."

Now she saw where all this was leading. The payment would soar to whatever heights he thought he could reach.

"Tell me your price," she said quietly. "I need many bottles of spirits, brandy or whatever you have. And laudanum, as much as you have. Just name your price."

He looked thoughtful. "What will you pay?"

It was a deadlock, and yet not quite. Alex reached behind her neck. For Fraser, her beloved, she would sell her dearest possession and never think twice.

"These pearls belonged to my mother. They are flawless and worth a king's ransom. I will not bargain with you. I will trade with my mother's pearls, and I want a fair exchange of goods."

She saw the greedy eyes narrow and knew he recognized quality when he saw it. She would get no more than a pitiful fraction of their worth, but it was the best bargaining power she had. And Fraser's life was infinitely more precious than the coldness of pearls around her neck. As for Constance . . . she knew that Constance would understand and approve.

"Very well. We do business," the man said.

He pulled a cord, and part of one wall of the room slid back to reveal a vast room behind, where bottles and packets and boxes were stacked ceiling high. Alex gaped at the sight of it all. It was like an Aladdin's Cave . . . and bitterness washed over her that this odious man could charge the earth for his goods to those who were desperate.

But it wasted time to think of such things. There were more urgent matters. Within half an hour, the merchant's assistant and Niaz had carried the crates of brandy and the precious laudanum supplies down to the waiting ekka, hidden in the small courtyard below. And then came the unnerving ride back to the hospital. Alex was bruised by the rattling crates as Niaz drove the donkey forward through the torrential rain that flooded the streets and made the wheels spin.

The street battles still raged, the rains continued relentlessly, and with every turn of the road there were strangled shouts as shots found their targets. At any moment, Alex thought it must be the end for her . . . but somehow they got through, and at last she heard Niaz shout that they had entered the Baillie Guard Gate of the Residency, and they were safe. As safe as anyone was in these turbulent times . . .

She ran into the hospital, informing Surgeon Wade that she had everything he required and that when Fraser's needs were fulfilled, he could have the rest and welcome. He looked up from his operation, startled at the defiant look on her face. Young and beautiful and desperate in her Indian sari, as he had never seen her before. The young Mackinnon was to be envied after all, he thought. He nodded abruptly and shouted for an orderly to unload the supplies and lock them safely away.

Alex was now given the duty of caring for Fraser during the day. She washed the livid wound with brandy, and it took all her courage to see Fraser's hands clench as the spirit bit into the raw flesh. The laudanum lessened some of the pain but was never enough. He tried to make no sound while she was there, and only in the night did his fellow sufferers hear his agonized shouts, which they knew were no more than their own.

"You don't have to do this, my dearest," he gasped out time and again. "Let someone else—"

"You would do it for me," she said quietly and continued, hiding her tears as best she could.

But at the Arbuthnot house, she let them flow freely in the sympathetic lady's arms.

"How can I bear to see him so broken?" she wept. "I wonder if I was wise to stop Surgeon Wade operating on him. I could have persuaded Fraser, if it meant saving his life. He seems to get no better—"

"He knows you now, Alex, and that's a great improvement. And if the leg gets no better, then at least it gets no worse. Have faith, my dear."

"I try," she whispered. "But it tears me apart to see him in so much pain. I love him, and I hurt him every day—"

"You're both strong, my love. And if love will pull him through, then Mr. Mackinnon can thank God he has you."

Several weeks later, when Alex reported to Surgeon Wade for her morning duties, she thought he looked at her oddly. Sometimes she suspected that he insisted she go to him first in case anything terrible had happened during the night. She saw at once that there was something different about him today. Then she realized. It was the first time she had seen him give a proper smile.

"I did a fine bit of surgery early this morning," he said cheerfully. "You'll find your patient in the recovery corridor, and get that worried look off your face. All his bits and pieces are intact—"

Alex didn't wait to hear more. She rushed to the recovery area, where Fraser lay sleeping. His face was white after the surgery, the lines of pain smoothed away. And he looked almost as Alex had first seen him, so long ago on the docks at Tilbury, when she had thought he looked so much like the beautiful and dashing Prince Albert . . .

She looked further. The gaping wound in his leg had been neatly stitched, which meant that Surgeon Wade was satisfied that all infection was finally gone. There would be no amputation.

The blood pounded in Alex's head. The relief was almost too much . . . too much. . . . She leaned forward and kissed Fraser's sleeping mouth, her throat

271

tight with tears. But now at last, they were tears of joy and silent thanks.

"Get well, my love," she whispered and left him to sleep. There were others who needed her.

Once the healing process began, Fraser became fractious with the enforced inactivity. On one of his periodic examinations of his handiwork, Surgeon Wade told him bluntly that he must not rejoin his unit, that there would always be some pain in his leg and his walking would be somewhat impaired, due to permanent damage to the muscles, where the grapeshot had gone so deep.

"God knows where my unit is now, anyway," Fraser said bitterly. "I'm pretty well useless then. Is that what you're telling me?"

"I didn't take you for a fool, Mackinnon. You've still got two legs, thanks to that young woman of yours. One that's good and one that's adequate is better than most of my patients end up with! No man is useless until he's dead, and you're far from that!"

"Aye, you're right," Fraser muttered.

"You'd have had less of an infection if you'd got to the hospital sooner. What delayed you, man? You rambled about being outside the city. I'd have thought a clever scout like yourself could have found his way in."

He frequently needled his patients into accounting for themselves. Fraser scowled at him.

"So I could, but I had to warn our men. They were in danger of being ambushed. I'd got wind of an enemy patrol about to pounce on them—"

"So you played the hero instead of getting your wounds seen to," Surgeon Wade commented.

"I'm no hero. I had a job to do and I did it—"

"You're all heroes," the other said bluntly. "If we ever get out of here, I'll make it known, Mackinnon. There'll be plenty to verify your words."

"I want no glory—"

"What *do* you want?" Wade demanded. "If you take my advice, you'll get out of here as soon as this city is relieved, take your young woman home to Scotland and marry her!"

"That's your advice, is it?" Fraser found himself grinning at the terse words. "I can't say I find it altogether unattractive."

Surgeon Wade snorted, looking down at this obstinate patient with a defiant glint in his eyes. Heedless of his own injuries this man had gone on to save a tattered regiment. And now this appalling wound in the patient's leg had put him nearer to death than he'd revealed, either to the man himself or to Alex. The kind of man Surgeon Wade respected enormously.

"If I was forty years younger, man, I'd marry her myself."

He strode off to deal with the new arrival of wounded, his sweat-stained coat flapping around him like a banner.

Chapter Sixteen

FRASER WAS DISCHARGED AS SOON AS POSSIBLE FROM THE
hospital. His space was needed for those worse off than
himself. His leg healed quickly, but muscle damage
could never be repaired, and mental scars would take
longer to heal.

The Arbuthnots welcomed him into their house.
Alex continued working at the hospital with the other
women each day. She hated to spend so much time
away from Fraser, but her conscience wouldn't let her
desert her post.

But if she was frustrated by the hours they were
forced to be apart, then so much more was Fraser. He
had been powerfully active all his life. Now he walked
adequately well, but sometimes the damnable weak-

ness in his leg made it give out, and he cursed volubly when it happened.

He admitted bitterly that Surgeon Wade had been right. He was no use as an army scout now. Whether he wanted the job or not wasn't the point. It was the fact that he was unable to do something for which he'd been so admirably suited that smarted and shamed him.

"How can you feel shame?" Alex snapped, exhausted after a long, wearisome day at the hospital and in no mood for petulance. "You did all that was expected of you. It's honorable to retire gracefully—"

"Damn it, Alexandra, if you were a man, you'd understand!" He glared at her. She felt tears cloud her eyes. She was so tired, aching in every muscle, and suddenly all the tenderness between them seemed to have vanished in a mist.

"You've never called me by my full name in anger before."

"I'm not angry with you, only myself," Fraser raged, not even seeing the significance of her words.

She had always loved to hear him say her name, with that faint Scots burr that had always enchanted her, but this time it held a different nuance.

"I should never have brought you here," he went on. "I should have had more sense and done what I'd intended."

She whipped back at him, "If you had, you'd be trying to live with only one leg by now—if you were alive at all!"

Her words silenced him, but it wasn't a comfortable silence. They argued so much these days, and the arguments always ended this way. Incredibly, Alex sometimes felt that he resented the fact that she had been the one to stop the amputation. She had thought she knew him so well. Now she felt she didn't know him at all. She loved him, but she couldn't reach him. And it came near to breaking her heart.

"Give him time, my dear," Mrs. Arbuthnot said sympathetically. "Once the nightmares stop—"

"Will they ever stop?" Alex cried as they hurried through the wet streets to the hospital one September morning. "Will all this ever stop? Why don't they end it all now? Why not open the gates and let them murder all of us, as they've done to so many others! We're all feringhis. At least I agree with Fraser about that. It's their land. They've won. We should all get out—"

Her voice rose in panic as a shell blast ripped out the front of a house not ten yards from where they were. She almost wished she'd been inside it. Then she wouldn't have to concern herself anymore with holding the hands of strangers who looked at her mutely for help, while both of them knew death was only a few days away. Such thoughts were hysterical ones, but she had them more and more often these days.

Outwardly, she was strong, but inwardly, she was still a frightened child, wondering what was happening to a world she had once loved . . .

"I never thought to hear you say such things, Alex." Mrs. Arbuthnot picked up her skirts and ignored the flying debris as she pulled Alex's arm and got the seemingly bewildered girl away. "We have a job to do, and we can't let our poor boys down."

Our poor boys . . . Alex swallowed her fears yet again and trudged the last yards to the banqueting hall. Was ever anything so inaptly named now! There was hardly any food in the city, except for those willing to pay.

She still had money, given to her by Miles Thompson, but she hoarded it for something more important than food to fill her belly. Once she and Fraser got to Calcutta, if they ever did, he would go to the East India Company Office and collect money held in trust for him there. Fraser was a canny Scot and had taken precautions a long while back.

But Alex didn't have that strong a belief in John Company anymore. They were seeing it crumble about them. She kept what money she could, to pay for the passage home . . . as the thought came to her mind, she knew she hadn't quite lost all hope.

At night, when Fraser's nightmares ran their frequent course, it was Alex who went to his room and smoothed his damp forehead and tried to calm him. It was then that she felt the full horror of native saber attacks, as Fraser relived them, telling of the terrible atrocities done to women and children and of the retaliation by the outraged British troops. Neither side was victorious in terms of decency and humanity. They should all feel shame.

During those bad nights, Alex could only hold Fraser close to her, cradling his head in her arms and crooning softly to him as if he were a child. And blessing the Arbuthnots for turning a blind eye to the time they were alone together.

Not that anything could be more innocent, Alex thought sorrowfully. Did the lovers they had been even exist anymore? Had they been through so much, changed so much, that they would never be able to recapture that ecstasy they had once known? She prayed it wasn't so. She loved him so much, and she wanted her lover restored whole to her again.

And gradually, the nightmares grew less vivid. At the same time, there was a strong thread of hope running through the British stronghold at Lucknow. There was the triumphant news that Delhi had at last been relieved after all these months of bitter struggle and hardship, and people could walk the streets in comparative safety again.

More importantly for Lucknow, news of General Havelock's imminent arrival at the city was enough for premature celebrations to begin. There had been false rumors before, but surely this time the rumors must be true.

By now, most of the buildings where the British and their loyal native regiments were besieged were shattered or badly damaged. Rain seeped into everything, and the weather was hot and humid, disease rife. They frequently felt they had been forgotten and were doomed. But with British optimism, spirits soared quickly when it was reliably reported that a substantial army under General Havelock's leadership had crossed the river Ganges and would be at Lucknow any day.

It was the 25th of September when the enemy finally realized they were the ones to be cornered. The brave remnants of the Lucknow siege still had some fight in them, and they were joined now by Havelock's determined and vigorous men. The rebels began to panic and flee.

Alex and Fraser were among those who flocked to the Baillie Guard Gate at six o'clock that evening, when Havelock's victorious army broke through. There were many Highlanders among the regiments, and Fraser hugged one bearded friend after another. People went wild with relief at the sight of their saviors. They were all ragged, weary, near to starving, but at that moment they tasted freedom, and it was very sweet.

"The siege goes on," Captain Arbuthnot said angrily, days later, when the first euphoria had died down.

"The devils aren't done with us yet after all. It's wise for those who can get away to do so. I mean you and Alex, Mackinnon."

"I can't leave!" Alex said at once. "I'm needed at the hospital. The wounded still arrive daily, and there's dysentery and cholera among the men and the families—"

"The place is awash with nurses now," Captain Arbuthnot said bluntly. "You know it as well as I. The two of you have done enough. Go home and make a life of your own, and stop being a drain on the food supplies here. We've little enough."

Alex looked at him in astonishment. He'd never said such things to her before. She couldn't tell if he was serious or not. But he spoke honestly. Food was still not plentiful, the merchants still unwilling to be too friendly to the British victors. They swayed with the breeze, Alex thought bitterly, yet she could hardly blame them.

"Ye're probably right, man," Fraser said roughly. "We've outlived our usefulness here—"

"I won't listen to such talk!" Mrs. Arbuthnot said in agitation. "Charles, how can you be so thoughtless?"

"I'm talking sense, woman," he grunted. "Mackinnon's a practical man and sees that. His brain's not cluttered up by female softness. A good scout always knows when to be still and when to move."

Fraser gave a humorless smile. "And now is the time. Do ye have the stamina for it, Alex? If so, we'll go tonight. Darkness will see us more safely out of the city. We'll still need to be on our guard."

She stared at him, her heart sinking. He was so hard, so insensitive, so changed . . .

"Am I to be given no time to think or to say good-bye to Surgeon Wade and my friends at the hospital?" She tried to ignore the shrill tone of her own voice, knowing she was scared at the prospect. Scared at everything now.

"There's no time for that," he said shortly. "If we go, we go tonight. We'll not be the only ones on the Calcutta road."

She knew that. Ever since the first relief of Lucknow, there had been clamorings to get away, to make the long, overland journey to Calcutta, to find a ship bound for England and home.

A wave of homesickness struck her sharply and unexpectedly. Oh, she wanted to go home so much . . . so much . . . but with this stranger who expected her to do his bidding? She had longed for him as if with a fever, but his eyes were so cold, his voice so abrupt.

She felt tears stab her eyes and blinked them angrily away. There was no time for crying. Fraser had dictated it so.

"I think you should do as Mr. Mackinnon says, my love," Mrs. Arbuthnot said gently, seeing Alex's distress.

The poor girl herself needed time to recover from the ordeals at the hospital all these weeks, the lady thought. Did no one else see that? Alex had done enough. She saw her give a tremulous nod.

"All right. We leave tonight," she mumbled.

Why not? They would probably be killed on the road, anyway. All this would have been for nothing. She couldn't think beyond that. She let herself be propelled in whatever direction people pointed her. She had suddenly lost all purpose, as if the ground was moving beneath her feet.

If all went well, they would be safe at last, and yet she felt nothing at the thought. No elation, no happiness, only a deep sorrowing emptiness for what was left behind. For India, for all of that lovely burnished land that had become a cauldron of hate.

The journey east to Calcutta was a different sort of nightmare. It took weeks of traveling. They left Lucknow by its maze of alleyways and were miraculously well away from the city before the first spasmodic firing of the night was heard. No one challenged them. No native patrol pounced on them with murderous screams and gleaming sabres ready to run them through.

The curtained ekka proved its usefulness again. They paid a native boy a few coins to ride the donkey until they were well clear of the city, but it was Fraser who directed him with low words of instruction.

Fraser had been an army scout for too long to be caught by surprise. They paused, they listened, they moved stealthily like thieves in the night. And once well away from the simmering danger areas and into the less populated countryside, it was to discover that much of India's people carried on as imperturbably as before and that the fiercest resentment against the British was confined to the dense central pockets of the country. They paid off the boy and let him find his own way back to Lucknow or go where he pleased.

They soon realized that though the fighting was over for them and their journey to the east of India was peaceful, there was not the same feeling towards the British now. The great and wonderful British John Company could be defeated, and Fraser commented harshly that its days were numbered, at least in its present form.

"So my father would probably have retired to his tea estate eventually," Alex said with unconscious bitterness. "He would have made a fine tea planter, Fraser. I hope the Forbes family enjoy life there. I wonder if we'll ever see them again."

"Why not? They may visit us in Scotland. Or we may come back here. You still have your own ties with Krubah Tea, Alex."

She shook her head violently. "I'll never come back! You can never recapture a dream."

"Aye, maybe not." He didn't argue with her.

For him too, the dream was long over. But he became more alarmed by Alex's apathy as they traveled. He never attempted to be more intimate with her than etiquette allowed. Somehow this brittle, slender girl, with her beautiful sad eyes, unnerved him a little.

Fraser Mackinnon had never been unnerved by anything, but sometimes Alex seemed as remote from him as a nun. In his mind, the thought threatened to emasculate him, and he hoped with a brutal male frankness that the feeling would soon disappear. He wanted his warm and passionate lassie again, and he wanted her to come to him freely.

In her present state, he dared not risk tipping the delicate balance by trying to seduce her, however sweetly and tenderly. But these weeks of close contact, in the ekka and the resting-houses where they stayed, had sorely tested him.

Arriving at Calcutta at last, they were met with new frustrations. Already, it seemed that half the British in India had converged at the port, seeking a passage home. And there was no ship expected for several days yet. There was still more delay, and no one had any priority when it came to boarding the ship. And the smell and sight of the river, running out to the sea, had begun a nostalgia in Alex that was sharp and poignant.

"It's cruel to be so near and yet so far!" She felt like weeping. "We look like scarecrows, and the people resent us—"

"We can do something about that," Fraser retorted. "We'll find a bazaar that sells secondhand clothes, and at least we can go home looking decent."

Alex knew they would almost certainly be dead men's clothes, but she made no comment. Any activity was better than doing nothing.

"Can we telegraph to Krubah Tea to let them know we're safe?" she said suddenly. "There's a telegraph office thirty miles from the tea estate, and I'm sure they'd take the message. Mr. Thompson probably thinks I'm dead by now."

"I doubt that. You're a survivor, Alex."

"Am I? There were times when I felt like a rat caught in a trap, and it's hard to shake off the feeling." She bit her lip to stop its shaking.

"Let's send that telegram," Fraser changed the subject. "We may get a reply before we leave. It's something to look forward to."

Alex could hardly remember how that felt. It was so long since she had been able to be enthusiastic about anything. Becoming excited about a new ball gown or a party, or wearing a new piece of jewelry.

Unconsciously, her fingers touched her bare throat. The only jewelry she owned in the world now was Fraser's ring on her finger. It was the most precious thing of all . . . A small thrill ran through her veins as she caught his glance.

He leaned forward and kissed her, his mouth warm on hers, and she responded with a fervor that surprised them both. She clung to him in the small, stuffy resting-house room, her arms tight around his neck, the musky scent of her rousing him unexpectedly.

"I wish I could say all that's in my heart, Fraser," she said threadily. "Somehow I seem to have lost the words. I thank you and I love you, and you mean the world to me, yet I can't seem to feel anything. I want to feel, Fraser. I want to be the old Alex again. And I'm so afraid that she's gone forever."

"No, she's not. Have faith, Alexandra."

The simple words ran through her head like a litany as they left the resting-house and did their errands.

First they sent the telegram to Krubah Tea, arranging to call back every day to see if there was an answer. Alex prayed there would be. She and Fraser seemed so rootless. A link with the Thompsons and the Forbeses would be more precious than gold right now.

The desire to be at Fraser's ancestral home was suddenly very strong. There, they could put down their own roots at last . . . they could begin to found a dynasty.

They went next to the Company offices, where some of Alex's dwindling faith in everything was restored. Felix Truscott had been known to the officials there, and they treated her with respect and expressed their sadness at her father's fate. Fraser's own affairs were in order, and he left with a satisfying bundle of British money.

To cast off some of the gloom the visit had evoked, they went next to the bazaars, with their colorful hotchpotch of goods and exotic spicy smells and a plentiful supply of secondhand British clothes. Both of them guessed they had been sold to the bazaars by escaping families who still had clothes on their backs but no money to pay for a ship's passage.

It did no good to dwell on such things. They bought what they needed and no more. There was no time to have clothes made for them. Time enough for that when they reached Scotland and resumed a normal life again. But at least they wouldn't board the ship looking like paupers.

And at last the news ran through the British, flocking to the quayside each morning, that a ship's arrival was imminent. It would make a direct journey to Tilbury docks in London and continue to the east coast of Scotland. Fraser had to fight his way through the crush of people to book their passages, but he returned triumphant.

At last, they were going home. This time tomorrow, they would be on their way. They could hardly believe it. Alex wept in his arms with sheer relief. They had already been to the telegraph office that day and joyfully found that an answer to their telegram was awaiting them.

"Thank God you're both safe. All well here. Forbes family happy. Ellen expecting a child next spring. Contact us again from home. We love you. Miles and Louisa Thompson."

Alex had wept over the telegram, and when the paroxysm was over, she had squared her shoulders and decided there had been enough tears. She could fill an ocean with them, and they had to stop. It was time to stop looking back and look to the future, hers and Fraser's. They were going home.

Their new clothes were stuffed into carpetbags, and they reported early to the ship the next morning. But not early enough. There were hundreds ahead of them, some with tickets, others begging to be allowed on board in return for work. It shamed Alex to see even ladies of obvious quality reduced to such begging.

"We could help them, Fraser—" she muttered. He pulled at her arm, guiding her quickly onto the ship.

"If we helped one, we'd have a riot about us in minutes," he said. "We must see to ourselves, Alex."

She obeyed mutely, knowing he was right. The day was hot, the conditions on the ship appalling. Seizing every chance to capitalize, the owners were exacting extortionate prices from those who could afford them. The others could rot on the quayside for all they cared.

Alex and Fraser pushed through the passengers to ask directions to their cabins. The seaman laughed coarsely. "Women on one deck, men on another," he slurred. "Four to a cabin, and take potluck who you share your quarters with—"

"Miss Truscott is a lady, you scab, in case you're so rum-soaked you don't recognize one anymore," Fraser said furiously. The seaman looked Alex up and down, swaying on his feet, and she shuddered at his leer. The thought of sharing a cabin with three unknown women for weeks at sea, with the likes of this lout as crew, was nearly enough to make her turn tail and flee the ship.

"A lady, is it?" He gave an exaggerated bow. "There's no difference between trollops and duchesses on this ship when it comes to allocating cabins. Think yourselves lucky to be on board at all. There's plenty who ain't."

"Where's the captain, you bloody leech?" Fraser suddenly jerked at the man's shoulders, pulling him near. Alex screwed up her nose at the reek of him. Rum and sweat and worse. She remembered the gentility on the SS *Arabella* that had brought them out to India and felt near to fainting at the prospect of the weeks ahead. She clutched at Fraser's arm, her fingers biting deep into his skin.

"Captain Gibbs ain't available," the man snarled.

"Not unless you've got money to pay for a special cabin, o' course."

He winked meaningfully. Fraser let him go so suddenly the man staggered backwards, against a large, hard-eyed man who was instantly recognizable as a ship's captain.

"Get about your business, man," he barked at the seaman. "What's to do here? Passengers get below and find yourselves cabin space. We've no time for special treatment—"

"Have you time to marry us, Captain?" Fraser snapped. "We'll not be separated for the journey. We require a cabin to ourselves, and as two who have fought bravely against the mutineers in past months, we demand fair treatment. If 'tis extra money ye need for the privilege of newly wedded privacy, we'll pay gladly. Name your price."

"Demanding, are you?" Captain Gibbs growled, and then he glanced at Alex's pale face, flooding with sudden color at Fraser's words. "Have you asked the little lady if she wants to marry you aboard ship? Tain't the finest of hotels, and if you've a leaning towards the sickness, tain't the best way to start wedded life—"

Alex hardly heard him. She became aware of Fraser's hand tightly holding hers as they were jostled on all sides by passengers coming and going on the sweltering deck. She saw all the love in his eyes as they sought an answer in hers and was close enough to feel his heartbeat, rapid as her own. His fingers pressed the engagement ring into her palm.

"Well, Alexandra? Do we wait to get home to Scotland to have a fine big wedding? Or do we ask Captain Gibbs to marry us now? It's your choice."

She heard the caressing way he spoke her name, and there was no choice. All they wanted was to be together. All she wanted was to be part of him. She nodded, her voice tremulous.

"I don't need a fine big wedding, Fraser. I just want to be your wife."

"Can't be done till we steam out. If you've money to pay for it, you can have a small cabin to yourselves, but it'll cost you, man. No doubt you'll think 'tis worth it. I'll arrange it, and you can find some deck space till we're clear of port."

Captain Gibbs spoke brusquely, suddenly aware of the luminous light in the girl's eyes. He had thought her a pale, wan little thing, but that was due to the cheap clothes she wore and the lankness of her hair. With some color in her cheeks and that sudden radiant look, he saw that she was beautiful. And even Captain Gibbs, who wasn't moved by much anymore, was moved by the surge of love in the girl's eyes. He cleared his throat.

"There are a few old wedding rings below, if you can find one to fit. If we have a deal, we'll go below and settle the details."

It was all a dream, Alex thought. They followed the captain down a short companionway to his own cabin, where he shoved a box of rings towards her. She wouldn't think how he came by them. She found one that fitted her finger and removed it again quickly. Fraser paid the enormous sum demanded for the captain's services and the private cabin and kept his own savage thoughts to himself. At this rate, every sea captain who sailed the Indian Ocean would end up a millionaire . . .

The ship steamed away from Calcutta that evening. By then, word had got around that there was to be a ship's wedding aboard. To many of the British passengers who had had nothing but terror in their lives for weeks or months, the small excitement was a brief respite in the struggle just to stay alive.

Most turned their backs on India and watched as Captain Gibbs performed the brief ceremony that bound Fraser Mackinnon to Alexandra Truscott, for better or worse, until death did them part. To the two people most concerned, the words were as binding as if said over them by the most devout priest.

Fraser slid the old wedding ring onto Alex's finger, and she felt the coolness of it against her skin. The captain finally pronounced them man and wife, and as Fraser pulled her into his arms for their first married kiss, the cheers of the other passengers rang in their ears.

There was a sudden feeling of gaiety and laughter, and in the absence of anything more appropriate, some of the passengers tore up bits of paper and pelted the newlyweds with the pieces as they made a dash below for their cabin.

There was no wedding breakfast, no flowers or finery, but it didn't matter. There was no wish to remain on deck and watch the glimmering lights of Calcutta recede into the distance as the ship steamed steadily southwards. All that mattered was that Alex was no longer Alexandra Truscott, but Alexandra Mackinnon. The new life had begun.

Fraser pulled her slowly into his arms. The need of her was like a flame searing his blood. The past months, the horrors, the pain, the partings, all were gone. Beneath them, the ship's engines pulsed with a low throb. The movement of the ship was a sensual, rhythmic accompaniment to the flowering of love between them. The night was hot, the bunk small and cramped, but they were together.

And yet, Alex knew that she was not as totally relaxed as she longed to be. This was her wedding night. She lay in Fraser's arms, wanting to give herself as rapturously as she had done once before in the fragrant surroundings of the Krubah Tea estate.

Their loving had been passionate then, even though it had been a clandestine night. Now, when they had every right to be together, Alex was aware of an odd restraint. She was unable to be all that Fraser wanted her to be . . .

"I'm—I'm sorry, dearest," she whispered against his bare shoulder. "It's all so unreal—everything's happened so fast—please be patient with me."

"It's all right, my love," he calmed her. "We don't have to rush things. We have all the time in the world."

But for him, every moment wasted was a moment of torture. He needed her so much. But she seemed so fragile. In the swaying light from the ship's lantern, the shadows beneath her eyes were made deeper; her perfect oval face seemed smaller with the golden spread of her hair on the pillow.

He twisted a tendril of it in his fingers and pressed his lips to its softness. God knew he ached for her, but if she was not ready, then he'd wait, though it killed him by inches to do so . . .

Alex felt a desperate fear that she might never be able to respond to him again. She loved him beyond reason, and yet she seemed unable to feel, to experience, as if all sensation in her had been frozen by the last terrible months. She couldn't bear it to be like that. Even if he hurt her, it would be better than this numbness that terrified her.

"Fraser, please love me." He heard her ragged, whispered voice. Her fingers played up and down his broad back, and he shivered at her slightest touch.

Beneath him, her full white breasts gleamed like marble in the lantern light. Against the rough male hair of his chest, their touch stimulated and aroused him.

Tentatively, his hand strayed over the curves and hollows of her body, while his lips remained on hers, kissing, tasting, exploring. He heard the indrawn little sound in her throat as his fingers reached her inner thighs, and he felt them part, warm and soft and inviting. His fingers moved inwards, and he felt her yield for him. Her heart throbbed under his.

"Oh, God, Alexandra, I want ye so much," he groaned against her mouth. "I've waited so long. God help me, but I can't wait any longer for my wife!"

Fraser caught her up in his embrace so that she rocked against him for a second, her spun hair spilling out behind her. And then he lay her back on the bunk, his arms still around her, and she felt him enter her, filling her until her softness enveloped him totally.

He lay without moving for a few seconds, his breathing labored with the sheer ecstasy of being where he had so ached to be. And then he began the gentle movements that were complemented by the ship's engines, a deep, slow pulsating of flesh against flesh, heart against heart.

And at last all the ice in Alex's soul began to melt, and sensation came rushing back with an exquisiteness that was beyond pain or pleasure. She clung to her husband, panting with him, rising to meet him with a hunger and passion that exalted him.

He slowed his movements to a sensual rhythm or thrust at her when intuition told him of her needs. She knew all of his power and tenderness and, most of all, his deep love for her. She matched him in perfect unison, until finally she sensed the moment of climax was near.

She clung to him, moving with him as his seed flowed into her. Her own body reacted with stunning response, the radiating waves of pleasure making her gasp with wonder and a sudden gush of tears dampening her face.

"Why do I cry, when I'm so very happy?" she whispered tremulously.

"It's often so," he said thickly, still bemused with the blaze of passion they had shared, more beautiful than he remembered from the last time, far more than he had expected on this traumatic night. "Tears can be for great joy or great sorrow, my lovely wife."

"I feel truly your wife now." She was wrapped in his arms, still wrapped in love, her heartbeat still indistinguishable from his.

"And so ye are, for all time, Alex." He held her protectively close. "I want to tell ye at last the legend of Jamie and Katrina, told only to a Mackinnon husband or wife and handed down. Katrina Fraser Mackinnon would think ye a worthy successor, my Alexandra. Ye've the same spirit, the same strength."

"Have I?" Alex twisted in his arms, some of the intense glow of their lovemaking inevitably beginning to fade and a feeling of drowsy contentment taking over. "What did she do, this ancestor of yours—of ours—that was so spectacular, Fraser?"

She heard the low rumble of his laughter at her spark of skepticism. It seemed so long since they had laughed freely together. It was a good sound. She snuggled close to him and reveled in the soft Scottish burr of her husband's voice as he related the beautiful and incredible events that had made Fraser's lovely ancestor known as the Scarlet Rebel.

A name bequeathed to her by a prince who was every bit as charismatic as the most fabled princes of India. And as beautiful as Prince Albert of Saxe-Coburg himself . . .

Chapter Seventeen

THEY SLEPT IN EACH OTHER'S ARMS AS THE STEAMSHIP moved steadily south during the night. Alex awoke with a feeling of nausea and the realization that this ship was very different from the one her father had carefully chosen for herself and Aunt Maud on their journey to India. The *Sea Star* was smaller and older and filled to capacity with passengers. And the weather became atrociously bad as soon as they had left the coastal waters. The ship rolled and pitched, and Alex's stomach lurched with it.

"I can sympathize with poor Aunt Maud now," Alex gasped for the hundredth time in the first week, when Fraser wiped her mouth and forehead in the musty cabin and tried to make her eat some dry biscuits to line her stomach.

"How can you act so normally, when every movement wrenches my head and stomach so?" she raged at Fraser by the second week, when he still seemed impervious to the storms and gales lashing the ship. She resented his stoicism, his good health, even the fact that his wounded leg seemed to give him little trouble in moving about the ship while others clawed their way from railing to railing.

Alex had nightmares almost every night as the ship tossed about in the darkness, and even the charm of the Mackinnon legend that Fraser continued to entertain her with began to wear thin. She questioned whether the dashing Bonnie Prince Charlie had stayed in a secret room in the Mackinnon house, and she doubted that Jamie and Katrina had aided him so much in his escape to France after the Uprising of 1745 as Fraser insisted.

She was incredulous that Katrina had disguised herself in the red cloak of an old madwoman of the glens to seek out news of the ship that was to take the prince into exile from the Scotland that he loved and the hated English Duke of Cumberland who was after his blood. The mission that was to earn Katrina the name of Scarlet Rebel from the prince's grateful lips.

Alex was in no mood to believe in anything anymore. It was one more story to add to the list of fortune-tellers' tales, and she had heard enough of them during her time in India. Every bazaar was full of storytellers, and each tale being told was more fantastic than the last, in the hope of extracting a few rupees from gullible listeners.

She wasn't aware that she had ridiculed the Mackinnon legend so often and so forcefully during her thrashing about on the bunk in near delirium while the nausea was at its worst. Nor did she notice Fraser's tightening lips or the anger in his eyes as her comments offended his fierce clan pride.

She was unaware, too, of the ribald comments her absences evoked among the seamen and of the knowing looks from the less genteel passengers, until the day when the storm lessened and she finally ventured up on deck. She leaned heavily on Fraser's arm, feeling the deck move beneath her feet and her stomach surge uneasily to match it.

"How good to see you, Mrs. Mackinnon," one and another said archly to her. "Are you enjoying the voyage?"

She muttered an answer, knowing she had never enjoyed anything less. She yearned for the solidity of dry land again, and this journey seemed an endless nightmare. Even Fraser seemed less loving towards her, she thought suddenly. He tended her needs as a good husband, but in the ways of a lover, all the special feelings had vanished.

Was this how it was when a lover became a wife? she thought miserably. She couldn't believe it, especially of two passionate people like themselves. She had felt too ill to consider it until now, and it wasn't in her nature to brood on things without demanding answers. One starlit night when the weather had calmed at last, they walked on deck with their arms entwined, and Alex leaned her head against his shoulder.

"What have I done wrong, Fraser?" she said in a small voice. "You seem so distant from me, when I thought we were to be so close. Was it so distressing to you to see me so ill? I saw far worse when I nursed the dying in Lucknow."

Her words weren't meant to be a reproach, but he took them as such. She saw his jaw harden, and she glanced away quickly. Far below, the ship scudded against the waves foaming white against its bow. Every wave took them nearer home, but Alex hardly knew where home was now. She had none of her own. She went to her husband's home, and her husband was a stranger once more.

"Do you really think my family legend so foolish, Alex?" His words took her by surprise. "Do you know you're the first one ever to ridicule it?"

"I don't ridicule it!" She was aghast. "I think it's charming—"

"Aye, like a fairy tale," he said bitterly. "I thought we two were so alike, but maybe I was mistaken. Maybe that was why you had to go to India after all, to see for yourself, rather than believe your parents' tales. You need proof before you can believe things."

"Is that so bad?" She was angry at him now. "I think that's better than putting my faith in astrologers like Prince Shunimar. I'm able to think for myself."

"They saw the blood in the stars, and they were right," he said coldly.

"We should all have seen the signs, if we hadn't been so blind and thought the Company was invincible," Alex said, shivering.

What was happening to them? Why were they arguing about such stupid things? Yet none of it was stupid to Fraser. She realized that somehow she had insulted his family pride, and she had no idea of how or when. It seemed impossible to put things right without seeming to indulge him, and he wasn't a man to take kindly to that.

"We all make mistakes," Fraser said harshly. Alex looked at him sharply. His face was so handsome in profile, his stance so elegant in his Scottish attire. He was so dear to her, and yet so distant. She felt the sickening beat of her heart. Was he hinting to her that their marriage was a mistake after all? Did she remind him too poignantly of India and all that he was leaving behind him?

"We'd best go below. You're cold," he said abruptly. "The nights are chilly now. 'Twill be far colder when we reach home."

She twisted to face him. "Do you really want to go home, Fraser? Or is your heart still in India?"

He bent to kiss her lips, regardless of who saw them. "My heart is wherever you are," he said simply. "I didn't think I needed to tell you that, Alex."

Such moments were precious to her, yet she still felt so lost, so purposeless. She had wanted India, and the dream was gone. She had wanted Fraser, and he was here by her side, her husband, and yet she still felt as though she moved in a dream. Nothing was real. Least of all, the story of two people of a century ago who meant nothing to her.

It should be, of course. It made her guilty to know it. The legend was clearly part of the Mackinnon tradition. She was now one of them, and she felt nothing for it, except to enjoy it as a fairy tale. Fraser was right. And until she could accept it as proudly as he did, she would never feel a true Mackinnon, either to herself or her husband. The shock of it was like a blow.

Alex refused to believe that her skepticism colored their relationship. During the rest of that long and wearisome voyage, they met and talked with other passengers. They compared stories of escapes from Delhi or Cawnpore or Lucknow.

At night, in the privacy of the tiny cabin, Fraser took her in his arms and made love to her, and she re-

sponded at last with a joy that delighted them both.
And yet, there was still that small cloud between them.

It was mid-February when the *Sea Star* docked at
Tilbury, and a great mass of passengers disembarked.
They had steamed up the English Channel during
darkness, and they awoke to familiar smells of the
London dockside. They were home at last.

Waves of memory ran through Alex as she watched
the dismal dockside, made fresh and untainted that
morning by a thin covering of snow. It was bitterly cold,
and Alex was glad of the cloak one of the kindly ladies
aboard had given her.

The last time she had seen this area, Aunt Maud had
been flustered about boarding the *Arabella* for the
great adventure. And Alex had met Fraser Mackinnon
and thought him the handsomest man she had ever
seen, with his likeness to Prince Albert—and the
rudest, snatching her back from an imagined watery
grave. She felt his hand cover hers as they stood at the
ship's rail.

"Don't look back, dearest," he said gently. "We
can't change things."

"But I can remember! If I don't, it's like denying that
they ever existed—Father and Mother and Aunt
Maud—"

She bit her lip. Wasn't that what Fraser tried to do
with his legendary ancestors? But did they ever exist, or
was it just a good story to share with Mackinnon
children to make their eyes grow round with wonder
and pride?

Alex stared unseeingly at the crowds surging off the
ship with cries of thankfulness. When had she grown so
cynical? When had the wonder of childhood left her?

She knew she had changed through the experiences of the last year, but it seemed so irretrievable, that feeling for life that her mother had never lost. Aunt Maud used to call her a romantic, a dreamer, but what happened when the dreams were shattered?

"If I have one wish to bestow on a daughter . . . it would be that all her senses are alive to every God-given pleasure on this earth."

Constance's voice seemed to float in and out of her head, and she couldn't even recapture that glow that the words had always given her.

"We'll go ashore for a couple of hours," Fraser said abruptly. "The ship doesn't leave for Scotland until late this afternoon. We'll find a tearoom and have some food and buy some newspapers. I also want to send a telegram to my solicitor to tell him of our arrival. He can inform the household at Mackinnon House."

Alex hardly heard the last sentences. Newspapers? Why would he want newspapers? At her vacant look, he spoke deliberately, as if she was a child.

"We've had little news of India since we left, lassie, and I've a wish to know what's happening. 'Twas part of my life for a long while, and I grieved as much as if 'twas my own father when we heard that General Havelock had died from the cholera."

They differed again. He wanted to cling on to India. She wanted to let it go. She couldn't bear to remember, and she couldn't even tell him of her feelings. She wanted to remember the people but not the country . . .

Somehow they had grown apart, and the rift seemed more terrible by its subtlety. Fraser didn't even seem aware of it. She followed him numbly, until they had left the ship behind and found a cab. Its wheels crunched through the crisp, snowy streets until they were well away from the docks and were able to send the telegram and then find a busy tearoom.

London was still the same, Alex thought nostalgically. The voices all around them now were rounded, cheerful, Cockney voices that were as familiar as the river Thames. This was home, and she was leaving it almost immediately to go to another strange land. Scotland was as unknown to her as India had once been.

"Are you all right, Alex?" She heard Fraser's voice as if from a distance and forced a weak smile.

"Just a feeling of nausea again," she said faintly. "Surely it should have gone by now after all these weeks! I feel as though I'm still on the ship."

"That will pass, my love. It often happens. Some good strong tea will help."

He ordered food and tea, and Alex made herself eat and drink, though every mouthful was an effort. Fraser had sent a boy to buy the newspapers for him, and when they were delivered, Fraser searched them for news.

"I can't believe it!" he exclaimed. "Hardly a space given to such important items, and instead we're told at length of the Princess Royal's marriage to Prince Fritz of Prussia and their honeymoon on board the royal yacht *Victoria and Albert* en route for Berlin. Is this the sum total of the country's interest?"

"Dearest, people are looking at us," Alex said nervously as his voice rose.

"Let them look! They'll see a survivor from a war, not a peacock dressed up for a royal wedding!"

"You can't blame them for being more interested in home affairs than those of a country very few of them will ever see, Fraser. Only families who have ties with India will have any idea of what's been happening there."

It was a cruel truth. Would Alexandra Truscott have been so enchanted with India if her parents hadn't been so much a part of the country's life? She doubted it. India would merely have been an area on a globe, studied briefly during geography lessons at Lady Margaret's Academy.

Fraser continued to feel angered by the lack of newspaper reports, as though he himself were slighted, though Alex knew he grieved for all the British dead and wounded, army and civilians alike, who were caught up in the massacres. And for the loyal sepoy regiments too, whose loyalty must have been sorely tested.

She was thankful after all when they returned to the ship, preparatory to the last stage of the voyage to Scotland. It grew colder as they journeyed northwards and finally docked south of Inverness. They were obliged to stay the night in the town, while Fraser sent another telegram to inform the household of their arrival by hired carriage in a few days' time.

Alex was acutely conscious of the cold. It seemed to penetrate her bones, and Fraser quickly found the name of an emporium that sold ready-made clothes, made of softest Shetland wool. They purchased several warm dresses and shawls for Alex and Highland garb for Fraser, and she immediately felt more snug and able to face the last stage of the journey to Mackinnon House. She still felt strange, somewhat light-headed, and the detachment she had felt on board ship still lingered.

"Once we get home, you'll feel differently, dearest,"

Fraser promised. "Once we settle to a normal life, all of this will seem like a bad dream."

His words were ill-chosen, but she said nothing. Nor did she question what form a normal life was to take. It seemed an eternity since either of them had led a conventional life. Would they ever be able to settle for the way other people lived? They had seen the exotic, the fabulous, the bizarre . . . and also the depths of pain and degradation and near-starvation. Could people whose strengths had been stretched to the limits ever adjust?

They left Inverness early the next day in a closed hired carriage to keep out the bitter winds and flurries of snow. Yet for all the cold, Alex, ever aware of beauty, could not ignore the splendor of the country through which they passed. The great towering mountains with their snowcapped peaks, the deep glens and plunging waterfalls, the occasional sight of a stag or a flock of hardy mountain sheep steadfastly weathering the cold.

"It's beautiful, Fraser," she murmured, her eyes following the ever-changing layers of blue-hazed mountains ahead of them.

"We follow part of the route that Jamie and Katrina took when the bonnie prince ordered his brave Jacobite army to scatter and save themselves," he commented without expression. "They traversed on foot from Ruthven barracks, south of Inverness, and made their way home to Mackinnon House. Charles Stuart was hidden from that day on by every crofter and laird who believed in Scotland's past and hoped for the future—"

"But it had all failed by then!" She knew enough of history to know that the so-called Jacobite Rebellion had failed and Charles Stuart, Bonnie Prince Charlie, had escaped to France and ended his days in exile.

"Maybe the cause had failed, but the man still lived, and still lives in true Scottish hearts today. There was a price on his head of £30,000, a fortune in those days, but he was never betrayed, though the crofts burned about the Highlanders' heads. It says much for the man, and for Highland faith in his cause."

Her interest was aroused. To Fraser's relief, she seemed more alert than she had been in weeks as he pointed out places relevant to the history of those turbulent times. As turbulent as any they had seen in India.

Perhaps it was only now, seeing it all through Alex's eyes, that he admitted as much and shared some of his own father's fervor for the Mackinnon heritage and realized why old Guthrie Mackinnon had been so loath to see his son leave his homeland. He was the last of the direct line. If he had died, the legend would have died with him.

Others in the clan knew the outline of the history, but none had access to the secret room where Charles Stuart had waited for news of his ship. Even the kinsmen who would by now be leaving the house to return to their own knew nothing of its existence. There was still much to share with Alex. The nearer they came to their own glen and to Mackinnon House, the stranger became the stirrings of clan pride in Fraser's blood.

At last, he called the driver to stop the carriage and pointed ahead. The day was fine and sparkling now, the sky a clear blue, the snow peaks glinting in the sunlight. Alex saw a beautiful, still loch, the mountain peaks mirrored in its surface. It stood in a deep glen, surrounded by a circle of protective mountains. There were several tiny crofts dotted about the glen and a large and impressive house at either end, the two of them only seen together from a distance.

"There's Frashiel House, where Katrina Fraser was born." Fraser pointed to the right. "But we go to the other one, to Mackinnon House." His voice thickened as he caught at her hand and put her fingers to his lips.

Alex felt a lump in her throat. It was impossible to be unaffected by Fraser's own emotion, whether he admitted to it or not. She knew him too well not to sense it. The last time he had been here, it was to watch his father die and to become keeper of the Mackinnon lands and legend. And she had dared to ridicule that legend . . .

She wanted to say something to restore that closeness they had once had. To do it now, this instant . . . but already he was telling the driver to move on, wanting to be home, wanting the solid gray walls of Mackinnon House to enclose him once more. To be master, laird of his lands . . .

He remembered briefly that the earnest family solicitor had once said he might be glad to come back to Mackinnon House, to think of it as a sanctuary. But he didn't think like that. To his own surprise, Fraser knew that he came back triumphant. For him, the glory of India was past, and he wanted desperately for his lovely Alex to feel as passionate about this land as he did.

It was still strange to her. There seemed to be so many people there, wanting to shake her hand or kiss her and to wish her and Fraser well. People with lilting accents she couldn't always follow that were her kin also now. She had an entire, vast family, and they were all strangers.

Douglas Rothwell, the family solicitor, had informed

them all that the laird was coming home, and they had all come to meet him, including Rothwell himself. With tears in his old eyes, he had shaken Fraser's hand furiously to hide his emotion.

"I wish your faither could be here to see this day," he'd said in a choked voice. "He'd be fair proud of ye, Fraser, and so happy to meet your lovely bride."

How long was it since they had left Calcutta and gone through that oddly emotional wedding ceremony performed by Captain Gibbs? Time seemed to have lost all meaning. Was it two months, or three?

All through the celebrations, the feasting and drinking arranged by the kinsmen, Alex smiled and nodded and felt completely lost among all these well-meaning Highlanders. She suddenly longed to be alone with her husband.

And at last they had all gone, back to cottage and croft and farm, and Mackinnon House was in the hands of its rightful owners again. The servants had retired to the kitchens to deal with the ravages of a clan feast, and Fraser took his wife's hands in his.

Here in his own domain, he seemed the epitome of a clan chieftain, descendant of a proud past, and Alex felt a sudden extraordinary shyness wash over her. She wanted to say she was sorry for all her doubts, for her wretchedness during the voyage, for all the extra burdens she had put on Fraser, yet she still couldn't find the words.

"Now I'll show you our home, Alexandra," he said quietly.

He held her close for a moment. She was still so fragile. Douglas Rothwell had seen that too, and had suggested asking the family doctor to Mackinnon House on an apparently routine welcome visit. Fraser had privately asked him to see to it, knowing it would relieve him to know that Alex was in good health after the trials of the past year.

"Are you going to take me on a tour of the place?" she asked, her eyes oddly bright as though with unshed tears.

"Of course. We'll start upstairs, and ye can nod acquaintance with the family portraits as we pass."

He made himself sound more jocular than he felt, as if this showing of the house was not of vital importance to him. Why he should think it especially so, he didn't really understand.

They paused on every few stairs for Alex to view the past Mackinnons whose portraits adorned the stone walls and looked down on her approvingly or otherwise. Some were stern, dour faces, others gloriously pretty, and all with the strong Mackinnon character in evidence.

The last portrait was a strange one. Depending on which angle it was viewed at, it showed the face of a man or a woman, both with fiery red hair, both handsome, passionate characters, evident from the piercing eyes and full, sensual mouths. Alex studied it, frowning a little. Who would want such a portrait?

"Jamie and Katrina Mackinnon," Fraser said. "Their lives were so intertwined, they chose to be portrayed in this way."

"As if they couldn't bear to be parted, even after their deaths," Alex murmured.

The sentiments were charming if unusual. But naturally, these two would choose to be unconventional. Alex surprised herself at her sudden intuition about Fraser's ancestors.

They continued on their tour of the house, but the

image of Katrina Fraser Mackinnon grew more vivid in Alex's mind. Until now she had been a shadowy figure, a legend, no more. Now, in this house, she assumed the mantle of a beautiful, living woman who had loved her man as passionately as Alex loved Fraser.

"This is a very special room." Fraser paused, his fingers feeling along a hidden shelf for an ancient key. He turned it in the lock and a small room was revealed, without windows and barely furnished.

"This is the room where they hid Charles Stuart," Alex said slowly. She had hardly believed it until now. Did she believe it yet, or was it all a fairy tale? Her feelings were mixed, and yet she couldn't deny the charge of emotion she felt in this room.

Was it the ghost of Katrina and the loyal Jamie Mackinnon and their quest to save their bonnie lad . . . ? There was a presence here, and not an unhappy one, but Alex was still glad when they re-locked the door and went downstairs to explore the rest of Mackinnon House.

"Do ye still have doubts, Alex? Have I not convinced ye yet?" Fraser said, half in jest. She spread her hands in helpless uncertainty.

"I want to believe it. It's all too fantastic to be true, and too fantastic not to be—"

"Come outside the house. Wrap your shawl around you. The day grows colder," he said abruptly. She obeyed meekly. She ached to be all that Fraser wanted of her, and yet she knew she still failed him. She followed him outside the house. The air was as clear as wine, the scents of an early spring already in evidence despite the lingering snow.

This glen would be beautiful in the spring. She thought of Jamie and Katrina running to meet one another through the long grasses and felt as though she almost recaptured their sweet pleasures. Was she going mad after all?

"Do ye see the marks, Alex?" Fraser spoke roughly, as if he felt something other than the pleasures of a past love. He pointed to the old stone walls, where the faint red crosses could just be seen.

"What are they?" Alex said, her heart thudding.

"The English soldiers daubed the house when Katrina fooled them into thinking she had the cholera. After that, the hated redcoats kept well away. 'Twas partly why they were able to keep Charles Stuart well hidden in the house. If ye want proof, then there's your proof, my doubting Englishwoman!"

For a few seconds, Alex felt the earth spin. She felt that queasiness again and held on tightly to Fraser's arm. She felt more. She felt a strange and loving empathy towards this brave and spirited ancestor of his—of theirs—as though the ghost of Katrina suddenly held out her arms to Alex, the newest Mackinnon wife.

It was as mystical a feeling as she had felt once before, when she had sensed her mother holding her and letting her go, releasing her from childhood. She turned to tell Fraser so, but it seemed she hardly needed to tell him anything. He looked into her face and saw all that he needed to know.

"Welcome home, Alexandra Mackinnon," he said softly.

The sound of hoofbeats stopped any further conversation, and Alex felt briefly annoyed at the intruder. But Fraser welcomed him so amicably, she knew she must be the dutiful wife of the laird and offer hospitality like a good Mackinnon wife.

She became more charmed by the minute with her new role and enjoyed the company of this newcomer, introduced to her as Doctor Fergus. He asked them many casual questions about their voyage, and as he rose to go, he offered Alex a potion to help rid her of the persistent nausea.

"I'll take it, though surely it will pass now that all the traveling is done at last," she said dubiously.

Doctor Fergus laughed, his eyes twinkling. "Dear lassie, what ails ye is no more the travel sickness than the plague! My diagnosis is that ye'll be bringing a bonnie wee bairn into the world in September! My congratulations to ye both, and I'll be calling to see ye again in a week or two to see how ye fare, Mrs. Mackinnon."

They could hardly wait for the doctor to leave. Why had they not considered the possibility of a child before this? The shadows grew long as the day closed in, and the servants had lit a fire in the bedroom they were to share. Yet still they had much to talk about in warm contentment.

"What happened to Jamie and Katrina when the prince had gone?" Alex asked, when they had exhausted all the dazzling plans for the future and the son they were sure the baby would be.

"They had a child the following year," Fraser told her. "They called him Charles after the prince, but they dared not do so openly. It was his second name."

They looked at each other, and Alex felt as though her heart would burst with love. They had as much to live for now as those other two. They had shared something very special with Jamie and Katrina. Dangers and fears and deeply abiding love . . . and the continuity still lived on. Perhaps one day they too would hand down their own story to add to the legend.

"If our child is a boy, I'd like to call him Charles too," Alex said softly. "But this time we'll name him with pride instead of secrecy."

310

In that instant, Fraser knew that she believed implicitly all he had told her of his ancestors. They were united in spirit from that moment. But for two such as themselves, it was not enough . . .

They moved towards the stairs together, their arms entwined. They passed the portraits of other Mackinnons, who suddenly seemed to look down on them both benevolently, and then went into the master bedroom that had once been Jamie and Katrina's, and was now Fraser and Alex's.

He pulled her into his arms and began to remove her clothing with sensual patience, knowing they had all night. Knowing they had the rest of their lives . . . He kissed each new area of flesh as it was revealed to him, his hand caressing the softly rounded belly where the evidence of their love grew and blossomed.

"My lovely, lovely wife," Fraser murmured huskily. "Could our own story have any better ending than this?"

"But this isn't the end, darling, it's only the beginning," she said tremulously, as he lifted her in his arms and took her across to the bed, to lay her gently on the coverlet.

The room had been warmed by the fire, the flames throwing leaping shadows across her clear white skin. Her breasts were full and beautiful, her limbs long and perfectly formed. Fraser felt more aroused by her now, the future mother of his child, than he had ever realized he could be. Each of them was warmed further by the sudden desire that burned fiercely between them.

As Fraser bent to kiss the softness of her lips and to ease his body over hers, Alex felt a deep joyfulness that this baby should seal the love they shared and dispel all the doubts.

Almost at once, the memory of anything other than

311

her man faded in her mind in the intensity of pleasure he gave her. Every touch, every kiss, every caress was like the first time. She hardly knew where one sensation ended and the next began. She drowned in his love and exalted in knowing that she gave him back as much as he gave her.

His hands adored her, his lips sought and teased and drove her to the edge of ecstasy. When the final exquisite moment of release came, it was almost too beautiful for her to breathe properly. She clung to him, and it was moments before she could open her eyes. They felt so blissfully heavy . . . but when she did open them, she found him watching her.

"Your beautiful blue eyes darken with passion, my Alexandra," he said huskily. "No one but me will ever see them like that. It's a humbling thought. And no tears?"

She pulled him to her fiercely, still part of him, still the other half of him.

"I've no need for tears anymore, my darling. I've come home at last. This is where I belong. This is where the new dream begins."